The Things
We Don't
Forget

March 9, 2000

To Mary,

With warm

wishes —

Dianne Aquile

THE

THINGS

WE DON'T

FORGET

*Views from
Real Life*

Dianne Aprile

TROUT LILY PRESS

Published by Trout Lily Press
1260 Bassett Avenue
Louisville, KY 40204

Second Printing October, 1996
Library of Congress Catalog Card Number: 94-90345
ISBN: 0-9642802-0-5
The author and publisher gratefully acknowledge The Courier-Journal in which versions of these essays first appeared. Some chapters reprinted with permission of The Courier-Journal.

Book Design by Julie Breeding, Plaschke Design Group
Cover Photo by Marian Klein Koehler
Printed in the United States of America

Acknowledgments

In memory of Mary Helen Byck, whose wildflowers are my reminder of the things we don't forget.

When Anna Quindlen was writing her "Life in the Thirties" column for The New York Times features section, her husband once asked if she could get up and get him a beer without writing about it. His point is well taken: It's not easy living with (or near) a newspaper columnist. It requires tolerance and deserves recognition.

Foremost, I want to thank my husband Ken Shapero for his sense of humor, his ingenuity and wise counsel, his energy, honesty and courage. I am grateful also to Josh, our son, for teaching me the essentials of origami, rock collecting, ghost literature, insect life and, most of all, love.

Thanks to Ken's extended family and mine (especially my father Vince Aprile and my brothers Vince and Kevin) for putting up with my interpretation of our collective lives, and to all my friends (Kate Adamek and Mary Lou Hess in particular) for their encouragement and patience.

I wish to thank my readers: Your hunger for commentary by and about women and your willingness to speak up inspire me. You are the people I won't forget. I also owe my writing students a debt of gratitude for reminding me that sharing our stories is always a risk worth taking.

I am deeply grateful to the publisher of The Courier-Journal; to the editors who have shown continuing commitment to my columns in the Sunday features section; and to the colleagues who have given me vital feedback and support.

Brother Raphael Prendergast first suggested collecting my columns in a book. Thanks to him and the Abbey of Gethsemani for giving me a place to stay and rest a while.

Writing a column is a one-woman venture. Creating a book is teamwork. I thank Paul Plaschke, Julie Breeding and Scott Kelien of the Plaschke Design Group for their creativity, talent and flexibility, and Arlene Jacobson for her keen eye and enthusiasm while editing this book.

I am forever grateful for the blessing of a gentle father and a mother who taught me how to find the truth in poetry and the poetry in truth. Her instruction has shaped my writing and my life.

Finally, I thank Lucy and Jack Shapero: Jack for his trust in me and his generous heart; Lucy for the priceless gifts of her experience, her shoulder to cry on and her unconditional affection. Without them, this book would not exist.

For Ken

"I hope to risk things all my life."
—E.M. Forster
Howards End

Contents

Foreword

Change is the theme that weaves its way through the pages of this book. As a journalist, I am drawn to writing about change at its most elemental—birth, death, the way strong winds transform a landscape—as well as at its most political—shifts in our attitudes about homeless people, cigarette smoking, poetry, race relations, fatherhood, physical fitness, breast cancer, letter-writing, women's work.

To me, the most powerful way to convey change is through stories of personal experience: my own and other people's. Stories make sense of change.

The columns in this book reflect my concerns as a feminist, a mother, a wife, a friend and a hometown journalist. The opening chapter is a collection of personal essays written from 1986 to 1992, during my years as a staff writer for The Courier-Journal. After I left my job there, I began writing a weekly free-lance column that appears on Sundays in The Courier features section.

The remaining chapters of the book are drawn from those columns.

Though I have made some revisions, I have not updated the columns. Some of those whom I have written about have moved away, taken new jobs, retired, resigned, remarried. Some have died. But their stories remain unchanged. In this way, the columns remind me of photographs in a family album. Snapshots. Landscapes. Portraits of special people.

Views from real life.

Dianne Aprile
September, 1994

The Things
We Don't
Forget

Snapshots

(1986-1992)

A Door Closed

What I remember most about the incident was the door closing, closing, closing—as if in slow motion, canceling out my mother's face.

The last glimpse I got of her, she was standing, stricken, alone in the school hallway, perhaps on the verge of tears herself, trying hard to lie convincingly to her only daughter, a weepy puddle of 6-year-old misery shrouded in parochial-school blue and white. I was standing on the other side of that slowly closing door, in a classroom jammed with tiny wood-and-metal desks and rioting first-grade boys and girls, all of them grabbing, pushing, yelling and—what mystifies me most—looking truly thrilled to be there.

I was not thrilled to be there.

This was the first day of my school career, and I wanted more than anything to be back home in the quiet comfort of our little brick house on the outskirts of St. Matthews, where my mother rarely was farther than a shout away.

In those preschool days, I never really had to vie for her attention. She was a housewife who didn't believe in leaving children with babysitters, and my only sibling rival was already enlisted in first grade by the time I was old enough to sit up and take notice. The next child, another brother, wasn't to arrive for five more years. In my innocence, I never dreamed this cozy situation could change.

Until that day in September, 1955.

The morning started inauspiciously, with me bolting at the sight of the big double doors of Our Lady of Lourdes School, and my father trying desperately to lure me up the stairs to the first-grade classroom where a soft-spoken nun named Sister Rosaire ran the show. When the tears started, my Dad despaired and drove me back across Breckenridge Lane, down the gravel side streets, home to Mom.

My mother was plenty insecure about a lot of things, but motherhood was never among them. She simply followed her instincts. A ravenous and indiscriminate reader of everything from Emily Dickinson to The National Enquirer, she nevertheless liked to boast that she never cracked the pages of a child-care book and reserved her most scornful tones for those who did. My mother felt about Dr. Spock fans the way other mothers felt about Betty Crocker cake mixes: If you couldn't raise a child from scratch, you ought to forget it.

This was a woman who didn't buy into theories like separation anxiety and school phobia. Faced with an obstinate little girl who refused to attend her first day of classes, she simply did what she knew how to do best. She sympathized, cuddled, cajoled, encouraged, debated, threatened and—finally—hammered out a deal with me. If I would just walk back to school with her and stay the morning, she would return at lunchtime.

A fair enough deal, I thought, feeling a little braver as we trotted out the door. But once back in the classroom, the good sister swiftly—and secretly—negotiated her own deal with my mother. While I was busy keeping a cautious eye on my classmates, she convinced Mom that returning for lunch would only disrupt whatever adjustment, however tenuous, I might have made by that time.

Mom, having sized up Sister Rosaire as a decent soul, trusted her instincts and said goodbye. The door closed slowly. And first grade began. When lunchtime finally rolled around and Mom didn't show, Sister Rosaire took me aside and gently, but firmly, explained the awful truth.

I was going to have to make it without my mother, that was clear. But I was not thrilled about it.

Somehow I survived that day, and the days that followed. It has now become a memory, safe to think about and talk about and even write about.

But sometimes, at key moments in my life, that memory comes back in a flash and I can feel the same hot tears and panic I felt then. A year ago, when I left my then 1-year-old son for his first full day at his day-care center, torn with doubt and confusion about whether I was doing the right thing and secretly worrying about what my mother (who didn't even believe in babysitters) would have said about this, I suddenly realized how painful it must have been for her that September morning.

She knew she wasn't coming back when she said goodbye. She knew it was the first of many separations between us, both real and symbolic, the first of many farewells, some more wrenching than others.

My mother died eight years ago, just before dawn on what turned out to be a beautiful, bright yellow October day. I was with her when she drew her last, labored breath. I remember thinking, the door is closing again. And I am not thrilled to be here.

August 23, 1986

The Next Best Thing

Why is it that everybody makes the same crack when they stumble on a baby-in-the-bathtub shot while dutifully shuffling through snapshots of somebody else's kids?

Hang on to this one, they chortle, so you can haul it out the first time he brings home a girl.

Personally, if I should ever want to give someone a behind-the-scenes glimpse of my son, Josh, I won't have to resort to embarrassing old photos. I've got something much more revealing.

I'll exhume his toddler "report cards," the rectangular strips of pink and green paper his day-care teachers scrupulously fill out each day and I eagerly collect every afternoon.

At a time when math flashcards are fast replacing Winnie-the-Pooh mobiles as the yuppie crib toy of choice, you probably assume that Josh's daily reports are pint-sized versions of the real thing, complete with letter grades assigned to key subjects—A in block building, B in pudding painting, an Incomplete in potty training.

Far from it. The primary purpose of these "care-giver sheets," as they're officially called, is to give my husband and me basic information: how much ravioli our 2½-year-old scarfed down at lunch; whether he spent the day grumpy or sneezy or bashful or sleepy; how long he napped; and that most vital of statistics, how well and how frequently his bowels performed.

But at our house these scraps of colored paper chronicling the past 20 months of Josh's life are most valued for the "comments" section at the bottom. That's the part our eyes focus on first, the reason we display them day by day on the refrigerator door.

Scrawled in a hurry by busy teachers, these hand-written messages are our link to Josh's 9-to-5 weekday world. At the end of a long day without him, the notes give us a quick fix on what his day was like—the silly moments ("he pretended to be an airplane most of the day"), the poignant ones ("just wanted to be held") and the ones we're just as glad we missed ("couldn't get him to do anything without saying NO and starting to cry").

No question, these makeshift memoirs will offer a more interesting peek into Josh's past than any snap-shot would.

In fact, I can see how they might prove edifying to some future girlfriend. A young lady of non-violent bent, for example, might be dismayed, as I was, to learn that on a December day in 1985 "Josh did a lot of pushing...He's finally deciding to defend himself. I guess that's good?"

And like me, she might be heartened by a report last month showing a more rational approach to self-defense on Josh's part: "He did get hit in the head today with a (toy) hammer while playing…He used his words very well as he told the other child how he felt about what he did."

Atta boy!

On the other hand, for good measure, I might share with her one of my all-time favorite comments, appreciated as much for its vivid imagery as for the writer's judicious use of humor to get her point across.

"By the way, is Josh taking tap-dancing lessons? He's stomping his feet an awful lot these days. At me, of course, when I ask him to do something. (Smile.)"

One of the dozens of child-care books I committed to memory when I was pregnant urged parents to keep a daily record of their infant's activities. You'll be sorry if you don't, the author warned.

I liked the idea of documenting my baby's childhood. I imagined myself at the end of each exhilarating day of new parenthood, sitting by the crib, scribbling charming anecdotes into a baby book.

Then Josh was born, and my scribbles were suddenly limited to grocery lists on the backs of envelopes. By the time most evenings rolled around, I had a tough time remembering whether there had been any charming anecdotes, let alone summoning the energy to put them on paper.

A year passed. My leave of absence from work ended, and so did my opportunities for chronicling

Josh's everyday habits. He enrolled in a day-care center in our neighborhood; I went back to my job.

That's when I first found out about report cards for babies.

Like coolers filled with bottles of frozen breast milk, they are a phenomenon of our working-mother culture and its sidekick, the infant/toddler day-care center. A mother can't quiz her 6-week-old infant about how the day went, and it's out of the question to expect a personal consultation with his caregiver every afternoon.

Not all centers provide parents with these daily accounts; some do it weekly, some not at all. It's not a legal requirement, the way posting the daily menu is.

Maybe it ought to be. For starters, reports sometimes help clear up mysteries. Like the afternoon Josh was wearing someone else's clothes when I picked him up. The note explained: "Josh has on Tyler's pants. He got Cream of Wheat all over his at breakfast."

(Don't worry about Tyler. It was a "spare pair" from Tyler's cubby that Josh was wearing.)

Different teachers tackle the job in different ways, of course, with some limiting their comments to a line or two about games and activities while others write copiously about fears and joys and friendships, covering both sides of the paper and maybe even an extra sheet stapled to the back.

My husband says he likes Josh's reports for their comic value, and he finds humor as much in what's left out as in what's included. For example:

"Joshua loved helping make pudding. He was in fact the only one that slyly put his whole fist in the bowl.

We talked about things that are brown."

I appreciate the humor, knowing that it's a commodity often hard to come by when you're coping with kids all day. I marvel at the enthusiasm that goes into those notes, realizing there's so much competition for time and energy.

If I ever want to get back to that baby book and fill in the gaps, I have plenty of good material. Sometimes when I reread the reports, I am amazed at how much intense emotion and complex behavior have been distilled into a few spare, straightforward sentences.

As the pink and green sheets slowly take over my kitchen, piling up in drawers, sliding off shelves, I often vow to throw them out, but I can't. Instead, I pull one out, randomly, and read a line or two from it:

October 13, 1986: "Josh had a good day. Very active and happy. Didn't eat much at meals because he just couldn't keep still long enough…We sat outside on the steps this morning and watched cars and buses go by."

I think to myself this is not the same as being there. And then I carefully tuck the slip of paper back into its pile, knowing it's the next best thing.

October 23, 1986

Fear Of Flying

The basic dream is always the same. I'm outdoors. I look up and note an airplane in trouble. It's weaving or pitching or, worse, not moving at all. Suddenly, I sense the plane is going to fall out of the sky. I start running to get out of its path. The plane lurches violently, takes a sharp nose dive and, right before my eyes, plunges to earth.

In the dream, I always get away. I walk off feeling charmed, blessed, lucky as hell.

This scenario has been a part of my nighttime repertoire for 20 years. Long before my husband took up flying as a hobby. Long before his bedtime reading turned to postmortems of air disasters published in aviation journals. Long before we bought a house in a neighborhood whose skies are crisscrossed by airliners en route to and from Standiford Field.

And most amazing of all, long before I ever felt afraid to fly.

That's right, afraid to fly.

My name is Dianne, and I am an aviaphobe.

Unlike my dream, I am not obsessed with a fear of falling planes. What I worry about is being *on* a plane when it self-destructs. When it fails to gain speed on takeoff and shatters into a zillion pieces. When it over-shoots the runway on landing and erupts in flames. Or, my worst nightmare, when it collides in midair with another plane.

This anxiety probably doesn't qualify as a full-fledged phobia. I don't hyperventilate or black out or even sweat inordinately on planes. I don't take the Greyhound to Boston. I don't cancel flights at the last minute. I can still fly, and I do.

But now I hear this nasty little voice nagging me whenever I purchase a plane ticket: Is this the flight? Is this the one?

I used to be fearless about flying. I loved the adventure, the escape, the amazing perspective you could achieve nowhere else but six miles up.

I was the type who could hop across the Rockies in a 10-seater commuter plane, gazing out the window at the mountain peaks that looked close enough to touch, oblivious to the guys across the aisle sucking nervously at their oxygen. I had flown in two-seaters, helicopters and Third World airlines, all without a moment's hesitation.

Then, shortly after the birth of our son, the first symptoms surfaced. I worried for weeks before our first family vacation, a flight to Florida. Would the weather be bad? What about wind shear? Would the ground crews remember to de-ice the wings? Did the plane we were flying have a good safety record?

Other classic symptoms followed: the ability to spot a headline about an air crash at 20 feet and a corresponding compulsion to devour every detail.

There are ironies to my story. My husband started flying at my urging. He always wanted to get his pilot's license but didn't begin lessons until I encouraged him to during my pregnancy.

Before I knew it, my son, too, was an aviation fanatic, a kid who couldn't pass I-64 and Cannons Lane without demanding to stop and see the planes at Bowman Field. I guess I realized I was in big trouble when, at the age of 3, he corrected a day-care teacher when she pointed out the "steam" coming from an overhead jet.

"That's not steam!" he explained. "That's a vapor trail."

I can't speak for the other 25 million Americans whom the airline industry calls "fearful fliers," but I have my own theory about what triggered my anxiety.

And it fits right in with the analyses of a couple of colleagues who also get clammy at the thought of flying.

One reporter who had to make some 30 flights while investigating the Arrow Air crash, including numerous trips to Fort Campbell, Ky., in a single-engine plane, believes his fear of flying has grown as he's become more confident in himself and the direction his life has taken.

Why should he court disaster when things are

working out so well? Why risk everything for a quick trip through the clouds?

Another writer traces her flying fears back to the birth of her daughter eight years ago. She can't explain the link. Call it what you want: greater responsibilities, love, commitment, the recognition of one's mortality.

For me, it's all that and then some. Like a plane falling out of the sky for no apparent reason, much of what happens in life seems out of our control, capricious. That's the scary part of my dream—and what gives me the jitters when I hand over my boarding pass.

The fuller and richer life gets, the more vulnerable it sometimes feels. A satisfying job, a strong friendship, a good marriage, a child. The more value we assign to each of them, the less willing we sometimes are to tolerate the thought of losing them.

Of course, there's a reassuring message in the dream too. I invariably get out of the way of the falling plane just in time. One can shift course, change, grow. And that's why I keep flying. I can change. I don't have to stand still while fear does me in.

In the meantime, I no longer sit by the window. Instead I sit on the aisle, hiding in a book or a magazine. I no longer cavalierly tune out the flight attendant's safety instructions. Now I read the plastic card diligently, making mental notes regarding emergency exits and flotation gear. And I rarely drink: I want a clear head if there's a chance of survival when we go down.

When we land safely, I often think of photographs of the pope, bending down, kissing the tarmac where he's just arrived. It's a nice gesture. Someday I might try it myself. But for now, I just walk off feeling charmed, blessed, lucky as hell.

April 5, 1987

The Good Mother

The first Mother's Day I remember was May 12, 1957. I was 8 years old and making my First Communion. The dress I wore was white organdy embroidered with tiny roses, which my mother carefully starched and ironed so stiff that the skirt stood out like an open umbrella.

Weeks earlier, we had taken a bus downtown and tried on what seemed like every white dress that came in Size 6X. I fell in love with the first one I saw. My mother loved it, too, but she wanted to keep looking, to check out the other possibilities, to make sure there wasn't another dress somewhere that might make me even happier.

At the end of the day, exhausted and empty-handed, she dragged me back to the store where we had begun our quest and, laughing at her own stubbornness, bought the dress we both had wanted from the start.

Now that I'm a mother, this memory makes sense to

me. Because I know now what I didn't know then: Being a mother means feeling you can never do enough.

Mothers feel this way, at least in part, because that's the message they get wherever they turn.

A mother who stays home with her toddler fears her child isn't learning to get along with other kids the way day-care children do. She read that in a magazine. She also worries her daughter will grow up thinking only daddies work in offices. She heard that on a talk show.

The mother who holds a job outside the home feels guilty about not being home in the afternoons when her children's pals come over. She read a newspaper article about the dangers of hanging out with the wrong peer group. She also wonders if her baby will grow up cold and unloving because she's not there for him when he's sick during the day. She remembers a chapter on that back in high school psych class.

No matter how many definitions of mother a woman fulfills—teacher, playmate, comforter, chauffeur—there are that many more she *wants* to meet. Or believes she *must* meet in order not to jeopardize her child's chances for a good life.

Though I haven't yet felt the urge to purchase the perfect pair of overalls for my 3-year-old son, I understand my mother's compulsion to find not just an adequate dress for that special occasion but the best dress available. Is that so different, after all, from my own compulsion during pregnancy to give up all coffee— even that first little cup of decaf in the morning?

Whether searching for answers to a little boy's sleep

problems or planning a birthday party that will make the day magical, I know what it's like to doubt your gut choice—to feel compelled to look further, check out all the possibilities and occasionally return to square one.

Other mothers tell me it's the same with them. One spent weeks sitting in on preschool programs before feeling comfortable choosing one. Another uses her lunchtime to buy posters for her child's room at a day-care center to make sure the hours he spends without her are fun and stimulating.

I don't think it's hormones or guilt or Type-A Super-Momism at work here, generating a need to constantly measure up. I believe it's a natural response to growing up female in a culture that believes Blaming Mom is the answer to any social problem and many mental illnesses.

Consider the public's response to the courtroom battle between Mary Beth Whitehead and Elizabeth Stern for the custody of Baby M. Lawyers, therapists, social commentators and men-on-the-street all felt qualified—no, *entitled*—to judge one or the other, or both, of these women unfit to be a mother.

Such arrogance. Why?

Perhaps having each had one of our own, we all consider ourselves experts on mothers. Or maybe it's that Finding Fault with Mom has become second nature in our society, not only the basis for much of our psychological research on infant development, but an accepted and even fashionable national pastime.

During the Baby M trial, we heard experts pick apart each woman's reasons for wanting a baby, her way of handling Baby M, her sense of self-esteem and confidence. Was Mary Beth unworthy because she didn't cuddle the correct way or play the right baby games? Or was Elizabeth the bad mother for putting off pregnancy for a career and then later refusing to risk her health to conceive a child?

Are we getting carried away here?

If it's not a psychotherapist on a talk show, it's probably your neighbor raking you over the coals for buying your toddler a GI Joe or for leaving your teen-agers alone when you go to a movie on the weekend.

Consider the results of a nationwide random sampling of middle-class Americans conducted last fall for Better Homes and Gardens magazine by the Opinion Research Corp. of Princeton, N.J.:

Nearly three-fourths of the 2,000 participants were critical of other parents for not spending enough time with their children, and half complained that other parents generally shirked their responsibilities. Ninety percent of those who gave their opinions were mothers.

While I don't have data to back it up, I think it's a safe bet most of them were talking about other mothers—not fathers. With that many of us picking on each other, no wonder mothers today often feel overwhelmed, isolated and inadequate.

No amount of Mother's Day lilies and chocolate truffles can gloss over the fact that, other than on the second Sunday in May, mothers today get blamed for most things that go wrong in a family. Over the years, mothering has been cited—incorrectly—as the cause of numerous mental disorders from schizophrenia, autism and manic-depression to hyperactivity and homicidal transsexualism.

Psychologist Paula J. Caplan, head of Toronto's Center for Women's Studies in Education, reviewed a wide range of clinical mental health journals between 1970 and 1982 to see if the women's movement had resulted in a decline in Mother-Blaming research.

Not a chance.

Instead she concluded the practice continues in "epidemic proportions." In the 125 articles she studied, mothers were held responsible for 72 kinds of psychological disorders in children.

So how do women come up with their definitions of "good mother"?

One friend says she finds herself incorporating the best qualities of every mother she gets to know into her own definition. What she ends up with is an order too tall for any one person to fill.

My own definition is much the same—a combination of what I've read, heard, seen, been told and what I feel in my gut. Part of it I picked up from my mother, whose one inflexible rule of child rearing was "Love your children. Everything else will come naturally."

Sometimes when I need reassurance, I think of her words and feel comforted. It sounds like a simplistic philosophy. But it worked.

As a child, I never doubted her love. Why now should I doubt her advice?

May 10, 1987

2 Good 2 Be 4 Gotten:
The Class Of '67

A crescent moon, a lilting tune,
  a prayer that soars above,
Your daughters sing while vistas ring
  to honor the school we love.

We were three months into our high school careers, just getting to know one another, when the first shoe dropped. Rushing out from P.E. class on a blustery Friday afternoon, sprinting to English class from the old gym located on one side of the Ursuline campus to the brand-new classroom building on the other, we were stunned to hear the news shouted our way.

The president was shot.

We were Catholic girls, 14 years old, most of us fresh from neighborhood parochial schools, full of dreams, ideals and the promise of a safe, hopeful world in which to live.

And why not? Our church had recently flung open

its windows, in the words of its spiritual leader, to welcome the winds of change. Our nation had laid to rest a longstanding religious barrier and elected a young Catholic man to its highest office. Our new school was giving us the first glimpse of what women could do on their own—run a school, the whole shebang, from superintendent and principal to calculus teacher, basketball coach and science-club moderator. Here, at Sacred Heart Academy, our class officers, star athletes, chemistry-class whiz kids and state-champ debaters were all—get this—girls.

Everything was possible.

Then came the assassination of the president, the first challenge to our optimism and a sign that the world beyond our woodsy Lexington Road campus was not as peaceful as we imagined.

By the time we graduated in 1967, the whole world seemed to be in the throes of an adolescent identity crisis, not so different from our own. The chaos we felt within ourselves as teen-agers seemed to echo the turmoil in our culture, in our church and in the role young women were expected to play within both. Though we were too busy growing up to notice it, the rules we had started out with no longer applied.

By that day in May when we traded our threadbare uniforms for white caps and gowns, the Beatles' claim to greater popularity than Jesus no longer seemed shocking. Nuns and priests were leaving their religious orders in record numbers. The Pill was routinely stocked on drugstore shelves. The women's movement was bursting through the all-male doorways of Harvard, Yale,

Cornell. The Summer of Love was about to begin.

And the Vietnam War, for so long just another clipping in current-events class, was as real as the boy next door.

Dear Sacred Heart, school of my heart,
Lovely the virtues that set you apart.

I took a video camera to my 20th high school reunion a couple of weeks ago. The idea of taping my old classmates, live and in color, as they reminisced about the agony and ecstasy of Catholic girls' education in the swinging '60s, and then playing it back again and again on a television screen—well, it was an image I couldn't resist.

After all, this coming together of girlhood chums was about change, right?

About the evolution from our adolescence, which most of us Catholic schoolgirls experienced as one long exercise in delayed gratification, to our middle age in an era whose trademark very well could be the VCR and that most immediate of gratifications, the instant replay.

So I took the video camera to the country-club luncheon and trained it on 38-year-old women who, despite the gray hairs and the lines around the eyes, still seemed 16 to me. I asked them questions. They gave me answers.

Later, back home, I replayed the 20 minutes of jumpy videotape for myself and a former classmate who lives in Chicago. We hooted at the stories people told and marveled at the way so many personalities seemed untouched by time.

But one image stood out.

It is a close-up of someone from my freshman home-room, now an out-of-towner, answering my question about what she remembers most from our first year of high school.

"Laughter," she says. "Fun."

She glances away for a second, and you wonder, "What's she thinking about?" Then she looks back at the camera and with a bemused, almost wistful expression, says, "I'd like to go back."

I remember the laughter too.

But I also remember other things. Like friendships so intense they hurt, so special I thought they would last forever and which—granted, in a different way than I expected—have.

Still, I'm not sure I would want to go back. Even for a moment. I like the memory as it sits in my mind today: a picture grown fuzzy with age, the disappointments and awkwardness of adolescence worn smooth by the passage of time. We talked about that at the reunion. At a 10-year reunion, you're just getting started in life, still proving yourself, eager to present a successful image that will erase the insecurities of the past. But 20 years give you perspective. The worst memories of adolescence fade, while the best move into sharper focus.

It hasn't always been that way.

There was a time when I looked back and regretted having spent four years in an all-girls school, stuck in an unflattering uniform, socially blockaded from the opposite sex, instructed by women who lived together in a locked-up wing of the school that was off-limits to students.

This was about the same time I thought my mother was ridiculous for devoting herself to raising my brothers and me. Eventually, I recovered from both notions.

A friend I work with recently told me she used to look at Catholic girls, as they walked home from school together in their look-alike uniforms, and think sadly of how they were being stripped of their individuality, forced to conform. But I look at those blue-and-white outfits today as a noble effort to minimize the differences between girls who could afford to dress in the latest fashions and those who couldn't. Besides, how were our uniforms of oxford cloth and wool so different from the ones of madras and chino that reigned supreme at coed schools?

And isn't learning to look beneath the surface for one's individuality, beyond clothes and cars, a major part of the work of being a teen-ager?

I had lunch with a former classmate the day after our reunion. Though she long ago stopped following the letter of the church's law, she says what she learned about values and ethics in Catholic schools has served her well. That's why she sent her children to them too.

"They were good basic rules to live by," she says. "They never got me in any trouble."

For us you've striven, to us you've given,
Courage and joy and our shining start.

Sacred Heart had an academic-track system in those days, and I began as a freshman in a group known as the "top class." We spent our first year together in Homeroom 309, under the tutelage of Sister Mary Olga, and for the most part, we ended up in the same classes year after year.

Despite the school's despised nickname, Snob Hill Academy, we were solidly middle-class kids who hailed from a mix of old city neighborhoods and newer suburbs in eastern Jefferson County.

Sister Olga loved Peanuts cartoons and us, even after the day we were threatened with expulsion for passing around a primitive questionnaire, known as the "purity test," designed to measure our sexual expertise. The expectations for our homeroom were high; the standards nearly inflexible; the pressures ever-present.

Like siblings in a big family, we were intensely loyal to one another but competed like crazy. Before each test, we prayed to heaven for guidance. Then fought like hell to outscore each other.

What I did not value until much later was the social experience. In my 20s, the oddity of an all-girls Catholic education was something to rebel against, to joke about, to reserve for shock value or comic relief. We had to take ballet freshman year, for pity's sake, and if our hemlines didn't touch the floor when we were asked to kneel down for a spot check, we were in big trouble.

Everybody's heard the stereotypes of nun-run Catholic education. The hilarious stories of straight-laced sisters warning impressionable girls about the dangers of patent-leather shoes reflecting up. Or the horror tales of rulers wielded in the name of God.

In reality, I was taught by Ursuline sisters for 12 years, and I cannot recall a single mention of shoes— other than a suggestion that our well-worn Weejuns could use a shine. And no one ever raised a hand to me.

I'm afraid the image I carry with me today has little in common with Sister Mary Ignatius, the fanatical nun caricature in Christopher Durang's satire about growing up Catholic. Yet I suspect my recollection is, in its own way, as oversimplified and one-dimensional as the playwright's.

What I remember are women who were well-educated, self-confident, strong-willed individuals. Dedicated career women. They belonged to a woman's association that had been around since the 1500s, the first Catholic order established for the purpose of educating young women. Unlike most of our mothers, the nuns did not depend on men, financially or socially. Instead of chasing after children, they spent their summers working on advanced degrees, writing papers, doing research at far-away campuses.

How many other teen-age girls, in the mid-'60s, had that kind of role model?

Their motto was simple: "Those who instruct many unto justice shall shine as stars for all eternity."

Some took that promise more seriously than others.

One of my favorite memories is the time our plucky government teacher led a group of us downtown, placards in hand, to march in favor of a controversial open-housing ordinance before the Board of Aldermen.

Another special teacher taught a few of us a creative-writing course one summer. I can remember sitting on the school lawn every morning for weeks, we girls in our Bermudas and round-collared blouses and Sister in her black-and-white habit, all of us writing our hearts out.

Both these women left the order before I finished college—an indication that their lives were not so fulfilling as I wished to believe.

Other nuns remained in the order. They took back their real names, put on regular clothes, moved away, changed jobs. At the reunion, someone reported that our senior English teacher, a bright, poised, open-minded nun who expected and inspired our best, was in Guatemala, training for her stint as a Witness for Peace in Nicaragua.

I wasn't surprised to hear it. What she taught us was to think for ourselves, to ask questions, to speak out.

Most of our teachers were nuns—but not all. There were other women on the faculty, some married, some mothers, some not. The best of them, like the biology teacher who's still there, taught us the joy that comes with accomplishment. The only men were a handful of priests who came in from their parishes to lecture in religion classes.

Of course, you could argue that what we received in the way of early feminist training was more than offset by the absence of the opposite sex. School rules banned boys from even picking us up in the parking lot after school. Certainly we mourned not having them around at times, particularly when our school dances rolled around and we found ourselves in short supply of guys to invite.

But on a day-to-day basis, it was no big deal. Like wearing uniforms, the absence of boys was eventually accepted as a convenience. One less thing to worry about. One less distraction. Not that we weren't as obsessed as any other group of adolescent girls.

It is just that, in the classroom or on the basketball court, we were never tempted to defer to boys as keener intellects or superior athletes. I recall, years later, finding it humorous when girls' athletics made the big time in coed schools. It took a federal law to put it on a par with boys' sports—but hey that's OK.

It's true I missed out on the possibility of developing good, close, non-romantic friendships with boys in high school because I wasn't hanging out with them day to day. And true, I didn't learn to compete with them, *mano a womano*. But in the '60s that was hardly what the "real world" was about anyway.

Today, in a society where women can and do compete daily with men, you could argue that single-sex education is an anachronism, a throwback, an artifact from a best-forgotten era. Or you could ask yourself, "What's wrong with first learning what you can do on your own, then tackling the 'real world' armed with that knowledge?"

Loving you so, onward we go,
Setting the hearthfires and tapers aglow.

It happened more than half our lives ago. The

hockey games at Seneca Park. The Sunday night mixers in the Trinity High School cafeteria. The term papers. The proms. The graduation parties.

What happened in the course of the last 20 years is what you would expect: part triumph, part tragedy. Lots of children, lots of divorces, lots of remarriages.

In different ways, we each made peace with our common religious background. The place where I've settled is far from where I started out in terms of religious geography, though I guess you never leave your hometown totally behind. That's especially true if it was through learning the lay of the land there that you cultivated your own internal landscape of ethics and values.

Unlike classes before ours, the Class of 1967 did not produce an Ursuline sister, a sign of the times more than a repudiation of the individuals we knew. The class of 198 women did produce a child psychiatrist, a fertility specialist, a college financial administrator, a psychologist, an opera singer, a caterer, a dental hygienist, a flight instructor, several lawyers, small-business owners, social workers, nursing directors, landscape designers, secretaries, artists and teachers of every stripe. And an abundance of homemakers.

At the reunion, two women showed up pregnant, one for the first time. One extremely fit-looking woman showed off a portrait of her five sons—the oldest 19, the youngest a toddler of 2. Some had no children, either by choice or by fate.

And one arrived wearing the old uniform, still sporting legs worthy of a varsity cheerleader.

But details like these don't begin to tell the stories of people's lives. A carload of doctorates does not a successful class make. Nor do hordes of children or bundles of money. We all knew, as we glanced around the sun-drenched room at the glinting jewelry and designer outfits, that the worst pain and the greatest joy often don't show on the surface.

We learned that long ago, as schoolgirls, struggling awkwardly to find the deeper meaning beneath the surface of a poem, a friendship, a failure.

Not long after we left Sacred Heart, one of our classmates died in a car accident. I still think of Diane the way she looks in her senior picture—blonde, pretty, big smile. Her mother called me a little while before the reunion, asking if I'd take some pictures for her.

She said she wanted to see what we looked like today, how we had changed.

> *Fling we our colors to brighten the sky,*
> *daring to try, hearts beating high.*
> *We shall remember and love you,*
> *we vow, ever as now,*
> *dear Sacred Heart.*

Maggie and Jackie came to my house the day after the reunion. We ordered in pizza and, over beer and Cokes, picked through boxes of dusty photographs, old student handbooks and wrinkled notes passed 20 years ago in some forgotten religion or history class.

"Di, I'm kind of mixed up! I feel awful!...Call me tonight."

A rusty French Club pin, a yellowed tassel, a term paper analyzing the women characters of Tennessee Williams. A senior-prom dance card with a tiny white pencil dangling on a cord, the song title "Almost There" printed in script on the back, "Barefootin'" and "Midnight Hour" scribbled inside.

They were amazed that I kept this stuff. I was amazed they didn't.

Surely they knew then that someday, somewhere, on the floor of somebody's den, we'd be together again, trying to figure out what made those years so intense, so memorable.

Was it the secrets we shared? The absence of guys? The fact that we were somehow different, set apart, a bit of a mystery to our public-school friends? And to ourselves?

Maybe it was simply this: From our protected place in the eye of the storm that was about to touch down and rearrange the world, things looked calm and peaceful.

Who wouldn't cherish times like those?

August 8, 1987

Moving
Experiences

It'll be two years this month. Our second anniversary together. Though I am finally relaxing and letting go, I'll be the first to admit I was a little gun-shy about making a commitment.

I've been hurt before.

Most recently by a tall, dark Victorian type whose Old World charm won my heart in no time. I still think about the three wonderful years we shared. The summer nights on the patio. The moonlight filtering through the bedroom shutters. Moving in was easy. Packing up and saying goodbye was agony.

I loved that house.

That's right, house. The passionate ties I'm talking about are the kind I develop with places of residence—apartments, houses, condos.

When it comes to taking possession of real estate, I'm the kind of big-time bonder who makes Shakespeare's Juliet seem casual about her relationships. When I move into a place, I put down roots that a summer of '87 windstorm would have trouble unearthing.

As a result, I hate moving.

I used to think it was a reaction to the time and energy it takes to sort through and pack up the accumulated belongings of a lifetime. Or else I dismissed it as a distaste for spending good money on utility-company deposits, phone hookups, new checks and mortgage points.

But my last move proved that the problem is much more than one of wasted time and energy. It's the emotional expenditure that gets to me.

Moving from the yellow-frame Victorian house where my husband and I watched our son take his first steps triggered an ache down deep, beyond the pocketbooks and the calendar, in the territory of the heart.

For months I suffered withdrawal symptoms, longing for a fix—a glimpse of the stained-glass windows lit by the afternoon sun, or a sip of coffee at the kitchen counter.

The new house, full of other people's memories, suddenly seemed a cold, uncaring stranger. Though we moved a mere quarter-mile away from our old house, I felt that a chunk of my past was gone forever.

This is not a unique reaction.

A friend who moved last summer confided to me at the time that as soon as her bid was accepted on the new house, she became panicky about leaving the old one. She couldn't bear to abandon the site of so many special memories. Never mind that her marriage ended there. What about the hours spent watching the neighborhood kids grow up? She would wake in the middle of the night, in a sweat, thinking, "This is where I brought my baby home from the hospital. This is where the saplings I planted grew into shade trees."

A Realtor once told me it's common, on the eve of a move, for people to suddenly become obsessed with doubt. They worry they paid too much for their new house or they might have done better if they'd only looked around a little longer. There's even a name for it in the biz: "buyers' remorse."

But the anxiety my friend and I felt upon signing our real-estate contracts came from a different source. I call it "sellers' grief." It's not that we regretted moving on to a new place. That was the exhilarating, challenging part. It was that we mourned having to let go of the old place in the process.

Few of us ever begin an affair—whether with a lover, a job or a house—giving any serious thought to how much it might hurt when it ends. We dive in and give it all we've got, assuming we'll be together forever.

A while back I jotted down the words of a woman I was interviewing about gardening. She described a yard she cultivated at a house where she and her ex-husband once lived. It was strange, she said, seeing the garden again years later and finding it had flourished without her.

"At the time," she said, "I thought I'd always live there—you know, the way everybody always does."

There are exceptions, of course; times in your life when you know you won't stay put for long. A woman who moved seven times in five years during the fast-lane stage of her career says she never lived anywhere long enough to get emotionally attached. She learned never to let down her nesting defenses, to always stay at arm's length from her physical surroundings. Today she's settled—married, raising a child and intensely involved with a handsome two-story stucco.

Pop psychologists call the phenomenon the "moving blues" and rank it up there with the biggies on their lists of most-stressful life events. They warn that moving can bring on mild depression, loss of appetite, insomnia, lethargy and guilt. The guilt hits parents hardest. They're the ones who every year uproot and transplant 12 million young people under the age of 20.

By most standards, my parents were stay-putters. We moved only once from the house where I was born, then returned to it 18 months later. I was 4 when we left for Dayton. Over the years I've hung on to a tattered black-and-white snapshot taken by a Louisville neighbor on the day of that first move.

In the foreground, my mother, father and older brother stand stiff and unsmiling. I'm in the background: a tiny figure slumped against the front door of our house, head pressed melodramatically against a raised forearm.

But here's the odd thing: When we moved back to our Louisville house, which we had rented out during our absence, I did not want to leave Dayton. The red brick apartment complex had become my home. There's no photo of that moving day, but I'm sure I was just as unhappy.

I didn't move again until I was 22, several months into my first full-time job. Most parents would have been cheering by this point to have a daughter that age out of the nest. But my mother—who had lived in the same house until she married—wanted to know why in the world I would want to leave home and spend money on a furnished apartment when I had a nice room all to myself upstairs.

That was the last easy move I made. Easy because it was overdue and because I knew I could go back to that house whenever I wished.

In the 16 years since, I've moved five times—each time feeling as if I were losing a dear friend. We had been through so much together, those places and I. When I drive past them now, I don't see bricks or balconies or flowering cherry trees. I see tears and toasts, birthday parties and blossoming friendships, 4 a.m. feedings and infatuations.

In her book "Necessary Losses," Judith Viorst says "losing is the price we pay for living. It is also the source of much of our growth and gain. Making our way from birth to death, we also have to make our way through the pain of giving up and giving up and giving up some portion of what we cherish."

I think houses fit that category.

We've been in ours two years now and already I feel bonded to the woodwork. The wildflowers in the back yard, the front porch swing, the skylight above the third-floor bedroom—each represents cherished moments in my life. I wish, like the woman with the garden, I could believe I will always live there. I don't.

Losing is, indeed, the price of living. I know that, but I don't have to like it.

August 24, 1987

How
I Quit
Smoking

I grew up watching my mother smoke.

I can see her leaning over the gas burner at our kitchen stove, lighting up. I can hear her calling out to me, from whatever room she was in, to fetch her cigarettes and ashtray. I can smell the smoke swirling around her and, if I try very hard, I can even remember how I thought it smelled good because it smelled like her.

The first brand I remember her smoking was Pall Mall. The cigarettes came in a festive red package, lined with silver paper, like a Christmas present. I used to love to fold the shiny paper like an accordion and cut it so I ended up with a row of silver dolls holding hands.

Everybody in my family smoked. My father, my older brother, my uncles and aunts. Only my grandmothers abstained.

I put it off till I was 20. I had taken puffs here and there in high school. But my serious smoking didn't begin until my senior year in college, working on the campus newspaper. We spent long hours in a ratty, old, converted Army barracks, writing, pasting, gluing, chugging black coffee and smoking. A week after graduation, when I reported for my first full-time newspaper job, I carried along a pack of True Blues as a security blanket. It was 1971, and only one person in our office didn't smoke.

From the start, I considered my smoking a temporary habit. Not once did I buy a carton of cigarettes. It was always one pack—the last pack?—at a time. I didn't tell my boyfriend until he noticed the smoke in my clothes and hair. I didn't tell my mother for years. Though she had been my model, I knew it would disappoint her. She wanted to believe I was stronger than she, and I guess I wanted to believe it too.

I smoked mainly at work. I couldn't start a story without lighting up. I couldn't fashion a transition without a drag. I couldn't make it through an interview without a cigarette burning nearby.

In 1973, about the time I hit a two-pack-a-day stride, my mother discovered a lump in her breast. It turned out to be cancer. As my life fell to pieces, I smoked more than ever. At my peak, I was up to three packs a day.

A hospital official once told me he found it heartless to restrict smoking on patient floors—too many nervous visitors, he said. I was one of them: lighting up outside her door, sucking out of my cigarette whatever comfort I could get. At some point, I confessed to her that I smoked. She looked sad and said she understood.

I tried to quit several times after that, without success.

Then on New Year's Eve, 1976, at a party, I came down with a vicious attack of bronchitis. I left the party early, my head on fire and my throat burning. The bronchitis lingered for two weeks. It made me sick to even think of drawing smoke down my throat. It dawned on me that this was my chance. I decided to see if I could extend the two weeks' forced abstinence into a cigarette-free lifetime.

Work was hell. It took me twice as long to write a story. I felt lightheaded. My ears seemed plugged. I had constant headaches. I chewed gum and snacked as I had never done before. I gained weight.

But I stuck with it. After six months, I still craved cigarettes and dreamed about smoking them. On a trip out of the country with a girlfriend, I held an unlit cigarette in my hand after every meal, so as not to feel totally dejected while she enjoyed a smoke.

Eventually, I started noticing the benefits. I'd wake up in the morning without a parched mouth. Or walk up three flights of stairs without huffing, but most of all I felt I had taken some control of my life at a time when nothing seemed dependable anymore.

Sometime later, my mother quit too. She stopped cold-turkey, after more than 35 years. But she never had the chance to enjoy the benefits. She died in 1978.

Perhaps, if we had known we could do without tobacco during the most stressful time of our lives, we would have quit much earlier. I think we undersold ourselves for far too long.

There is an embarrassing old photograph of my younger brother that I run across now and then. He's about a year old, standing in the front seat of our old station wagon, an unlit cigarette dangling from his mouth. I'm sure we thought it was cute at the time, like a child "puffing" on one of those pink-tipped candy cigarettes.

Thank God, things change. Hardly anyone in my family smokes today.

Ironically, my younger brother is the only one who never took it up. Maybe it's because he grew up with a keener appreciation of how fragile life can be. When I was 13, my mother was full of laughter and energy and jokes about how much she smoked. When he was 13, she was dying.

January 3, 1988

All The
Right
Ingredients

One of my favorite holiday traditions is making plum pudding.

And one of the reasons it's so special is that it's not a holdover from my childhood. My mother baked fruit-cakes at Christmas time. My grandmother, the Irish one, made potato dumplings on holidays. And my Italian grandma served up meatballs, whatever the season.

Nobody in my family made plum pudding.

In fact, I grew up thinking of plum pudding—or figgy pudding, as it's called in Christmas carols—as a culinary artifact, a dish that went out with the Cratchit family.

Then, a few years back, while planning a holiday party, I came across a pudding recipe that sounded, oh, slightly exotic. That appealed to me; it was that kind of Christmas. I had inherited my mother's much-loved fruitcake recipe and had ceremoniously baked it each of the two years since she died. But mine never tasted as good as I remembered hers.

It took me longer than it should have to figure out that a key ingredient was missing—her.

Proust knew what he was talking about when he made the connection between the taste and smell of certain foods and the powerful childhood memories they evoke. One bite of a madeleine, and he was magically transported to the old gray house of his youth, happily enjoying Sunday morning tea and cakes with his beloved Aunt Leonie.

But there's something to be said, as well, for a food with no emotional history. One that doesn't take you back anywhere, but lets you stay put in the present, supplying fresh meaning to tastes and smells.

After all, as the holiday-stress experts tell us, we tend to overload this season with our idealized memories of childhood. Too much of a good thing can end up burdening us with unrealistic expectations—and a holiday season doomed to disappointment. Creating new traditions is a good antidote for an overdose of nostalgia.

That particular Christmas I was instinctively ready for something different, for an adventure.

And a pudding recipe that called for grating and chopping mounds of carrots, currants, raisins, dates, pecans, orange peel and just about everything else you can think of but plums, then mixing it with spices and staples like eggs and butter and milk and molasses, then steaming it in a greased pudding mold for hours and hours on top of the stove, then dousing the finished product with brandy and lighting it—well, it seemed to qualify absolutely as adventure.

At the time, I was living alone in a rambling, third-floor apartment on Douglass Boulevard. The place had more windows than I could afford to cover, and the light that filled it in December was warm and bright. The sun room opened into the living room, which flowed into the dining room, creating a great space for a party.

So I invited friends and family for a holiday meal.

With the help of a girlfriend, I somehow whipped that first pudding into shape. We started chopping early in the morning. By the time the pudding was ready to steam, we had earned new respect for the samurai waiters at Benihana.

By the time it was ready to eat, it was dark outside.

But that just added to the drama, making it easier for all to see the blue flames licking up the brandy as I presented the pudding on a silver platter to an appreciative crowd. Topped with hard sauce, it tasted as spectacular as it looked.

A tradition was born.

A few weeks later, at another party, I met a man with a background considerably different from mine. It wasn't until much later, after we started talking marriage, that we discovered that in one critical aspect our childhoods were the same. He, too, had grown up without plum pudding. And he was game to try it.

By the next Christmas, we had set up house together in another old, rambling apartment, this time on Cherokee Road. The living room had French doors that opened to a balcony overlooking a Tudor church.

The place cried out for a celebration. And for a tradition to call our own.

In some ways, making plum pudding together that Christmas was the true beginning of the tradition. The year before had been my trial run, setting the stage for a new holiday script.

Six Christmases have come and gone since then; six plum puddings filling our home with delicious smells. The tradition has survived two more moves, the acquisition of a food processor and the birth of our son, Josh.

Some years we've served our puddings at big, noisy Christmas parties, with kids and grown-ups vying for a view and a taste. Other times, we've shared it with two or three close friends at the coffee table in front of the fireplace. It's a flexible feast; we like it that way.

But what I've come to like most about making plum pudding is the ritual—the way we work side by side in the kitchen, starting early in the morning of the day we serve it. I find a comforting lesson in the way the pudding slowly takes shape. What begins as a cold and formless batter winds up as a festive dessert—solid, warm, satisfying.

Amazing the changes that time, patience and a long, slow simmer can bring about.

As with any ritual, we play our chosen roles. I'm the one who soaks the raisins in sherry the night before. He greases the pudding tin and fills the deepest pot we own with hot water. My job is to spoon the batter into the tin. His is to ease the tin into a rack inside the pot. We take turns fussing with the flame, adjusting it as needed.

And we both sigh with relief and delight, year after

year, when the tin slides effortlessly away from the finished pudding, revealing our fluted masterpiece. No question, the whole of a plum pudding is much more than the sum of its parts.

I still make my mother's fruitcake. But like shopping for a Christmas tree or hanging ornaments saved from childhood, it carries a complicated legacy of memories and expectations.

Plum pudding, on the other hand, is plum pudding. Its history is short and sweet. At least for now, for my husband and me.

Who knows what Josh will think of it, in years to come, when he's in search of adventure and a tradition to call his own. Will he remember the sweet, steamy smells filling the house? The fussing over the flame? Or our delight in tasting what we all worked together to create?

The proof will be in our pudding.

December 11, 1988

In The Beginning

October is a fine and dangerous season...The land is wild with red and gold and crimson, and all the lassitudes of August have seeped out of your blood, and you are full of ambition. It is a wonderful time to begin anything at all.

—*Thomas Merton*

Most mornings we take our time walking to the corner where the school bus stops. Just Josh and me.

Though the land's not exactly wild yet on Bassett Avenue, October is beginning to have its way. We pay attention to little things on our walk; mushrooms huddled in a patch of damp grass; a sudden hail of acorns on the hood of a parked car; squirrels circling a tree trunk in a game of tag—or is it hide-and-seek?

At the corner, we wait patiently until we hear the first distant squeal of brakes.

"Here comes Barney," one of us says, and we start counting. We know just how many squeals it will take

48

before Barney's bus pulls up to our corner.

We enjoy this new routine. We like standing on the corner, watching the pattern of the school-day morning unfold, like the accordion door on Barney's bus—opening us up to a fresh perspective on life.

Some days Josh wears a cardboard mask to the bus stop. He keeps it on just long enough to get Barney's reaction, then he hands it over to me, his prop mistress, and climbs blithely aboard Bus 8823.

Some days Josh is a dragon. Some days, a lion or a skeleton or a monster. I marvel at his moxie and fall in love with Barney for the way he smiles patiently and ruffles Josh's hair as he passes.

I try to keep my eyes on that mop of hair when the yellow door squeezes shut and Barney lurches off to his next stop. I watch it bounce just above the seat line as Josh travels down the aisle to the back of the bus. I wave at him madly, though he is all too quickly caught up in this other world to notice me. Only the older kids watch my hands flapping in the air, and none of them waves back.

I didn't think it would be like this.

Back-to-school, I'm here to say, is much more than a retailer's gimmick, a way to sell Crayolas and Thermos bottles and Ninja Turtle backpacks.

It's more than the end of summer.

Back-to-school is a beginning. It's a ritual, a cultural rite of passage and as natural a sign of the start of fall as the discovery of that first cache of leaves curled in a corner of your front porch.

Merton was right. There is something paradoxical—both fine and dangerous—about this season and the promise it holds out to children and grown-ups alike: knowledge, friendship, endless possibilities, a second chance.

Whether it begins with a bus ride or a walk to a neighborhood classroom, the start of school is more than a physical journey. For adults, especially, it is a spiritual trip too.

For kids, school is life. Opening day, they go live it. But for the rest of us, this rite of autumn consists of equal parts memory and great expectations—an uneasy alliance at best. We've been there, after all, and we want better this time around.

A pediatrician I know puts it another way: The mothers who worry most about their daughters' chewed-up fingernails are the ones who still gnaw at their own.

The first day of school this year, as I stood on the sidewalk with my husband and my next-door neighbor wondering how I could possibly have put my only son on a bus with a bunch of strangers—a concept that seemed perfectly reasonable before those yellow doors swallowed him up—I suddenly heard someone shouting my name. I looked behind the bus and there, in her car, was a neighbor whose daughter is also in Josh's first-grade class.

"Don't worry!" my neighbor yelled, leaning across the seat out the passenger's window. "I'm following the bus all the way to the school!"

A miracle had surely occurred.

A few weeks later, standing beside me by the punch-and-cookies table at Byck Elementary School's open house, my neighbor gave me a more mundane explanation. She had promised her daughter she would drive her to school the first day. But then she'd heard school officials say it's easier for a child to adjust to the bus ride if she makes the trip from Day One. This was her compromise.

When I think about it now, Josh wasn't the only one behind a mask those first days. He just happened to be wearing the kind you can lift up and look beneath.

If you could have done the same with my neighbor and me, you might have found the same person underneath: a jittery first-grader on the brink of a grand journey.

Everything—and just about everybody—changes with the first day of school. Rush-hour traffic snarls along bus routes and in school zones. Life's pace switches to a higher gear. A woman I work with believes that if more CEOs and politicians were in charge of filling lunch boxes and stocking backpacks with tablets and pencils, the first day of school would be declared a national holiday.

It might as well be anyway. A newcomer to back-to-school, I expected only parents like me, with first-graders, would get caught up in The Event. But for weeks now I've heard folks trading back-to-school stories and, in the process, recalling their own first-day experiences.

Occasionally, these stories help me connect with strangers—like the woman who works behind the counter at Josh's favorite rock-and-mineral store. I never really spoke to her until I overheard her talking about our neighborhood middle school. We found out we knew some of the same kids, same parents. Now when Josh and I stop by, we will have more to talk about than the going price of rose quartz.

Let's just say we have quietly bonded—not permanently, like fossil to rock, but as fellow pebbles along the same path.

Working for a newspaper keeps you in touch with seasonal rituals like State Fairs and Tractor Pulls and First Days of School—whether you truly wish to be in touch with them or not. So despite the fact that I have not been a full-time student in two decades, nor have I had one in my household, I've taken part in my share of back-to-school ceremonies.

There were a couple of autumns in the mid-1970s when I spent opening day and weeks after that hanging around schools—looking for trouble, hoping not to find it. Those were the years when local schools were in the throes of massive change: a messy merger of city and county systems and a court order to balance the racial makeup of our classrooms by busing students to schools outside their neighborhoods.

I remember, quite clearly, watching kids' faces as their buses pulled out of the Fairdale High parking lot, past angry adults shouting protests and carrying hand-printed placards.

I wasn't a parent back them. In fact, I was closer in age to the students on the bus than the people picketing around them. Though I never rode a school bus in my life, I could imagine sitting in those kids' seats, caught in the crossfire.

Maybe that's why I still think of their faces on mornings when it's so quiet at our bus stop that Josh and I can hear the wings, not just the honking, of the Cave Hill geese as they fly over us. The only placards disturbing our peace these days are the usual October campaign posters mounted in neighbors' front yards. A lot can—and happily does—change in 15 years.

Josh is bused this year, across town in the service of desegregation. He's too young, of course, to understand that "busing" has a meaning beyond its literal definition. It's how he gets to and from school. It's his world for an hour and a half each day. It's where he has made some new friends and learned some old jokes.

It's where he turns away from me each morning and doesn't look back, trusting I'll be there when he's ready to return. It's life, and so far he likes the ride.

We've now been to our first open house and paid our first PTA dues. The first report card arrived 12 days ago. Last week we made our first mad dash to catch a missed bus. Things are beginning to fall into place, to settle down.

And so I start wondering: When does "the start of school" become "the middle of school"? When do the changes stop happening? When does it become routine, old hat, predictable?

Sure enough, as soon as I begin thinking this way, Barney hops off the bus one morning and says, "See you around." I look inside and see someone else in the driver's seat. Barney is a substitute. I have known this all along but didn't know when the change would occur. As he climbs back aboard, I think of something that happened the first day of school.

After Josh's bus pulled away from the corner with him in it, my next-door neighbor—a former school-teacher—opened her arms and took me inside them. Her own three sons are grown now and live out of town. She didn't have to ask me how I felt, and I didn't have to keep my mask on. When I surprised myself by suddenly starting to cry, she just hugged me harder. Then she said something you could take two different ways, which I suppose was her point.

"It's only the beginning," she said. "Only the beginning."

October 15, 1990

At War With Children

A few nights after the start of the Persian Gulf War, a friend happened to catch her 6-year-old son in the midst of one of his standard wrestling matches with a favorite stuffed toy bear.

She didn't think much of it until she heard him mutter something about "killing" the bear. Her mind flashed instantly to the violent warfare she had been reading about and watching on television. She used the opportunity to sit down with him and talk some more about the war unfolding on the TV screen.

Her son listened and then promptly went back to his game. But before he resumed his tussling, he offered a compromise of sorts.

"Mama, this is my pet Snagglefrax," he said. "Let's pretend he can't be hurt or injured or killed, but he likes to pretend to wrestle."

Telling me the story the next day, my friend recalled how eager her son had been to get back to his game and escape what she labeled her "little moralizing sermon."

I could identify with her dilemma. What peace-loving parent hasn't felt the need over the past few anxious months to put in a plug for non-violence whenever possible?

On the other hand, my friend's son also has a point. Maybe there was another "moral" to this story, another "little sermon" to be heeded.

Perhaps it's not just our children who want or need explanations about why we're in a war, why people are trying to kill each other, why it's acceptable for grown-ups to behave this way.

Maybe the concern about the war's effect on kids' emotions has more to do with our own need, as adults, to make sense of the horror we are watching day by day on our television screens and front pages.

Maybe, just maybe, if an expert can tell us how to explain it to our kids, then it will become clear to us too.

Could it be we are looking for the "right" words to comfort our little ones so we can reassure ourselves as well?

Robert Coles, the Harvard psychiatrist who has written so sensitively and wisely about children in crises, was quoted last week in The New York Times, saying he was worried about the "condescending and patronizing messages" that have been bombarding American parents in recent weeks.

Coles was responding to the barrage of advice on helping kids cope with war that the media, mental-health professionals and talk-show hosts have been lobbing at parents since the war began.

There was, for example, last weekend's ABC call-in TV show aimed exclusively at children and their questions about the war. There are spot messages tailored to kids, starring Mister Rogers and broadcast on Nickelodeon and public TV. And there are count-less, often contradictory, tips from specialists.

"Don't Let Your Kids Watch TV News"..."Kids Need To See What War Looks Like"..."Wait Till Your Kids Ask About Violence"..."If You Wait Till They Ask, It Will Be Too Late."

Coles is skeptical of the value of such advice:

"It has been possible in the past for children in the United States to get through wars without the massive intervention of school psychologists and television personalities, and I rather suspect it will be possible in the future if we only give children a chance."

Citing his own family's efforts to help him deal with World War II, he expressed confidence in American parents' ability to "talk thoughtfully and intelligently to their children" about war.

Of course, this is not World War II. Although Coles didn't mention it, this is the first generation of kids to face a war saddled with parents whose formative experience with military conflict was Vietnam.

It's clear not all parents feel the same about the Gulf War. It's clear many adults are of two minds about it.

One way to handle the uncomfortable feeling that this ambivalence generates is to heed the best advice I've heard yet for coping with war anxiety, whatever your age: Remember it's normal to have conflicting feelings about war.

In fact, that seems to be the lesson in my friend's story about her son and his stuffed bear. He seemed at home with his mixed emotions, using his "pretend" skills to handle the internal conflict.

It may be that kids, in their innocence and genuine curiosity, can teach us in this war. Maybe we instinctively know that. Cole certainly does. His most recent work, "The Spiritual Life of Children," is one in a series of books based on respectful encounters with real-life kids and probing investigations of their built-in coping techniques.

Coles says many children, especially young ones, view war as totally unreal. It's only useful to them as a symbol for conflicts closer to home.

Kids who might have worked out their fears or aggressiveness with Ninja Turtles or He-Men a few months ago may now be engaging in "war talk" and war games or drawing missile battles and face-to-face combat scenes instead.

Coles' comment about the unreality of the war for children hits home for me. It's a word I've heard many adults use to describe the war as seen on TV and in newspapers.

There's a part of us that wants to keep it there— safely distant. But there's another part that believes peace won't come until war is exposed for the close-up, brutal activity it is.

Another friend of mine told me her 4-year-old son has repeatedly declared he wants to grow up to be a

"He-Man soldier and fight in the Gulf War." She patiently reminded him each time that fighting a war is not a game. He persisted.

So she let him watch TV news. "I thought he needed some sobering," she said.

Slowly, the message sank in. One night he asked, "When they fight like that, do the bad guys have to take a time-out?"

A couple of nights later, after seeing footage of an attack on Tel Aviv, he had another question.

"Is that red stuff *blood*?"

"Yes," she told him. "It's blood."

Anyone who spends much time with kids knows this: One of the best ways to uncover your own feelings about an issue is to try to answer an inquisitive child's questions.

Sometimes kids ask questions adults are too scared to ask.

My son, a first-grader, wanted to know three things the night war was declared.

He wanted to know exactly where Iraq was located. He wanted to know if we had any friends fighting over there. And he wanted to know details about the weapons being used.

After my husband supplied him with a few new vocabulary words, like Scud and Patriot, he had one more question:

"Will they use the atomic bomb? And if they do, will it reach us?"

Sometimes after you've answered the questions the

best you can and crossed your fingers, you find your-self stumbling onto a lesson your child doesn't even know he's teaching you.

Like my friend and her son's teddy bear fight.

Or like the drawing my son presented to me one morning last week. He said it had to do with the war.

Since he's a longtime fan of scary ghost stories and hair-raising sci-fi movies, I expected something fairly graphic—with a heavy emphasis on the missiles and bombs he asked so many questions about in the first days of the war.

Since I'm forever finding pictures of weird alien creatures and UFOs tucked inside his school folder, between the math papers and spelling tests, I expected a drawing or two of an evil-looking "enemy."

But what he showed me was something else again. It was an abstract drawing—a circle with a geometric figure inside, colored in soothing greens and blues and yellows. The figure had 1960s-style peace signs for arms, and they were stretched out at his sides.

"What is it?" I asked.

"The God of Peace, gathering peace," he said.

Later I asked if he wanted to draw a companion to his peace picture, something representing war. I told him we might run the two pictures in the newspaper with a story I was writing.

He wasn't interested. Peace was all he wanted to draw. Take it or leave it.

I had to smile at his stubbornness, and that's when I stumbled onto it. Maybe we're missing the boat by talking so much about war with our kids.

Perhaps we could all profit more by concentrating on the other side of the issue—the hopeful half of the equation.

Why not give peace a chance?

January 28, 1991

Friends And Teachers

Some of my best teachers are friends.

We met in classrooms in the '50s or '60s or '70s. We keep up through letters and holiday lunches and—this is one advantage of being a hometown girl—hellos waved across neighborhood sidewalks and grocery-store aisles.

Even those who died years ago come calling occasionally in memories and dreams. Sister Antonio, lover of Latin, still glides into my thoughts now and then, most often when I'm ready to give up on a challenge, when I need to be reminded of the poetry in perseverance.

She stands there, her beloved "Aeneid" in hand, smiling patiently at me as I enumerate the many reasons why I can't do whatever it is I'm afraid to try.

Her smile's what I can't resist. It's so encouraging, so full of the faith in me that I lack. I struggle on, though, and soon she's got me back in the rhythm of things, remembering the basics, the rules you can always fall back on:

Amo, Amas, Amat: Sometimes it's that simple.

I've been thinking a lot about this link between friends and teachers lately, as my son begins second grade and the soul-searching associated with school reform in Kentucky grows more intense by the day.

Do kids learn more when they're tested each year to see what they don't know? Are they more stimulated when they're grouped with students of other ages? Do summer vacations, once whiled away in back yards and now increasingly spent in pursuit of organized activity, only serve to interrupt a youngster's learning curve?

At the risk of being labeled naive, I would toss out yet another question: Does affection between student and teacher have a role to play in education?

I know, I know: You can't legislate friendship. It's intangible and serendipitous and you can't hold anyone accountable for not being good at it. But you can encourage it as a classroom goal worth striving for, acknowledging that it is at least as desirable as replacing desks with team tables. Months before my son entered first grade last fall, I called Byck Elementary, the public school where he was to be bused, and placed his name on a waiting list for a teacher whose reputation was outstanding and well-known.

My husband and I knew she had a long list of national and local teaching awards to her credit, and we'd heard testimonials from parents who raved about how much their kids learned from her.

It didn't take long for us to see that this fun-loving, upbeat, unbelievably well-organized woman was all she was cracked up to be as a classroom instructor— and more.

The "more" was this: She had the chutzpah to ask her students for something beyond academic achievement and good behavior. She asked for friendship. And, of course, she got it.

Kids can resist demands for perfect penmanship and they can fake cooperation, especially the bright ones. But they can't resist love, and they don't fake friendship.

At "Young Authors" night and the Christmas play, on honors day and the class camping trip, I could see these kids and their teacher shared a cozy camaraderie that was no accident. There were many inside jokes and nicknames in that class—the kind of easy ribbing that's only possible when kids feel confident and cared about and comfortable with their own and other people's eccentricities.

Dianne Barham did not wait for friendship to happen; she invited it.

My third-grade teacher recently sent me a card from South Carolina, where she lives in an apartment in West Columbia. When I knew her 30-something years ago, she lived in a convent in St. Matthews. Things change. But not much.

What I remember about this warm, wonderful teacher was how happy she seemed to be with us. Her laughter was deep and strong and, best of all, frequent. She liked to hug and tease and wanted to hear about our lives outside the classroom. Ballet recitals seemed at least as important to her as spelling bees or achievement tests.

She was a Southerner, through and through, and a singer. And that's what I remember most about that year—

the songs we belted out in unison, swaying on our feet, standing beside our desks. We roared those songs as she waved us on, pitch pipe in hand, arms swinging to keep us in some kind of time.

I honestly don't remember a single "instructional" moment in her classroom, although my report card from that year claims I mastered numerous subjects. The lessons I recall, and it seemed they were abundant that year, were informal, spontaneous, essential.

I remember learning about the painkilling power of humor in the first-aid room the day I came in in tears and embarrassment after skidding on my knees across the school parking lot at the climax of a crazed game of Red Rover. She treated my wounds with Mercurochrome and one-liners. I wish I could say I learned that lesson— The Healing Properties of Laughter—my first time out. In reality, it's one class I've had to repeat. But it was a memorable introduction to the subject, thanks to my dauntless instructor.

So when the envelope bearing her South Carolina return address arrived in my mailbox last month, I ripped it open eagerly. It was, as I expected, a big-hearted letter, full of delightful details. She spends her free time now swimming and—I have to smile—singing in a choir.

"I find them both uplifting," she wrote. Why does that not surprise me?

When I think of the teachers I've stayed friends with over the years, they are the ones who showed me that education is at its core a mutual encounter. A sharing, not a handing-down of knowledge and experience: a give-and-take among friends, a two-way relationship.

This summer one of these old friends from the mid-'60s was visiting in Louisville. We had lunch.

Though she long ago gave up the classroom and switched careers, I was caught off guard when she said she didn't like to use the word teacher anymore. In any context.

I asked her to explain.

She said she was uncomfortable with the implication that learning is bestowed upon us from above at the behest of certified experts, licensed practitioners of wisdom—society's designated "teachers." She thought it was wrong-headed, even insulting, to believe that education is so linear or one-way a process.

I knew what she meant. My mind flashed to the many times I've been humbled by how much I've learned from other people in the process of trying to teach them something. Children, especially.

Talk to children about death, for example. See how far you get before they disarm you with their insight and educate you with their questions.

Looking across the table at my friend and remembering the classroom we once shared, I found that her comments fit my memory quite comfortably. I could see that room clearly and her leaning precariously against the lectern, tilting it forward at what surely was a risky angle, moving as close to us as she could, tossing out questions as we argued uppercase issues—Civil Disobedience, The Great Society, Equality, The War.

I had no idea then, sitting at my wooden desk, that she and I would years later call ourselves friends.

But the truth is, we were even then.

September 5, 1991

The Things We Don't Forget

It's not that it hadn't happened to me before. It's just that there I was, once again, not prepared for it.

I was in my back yard this time, checking out the wildflowers in my garden, ticking off the names to my son as he pointed them out. Wild ginger. Dwarf iris. Blue phlox. Columbine. Bellwort. Poppy, trillium, May apple, bluebells.

"Over there! Look! Jack-in-the-pulpit!"

Then silence. We both stared at a stalk of white flowers rising out of a patch of ivy and ferns. Josh looked up at me, expectantly. I felt a rush of regret. I'd forgotten the name of the plant. I'd lost it.

And that reminded me of a deeper loss—of a woman who, in other springs, I could have counted on to fill in this gap in my wildflower vocabulary.

This is the first spring since Gran died. For six wildflower seasons before this one, she would sit on my deck, patiently feeding me the names of the flowers

I'd forgotten over the winter. Many of the gems now flourishing in my back yard came from Granny's garden, a wildly colorful patch of flowers that bloomed from early spring to late summer.

When I first got to know her, before I married her grandson, she walked me out to her flowers once and, pointing each one out, told me their names and a little bit about where they came from, what kind of weather they liked, what their full names were, as if introducing eccentric aunts and uncles to a newcomer.

One spring I brought a friend to visit Gran. This woman had grown up with wildflowers the way I grew up with jump ropes and bicycles; she needed no coaching on names. The two of them had a wonderful time together. Gran urged us to dig up whatever plants we wanted—the time was right, she said—and transplant them to our own yards.

And that's what we did. Year after year she encouraged me to take more. Spring upon spring my garden grew with her gifts. Eventually, a Sunday in May arrived when Gran sent me out on my own to look at that marvel of a garden in front of her house. By then, it hurt too much for her to walk. But she watched me through the glass storm door. I know this because I'd turn back now and then and catch a glimpse of her, straining from her chair to see through the glass, down the sidewalk to where I stood among her blossoms.

Last summer she stopped coming outside at all. She lay in her bed, big white pillows fluffed around her head and body, and flowers of all kinds—coral roses, lilies, bright daisies and irises—stuffed into china vases, spilling out of cups and bottles, some cut from her own garden, some brought to her bedside by friends.

She would slip in and out of dreams, sometimes forgetting where she was or who was visiting her. But she never forgot the names of flowers.

One night not long before she died, I couldn't resist burying my face in a big beautiful day lily on her nightstand. Of course, it didn't have a scent. What it did have was a rich, dark, moist pollen that clung to my blouse when I brushed against it. Straightening up, I flicked at the sprinkles with my fingers, thinking they would fly off like powder or dust. Instead, they smeared and turned darker, leaving a blood-red smudge like a wound over my heart.

I was sure the color would not come out in the wash, but it did. In some way, I regret that. With one washing, the stain disappeared—gone with no trace, like the name of the starry white flower in my garden.

In a psychology class a few years ago, I came across a sentence that's stuck with me: "Much forgetting is not just desirable; it is unavoidable." There's immense comfort in that line, as well as infinite sorrow.

I remember the day many years ago, shortly after my mother died, when I felt a craving for her delicious egg noodles, flat yellow strips of floured dough that my brother and I used to snatch from the cutting board whenever she turned to stir her soup. I had not committed her recipe to memory, though I had watched her make them many times. There was no need. My mother was my "Joy of Cooking," just as Gran was my Linneas.

That's how it happened that I was already on the

phone, dialing her for the forgotten ingredients, when it hit me: She would not answer.

The way I see it, there were two kinds of forgetting at work in my reaching for the phone that day: the forgetting of lessons learned in childhood, and the forgetting of death. I have to wonder—which is desirable and which unavoidable?

If it hasn't happened to you, it will. You will be laid off your job or spurned by someone you love or forced to move from your neighborhood, and suddenly you will wish with all your heart you had paid better attention to your mother's stories of coping with disappointment and tragedy. Or you will be sitting on the edge of your daughter's bed some middle-of-the-night, racking your memory for the story your Dad always told to soothe you back to sleep after a nightmare.

What you will want to have back in those moments will not be the words you've forgotten. You will want the people you were sure would always be there to supply them.

I could have called my friend today and asked her the name of the flower I couldn't identify. She'd know. Instead, I looked it up in a book. Rue anemone is what it resembled in a photograph. But rue doesn't sound right to me.

Someday I'm certain it will come back to me. I'll hear Gran's voice again reciting the names—coreopsis, mertensia, wood lily. She'll be whispering them to me softly, like secrets, like answers to a prayer.

May 19, 1992

Shifting Focus

Starting Over

When I left my job at The Courier-Journal six weeks ago to spend more time at other things, I knew the hardest person to break the news to would be Bernie, the butcher at my neighborhood grocery.

Maybe it was because Bernie is a newspaper reader of the old school—cover-to-cover—and never shy about sharing his reactions to what he's read.

Or maybe it's because of all we've been through together. My first leg of lamb. The countless pounds of hamburger, dished out over seven summers.

Once, a few years ago, Bernie was slicing turkey breast for me when his hand came too close to the spinning blade. The injury was serious enough to warrant a trip to the hospital. I saw him leave, his fingers bound up in white cloth. He didn't return to the meat counter for weeks, and I can remember wondering if he'd come back at all.

He did, of course. And when I asked about it, feeling

responsible in some way, he said these things happen in his business and this certainly wasn't the first time he'd been hurt.

Risk comes with the territory, Bernie said.

For nearly eight of the 21 years I worked at The Courier-Journal, part of my job was to produce a weekly column about health issues.

Bernie is one of the people who used to come to mind on the mornings I woke up believing I could not muster another syllable on the subject of heart disease or blood pressure or allergy medications.

Some of those mornings I'd look out my living room window at the neighborhood I love and wonder if I'd ever have the time to get to know each tree and house the way I knew the ones on the street where I grew up.

In the summer, if the morning looked promising, I'd daydream about playing hooky and taking my son to the woods for a hike.

In the winter, I'd think: "If only I could spend today at home, spinning stories out of my head and heart, or exploring questions instead of supplying answers."

But then I'd remember a note from a cancer patient, something she wanted to share after reading information I'd passed along in the paper. I'd recall a conversation with the parent of a depressed teen-ager who rang me up just because he thought I'd understand.

Or I'd hear Bernie, sending me off cheerfully with my white-paper packages and a mandate to "keep up the good work."

Shortly after I made the wrenching decision to give

up my full-time career in exchange for more time and flexibility, it dawned on me I was avoiding Bernie.

I was shopping only in areas safely out of his sight: bread aisle, produce section, frozen-pasta shelf.

Better to renounce life as a carnivore than to have to face Bernie.

But one day he tracked me down at the cash register. Hands on his white-aproned hips, he motioned me out of the line with a squint of concern in his eyes.

"Where've you been? I haven't seen you in the paper. What's going on?"

When I explained what I'd done and how I was eager for new challenges, he stared at me with disbelief.

That's the moment it hit—the full weight of 21 years, falling fast and hard, like a butcher's blade slamming through bone. I felt it disconnecting me from something vital, something visceral, something I'd spent half a lifetime nurturing.

Certainly I would miss my paycheck. I'd miss my friends at the office too. But what hurt most about leaving my job was the thought of severing the bonds I had forged with readers like Bernie—and with the many others I had never met but felt attached to nonetheless.

There are 50 ways to leave your lover but no words at all when you split with a reader.

My friends at the office gave me wonderful goodbye parties, which reassured me that leaving my job did not mean losing their friendship. But how could I tie up the loose ends with readers whose names I didn't even know? I considered taking out an ad or writing a farewell letter-to-the-editor.

Neither seemed right.

While I was still pondering the question, the answer arrived. You're reading it now.

Starting today, I will be writing a different kind of weekly column. From my own home. And from my personal perspective as a 40-something woman, a not–afraid–to–say–it feminist, a hometown girl, a mother, wife, daughter, sister, student, patient, neighbor and friend.

I'll be here each Sunday; I hope you will look me up.

But now you're probably wanting to know what lots of people asked me over the holidays: "What will you be writing about?" I can tell you I will *not* be writing about your blood pressure or your cholesterol levels— though I do intend to deal with matters of the heart, the flesh–and–blood issues we all struggle with, regardless of gender, skin color or the unique set of experiences and beliefs that determines how each of us looks at the world.

Leaving a job is one such issue.

No matter whether you're laid off, fired, forced to leave because of a family move or a better job some- where else, the emotional fallout is the same.

It's like leaving home. The same mixed feelings: sadness at going, excitement at the challenges lying ahead.

For two decades, I've lived by the journalists' creed: Stay on the sidelines, don't get involved in your stories, let other people speak, keep your own voice out of it, avoid becoming part of the trends you describe.

It's appropriate that now, as the new year begins, I'm breaking that habit.

I am a self-confessed "down-shifter," for example—one of those midlife Americans you read about who are trading high-demand, high-salary jobs for greater freedom and more time to spend on life outside work.

I also plead guilty to being a part of a small but steady movement of men and women trying to integrate work life and home life by combining them in the same space.

My office at Sixth and Broadway had a huge window through which I watched the new Commonwealth Place come to life, season by season.

Through that window, I watched ginkgo trees turn yellow in the course of one day.

And I'll never forget the afternoon I watched 679,000 fire trucks race up Broadway within a two-hour period. At least it seemed that way as I struggled to concentrate on the story whose deadline I'd already missed.

My office now is a second-floor room with a view of dogwoods and maples and oaks and magnolias. Instead of screaming sirens and calls for advice on treating hay fever, it's gas-meter readers and telephone vendors who interrupt my work.

Some work rituals remain the same: the sound and smell of fresh coffee dripping into a glass pot.

Others have changed dramatically. Between paragraphs typed into my home computer, I throw a load of laundry into the washing machine. At 3:30, rather than breaking for coffee in the cafeteria, I walk to the front door and watch my son skipping up the sidewalk from the bus stop.

Like my walls at work, the ones surrounding my home office are littered with calendars and notes and sayings that cheer me up.

"One doesn't discover new lands," reads my favorite at the moment, "without consenting to lose sight of the shore for a very long time."

When I first pushed my way through the revolving glass doors of the Courier-Journal building on a June day in 1971, the last thing on my mind was what I would feel like when I left.

I was fresh out of the University of Louisville, where I'd been a commuter student. It would be months before I even knew what leaving home was like.

It would be years before I learned that endings are as much a part of life as beginnings, and sometimes even the same part.

And decades would go by before I understood, as Bernie says, risk comes with the territory.

All I knew was that I wanted to write and I needed readers to write for.

So I hurled myself into that whirling glass circle of doors, trusting I would know when the time came to step out.

January 3, 1993

The
Invisible
Woman

What would you think if you unrolled your newspaper one morning and found the front page had become a literal No Man's Land?

Every name and every face belonged to a woman.

Every byline, photo, quote, opinion, reference, analysis and authority was strictly female.

My guess is you'd be suspicious. After all, women make up 52 percent of the population—not 100 percent.

If you were old enough to remember how most women reporters got jobs in the 1940s, you might even worry that war had been declared.

But what if the tables were turned? What if you stumbled on an all-male Page One? Would you notice?

Probably not. You'd be used to it. It happens routinely.

In the best of newspapers.

A major study earlier this year of 20 dailies, including The Washington Post and The New York Times, found women were mentioned or asked to comment only 15 percent of the time in front-page stories.

That means 85 percent of the time men were the focus of attention.

Even when the issues they were commenting on had the greatest impact on women, as breast implants and sexual harassment do, men's voices dominated front pages.

Men also wrote two out of three stories and appeared in two out of three photos. At least two newspapers ran all-male front pages.

TV network news fared no better: Men reported 86 percent of the nightly news. Three out of four interviews were with men. At least one day on each network, not one woman reported a story.

Shocking news?
Some of us thought so, when we heard it at a recent gathering of Kentucky journalists in Frankfort.

Junior Bridge, who conducted the study for the Women, Men and Media project, discussed her findings at a meeting sponsored by the Kentucky Commission on Women and the Bluegrass Chapter of the Society of Professional Journalists.

A project of New York University and University of Southern California since 1989, the study has consistently concluded that women are "significantly underrepresented."

Since Bridge didn't study Kentucky papers, the women's commission did its own research, using similar techniques—with similar results.

For three two-week periods, the staff studied front

pages of each section of the Lexington Herald-Leader and The Courier-Journal. The Kentucky Post was added last winter.

Though the findings may not be "100 percent correct" due to staff turnover during the study, commission executive-director Marsha Weinstein called them "alarming."

Last summer only 15 percent of stories on front pages of sections were about or by women. In the fall, it was 13 percent; in winter, 22 percent.

Hearing these figures was bad enough, but sitting down in small groups with colored highlighters and personally marking front pages for male and female references was the biggest eye-opener of all for me.

We used green markers for men, pink for women.

The conclusion in my group was clear: When it comes to front-page coverage, Kentucky's major newspapers are not always in the pink.

You may wonder what difference it makes who's on the front page most.

Listen to Nancy Woodhull, a USA Today founding editor and co-chair of Women, Men and Media:

"There is an act called symbolic annihilation. It means that if the press does not report your existence, for all perception purposes you do not exist."

It's called feeling "invisible," she told the group.

And it has consequences: If you can't find yourself reflected in a newspaper, eventually you stop looking.

That's exactly what a lot of women have done, Woodhull said.

In 1970, 78 percent of U.S. women read a newspaper on a given day. By 1990, that figure had dropped to 50.5 percent, she said.

Male readers also jumped ship, but their plunge was not so dramatic; from 77 percent to 64 percent.

To put this gender gap into perspective, Woodhull said that if newspapers could get women to read in the same proportion as men do, they'd gain 4 million readers.

She urged women to complain—not bail out—when they feel ignored. Write editors, call ombudsmen. Speak up when you feel included too.

Studies show that women readers want more than just-the-facts. They want "context." They want to know what the facts *mean*, how they affect people, what can be done.

As Pulitzer Prize-winning columnist Ellen Goodman says in a current interview in Ms. magazine, "Newspapers offer crime statistics instead of describing how unsafe women feel."

They want to hear voices they can identify with and trust.

But as Maria Braden, an associate professor of journalism at the University of Kentucky, found out when she led a panel discussion at the meeting, there is no consensus, even among women journalists, about how to win back women readers.

In her new book on women newspaper columnists, "She Said *What?*" Braden writes that while women journalists don't always agree on issues, "one fact stands out: women's voices often contrast significantly with those of men."

If newspapers fail to give expression to that contrasting voice, on the front page and every page, the trend is clear. Women will look for it somewhere else.

July 4, 1993

Pictures
(Of Women)
At An Exhibition

Somehow I missed the nude bather.

I must have walked past her a dozen times without noticing her awkward pose, the modest way she tried to cover herself, that look of surprise and embarrassment at being caught in the buff by a stranger.

This bronze beauty, sculpted a century ago by the French impressionist Edgar Degas, escaped my attention the first few times I visited the Wendell and Dorothy Cherry Collection, currently on exhibit at the J.B. Speed Art Museum.

On my last visit, however, I took a good close look at her. She was different from the other females in the exhibition. She looked timid and vulnerable, as if shrinking from public view—while her sisters in the show were busy striking poses that were bold, brash, even brazen.

Vulnerable is *not* the word that comes to mind to describe these others, regardless of whether they're in oil, watercolor, pencil, crayon, pastel, wool tapestry, gouache, terra cotta or marble.

The bronze figure offers a conventional view of women as meek and proper. The females in the other works (even those by Degas) defy such "female virtues."

While the bronze is called "Woman Taken Unawares," it's hard to imagine the other females *capable* of being caught off guard.

They dance alone and gossip together. They smirk, smoke, strut, stare, make music, make fun, make love and without fuss go about the business of defiantly rescuing the infant Moses from the Nile.

I'm no art critic, just an interested observer. But it seems to me, in the midst of such vibrant images of womanly spunk, it's no wonder the Degas bronze—striking as she is—failed to snare me.

This exhibition, which calls itself "In Pursuit of Excellence," makes a strong statement about women. Intentionally or not, it celebrates their vigor and vitality, even their rebelliousness.

You find no madonnas here, no serene domestic scenes. Here you find women who engage the viewer head-on, forcing them to question and wonder.

If you doubt this exhibition's perspective on women is anything out of the ordinary, then keep your eyes open as you exit it and head back to the main desk. Notice the paintings along the walls, drawn from the Speed's general collection.

See "The Convalescent," a portrait of a passive young woman in bed. Notice "Young Woman with

Japanese Screen," in which a demure ingenue poses sweetly by a table.

Turn the corner, and see sedate scenes of women in flower gardens or in cozy parlors embroidering. Note the stone sculpture of a mourning virgin, holding back her grief, and a tapestry of Anne of Brittany, humbly bowing before Charles VIII.

You get the picture.

On the first floor, the closest you come to anything like the compelling females in the Cherry collection is the monumental stone sculpture of a reclining woman by Henry Moore. Located outside the museum cafe, this self-possessed female appears to strain to see past the convalescents and embroiderers to where her sisters in spirit hang—the sensual Spanish dancer by John Singer Sargent, the provocative lovers of Egon Schiele, the girls huddled on a bridge in Edvard Munch's mysterious landscape.

Nearly all the show's 30-plus sculptures and paintings are portraits. There are no landscapes, and few still lifes. Of the portraits, only two feature men: a bearded gentleman by Rembrandt (or his assistant—no one knows for sure) and "Page Boy at Maxim's" by Chaim Soutine.

I'm no connoisseur, but I found Soutine's other painting in the show more interesting: "Woman Lying on a Red Couch." Wherever I stood in the room where she lay draped across velvety cushions, I found myself looking back for another glimpse.

Was she angry, exhausted, meditative, depressed, petulant, in love or dying? In this, his first painting of the female form, Soutine reveals the profound power that ambivalence can wield on others.

The Modigliani portrait of his lover, Jeanne Hebuterne, shows how, even on the edge of madness, this exquisitely sad woman dominates a room with the pure strength of her will. Rejected by her parents for bearing the artist's child, she leapt to her death—pregnant again—two days after he died of TB.

Room by room, the visitor is greeted by flashy actresses, a sneering socialite, proud ladies with fans, a girl playing a harpsichord, two Degas bathers much more at ease with their bodies than their bronze sister.

Degas was Wendell's favorite artist; Dorothy's was Egon Shiele. His are the only works in the show that are strongly sexual in content. His love scenes among lesbians, a subject that fascinated him, caused a stir in turn-of-the-century Austria, sending him briefly to jail.

Finally there is Eva Gonzales, star student of Edouard Manet and the sole female artist represented in the show. What stands out about her "Self Portrait" is its dignity. Her eyes are averted, not in modesty or shyness, but out of a willful refusal to give too much of herself away.

After selling "Yo, Picasso" for a record-breaking auction price in 1989, Wendell Cherry reportedly told a friend he no longer needed to own this self-portrait.

"I'll always possess that," Cherry told Eugene Thaw, according to the exhibition catalog. Cherry, a native of Horse Cave, Ky., was well-known as a world-class art collector at his death in 1991.

In some odd way, I feel the same about the women I met in this exhibition, the ones I spent time watching, trying to grasp what sets them apart. I, too, suspect I'll "always possess" them—though it's unlikely we'll meet again.

You see, the fate that awaits these extraordinary females ironically imitates that of many ordinary women through time.

After the exhibit closes today at 6, they'll be sold to the highest bidder.

April 17, 1994

Facing FAX About
Letter-Writing

Our Christmas tree is finally down, on its way home to the Hart County farm it came from, to be recycled and returned to the land there.

The holidays are now officially over.

What I miss most, already, is the mail. The holidays, let's face it, are the time when we're all most likely to get letters.

I mean *real* letters, not computer-generated epistles asking us to buy, rent, lease, donate, apply, subscribe, volunteer or pay-up-promptly.

Letters from old friends and scattered family. Handwritten letters. Letters you hang on to from year to year.

Pages crammed with the random details and rambling observations that rarely arise in long-distance phone calls.

Recently I was prompted to hunt down our household copy of "Letters of E.B. White," a fat collection of mail to and (mostly) from a fellow who could write almost anything—from fanciful children's classics ("Stuart Little" and "Charlotte's Web") to refreshing revisions of a small but timeless college grammar book ("The Elements of Style").

Reading the collection again made me think of a line from a John Lennon song: "Life is what happens while you're busy making other plans."

Most of White's letters are full of the mundane stuff of urban and farm life. White's city home was Manhattan, specifically the midtown offices of New Yorker magazine, where he met his wife Katharine; his country home was North Brooklin, Maine, where the couple farmed, raised a family...and wrote letters.

If you flip to most any page of this generous collection, you'll find a slice of White's life as told to a friend or stranger. A humorous recounting of a bout of pneumonia. A description of the "calls" of the bobwhite. Snippets of a dream about President Dwight D. Eisenhower having prostate surgery in White's home without benefit of anesthesia. Scenes of grandchildren throwing pea pods at each other. Even a wry account of a three-day centennial celebration in small-town New England, complete with floats and decorated bicycles.

One letter mentions Katharine's miscarriage. Another, longer one comments on the birth of his son, right down to a candid admission of feeling "the mixed pride and oppression of fatherhood."

Letters are like that. No other conversation between friends encourages such honest, thoughtful give and take. Once, a couple of decades ago, a good friend of mine moved from Louisville to Africa. We vowed to write, as friends always vow. For some reason we actually did.

We wrote furiously, nonstop, it seemed—letters criss-crossing the Atlantic at a rate surprising even to us.

She was married, living in Tanzania, raising a toddler in an economy of scarcity, playing full-time housewife for the first time. I was single, living alone in my hometown.

Our friendship grew in ways I doubt it ever would have if we'd stayed in the same city. Without interruptions or questions from the other, we could speak our minds frankly and move on.

It was the best and longest conversation we ever had. It lasted 11 years.

Three years ago she returned to Louisville. Now we live three minutes apart, as the station wagon drives. Our domestic lives have reversed: I'm the one with the husband now; she's single. But that's not all that's changed.

We talk on the phone in hurried snatches now, me banging about the kitchen, overseeing supper and homework, my friend on her way home from work to her daughter, now a college-bound senior.

We trade messages with each other's answering machines and voice mail. Or killing two birds with one stone, we talk as we walk, exercising our friendship and our bodies at the same time.

There are times when I miss our pen-pal days—the time we dedicated to writing each other, the care we took to find the right words.

White's last letter in his collection is a note to his stepson, Roger Angell, about a piece the younger man had published in the New Yorker on the dying tradition of small-park baseball. The article reminded White of his own sentiments about other aspects of American life also on the demise.

For example, he compared the patient pace of railroad travel to the (relatively speaking) immediate gratification of the supersonic Concorde. He theorized about why people would actually prefer the latter.

White's comments could apply to the dying art of letter-writing as well:

"It seems to be essentially a matter of the spiritual acceptance of What's New or What's Greater—as though there were something wrong or disappointing about what isn't new or what isn't greater."

"What's New" now is to FAX a friend or call her on her car phone and hear her voice fade in and out between interruptions from call-waiting.

"What's Greater" now is the distance we've traveled from the days when writing a note was not just a pleasure, but a necessary ritual.

What's wrong and disappointing today is that we hardly miss what we let get away. It's true that faster is sometimes better. And brevity may be the soul of wit.

But I doubt that friendships can grow deeper via voice mail.

And I am certain that even the author of "Charlotte's Web" would have trouble finding a publisher for "The Collected E-Mail Messages of E.B. White."

January 9, 1994

Learning Not To Look

Paging through my new-improved New York Times Sunday Magazine a few weeks ago, I stumbled on a "Style" feature called "No Peeking Zone."

It was about how office workers in Manhattan have achieved the ultimate freedom.

They can now undress on crowded city sidewalks and re-dress in tights and Rollerblades without anyone paying a lick of attention.

"No one seems to notice," the writer explained with unbridled civic pride. "People have learned not to look."

A photograph showed a pretty young woman sitting on a curb, lacing up skates as her fellow urbanites passed by unfazed.

"People spin a chrysalis of privacy around themselves. It's an aura. It's an attitude…a bubble of privacy."

It's scary, if you ask me.

In a cheeky celebration of this new "sidewalk

etiquette," the writer went on to give several examples from real life. The woman pulling off skirt and jacket and tugging on tights was one. A mother breast-feeding in a grocery line was another. A man using a sidewalk bank machine was the third.

According to the new etiquette, noticing any of them would be a major *faux pas*: "In each case, the observer, not the performer, is in bad taste."

In other words, you—the average Jo buying your frozen pizzas or walking to your bus stop—are supposed to pretend what's in front of your eyes *isn't*.

The clincher came next:

"This nuance of etiquette used to be reserved for the less fortunate: the derelict on the sidewalk, the ranting crazy on the train." But that's changing, the writer concluded buoyantly.

"Looking the other way has become a middle-class way of life."

Still reeling from this chilling commentary, I opened the same newspaper a few days later to find an item filed from the nation's capital.

It was about a homeless woman in her 30s—known only as Brenda—who died alone and unnoticed on a bus-stop bench across the street from HUD headquarters.

That's HUD, as in the Department of Housing and Urban Development, the federal agency whose top priority in the Clinton administration is the "homeless issue."

Brenda had been lying under a blanket throughout the early morning of Nov. 29, as commuters streamed past. (Presumably they practice the "new sidewalk etiquette" in Washington too.) She finally got noticed about 9 a.m., when a city worker tried to shake her awake and discovered she was dead—"of natural causes."

HUD Secretary Henry G. Cisneros cited the case as a sign that the public is growing callous to street people. He waved a Time magazine that coincidentally came out on the day of Brenda's death. The cover story described the "cruel backlash" that's building against the homeless.

"The sympathy of the 1980s that gave way to compassion fatigue is now an open expression of loathing for the homeless," the article said.

It would be nice if we could toss off these disturbing news items as the excesses of Mega-Cities. But we know better.

When I was a teen-ager my cousin Annette, who lived in Detroit, used to mail me the Top 40 list from her rock radio station. It would always be full of songs I never heard of. But if I hung on to it a few months, I found those unknown titles eventually hit the Louisville airwaves.

Today, in an age of instant communication, there's no lag between big cities and medium-sized ones, when it comes to music *or* social attitudes. As Manhattan and D.C. and Detroit go, so goes the nation. That means the new etiquette is already playing on a sidewalk near you.

Besides, looking the other way is nothing new, despite its ballyhooed arrival on the slick pages of trendy city magazines.

Psychiatrists have long had a name for it: Denial. Don't see what you don't like.

A few Christmases ago I made friends with a homeless woman who told me that people in Louisville walked past her as if they were looking *through* her, not at her.

She said she knew why: If they made eye contact, they would see themselves in her wrecked face, her bone-thin body.

What we're seeing now is the trickle-down effect of looking the other way.

You start by closing your eyes to the homeless man you pass every day on the sidewalk. You end up refusing to believe homelessness is a problem we need to face.

Or worse, you come to think that the homeless *are* the problem.

I refuse to believe that middle-class life has to become a long sad series of sidelong glances and shifting eyes.

"Stay awake. Be alert." Those are the lines that were read in churches around Louisville the day before Brenda's death, the first Sunday of Advent, the four-week period preceding Christmas that's better known as the holiday shopping season.

Translated, those Biblical lines mean "Keep your eyes open." Don't glance the other way. Find room for the men, women and children with no beds for the night.

This is also the season of Hanukkah, the eight-day Jewish holiday that is now halfway through its cycle. Hanukkah is a celebration of the victory of the weak over the mighty, the few over the many.

Each night this year as we light Hanukkah candles in my Jewish-Catholic household, I wonder if the weak stand a chance against a backlash of "loathing" and an epidemic of "compassion fatigue."

December 12, 1993

Landscapes

Place Of Peace And Paradox

"'Tis a gift to be simple, 'tis a gift to be free"...from "Simple Gifts," a Shaker song

The second time it happened, I paid attention.

The day was cold and rainy, a mid-October digression from an otherwise splendid Kentucky autumn. I was on my way to the Abbey of Our Lady of Gethsemani, driving south of Bardstown along a stretch of Nelson County road that dips and climbs and curls, always surprising you. I hadn't come yet to the turnoff at Culvertown, where you pick up KY 247—or Monks Road, as the locals call it.

Just minutes from the monastery, on my second visit in a week, I found myself wondering what it was that drew me back.

What was it about the life there that beckoned so strongly for me to understand it? A fascination with the spiritual quest that leads a man to leave friends and family and creature comforts to get closer to God? A curiosity about a lifestyle that could nourish a complicated artist like Thomas Merton even as it placed cumbersome restrictions on him?

That's when it happened.

Over the car radio, I heard a guitar rendition of the Shaker song called "Simple Gifts."

That same familiar melody was playing the first time I drove this road to Gethsemani. I smiled at the coincidence and couldn't help but make meaning of it.

Certainly these lyrics applied not only to the Shakers' philosophy but also to life at the monastery where Merton, the most famous of modern monks, lived and wrote for 27 years, the last three in a hermitage in the woods.

Simple and free.

During the month this fall that I spent visiting and revisiting Gethsemani, that tune stayed in my head, singing its way through the wooden doors of the abbey church, playfully harmonizing with the monks' solemn chanting of psalms, winging by me as I hiked the trails and inhaled the enchanting smells of fruitcakes fresh out of the oven and cheese aging in a cellar room—never letting me once forget that for all its celebrity and for all its computerized mail-order business and for all its 2,400 awesome acres of mostly uncultivated pasture and woodland, the point of life for the 75 monks at Trappist, Ky., is to be simple and free.

Complicated theology can be found in the abbey library that houses 30,000 volumes of mostly religious and philosophical books. But elsewhere at the monastery, the spiritual focus is more basic.

"In the best sense, this is an ordinary place to live," Brother Luke, the abbey's 40-year-old guestmaster, told me when we met. "The getting along. The surrender. The monotony. Very ordinary. It's a wonderfully prosaic life."

You frequently hear monks talk of the peace that can come from "accepting the life" and learning to find joy in the details of everyday tasks.

Not that it's easy; not that there's no struggle. Brother Benjamin, a 38-year-old Canadian monk, put it this way: "Nothing is expected of us except to be. That sounds great, until you have to do it."

On my first visit, Ben told me how he initially balked at the work he now does—an office job that involves programming the computer that processes orders for the abbey's catalog food items. It was a rough adjustment after working in the kitchen, a homey place where people come for nourishment and conversation.

A journal-keeper and poetry-writer with an interest in woodworking, Ben resisted the idea of typing at a keyboard because the task seemed too technical, too detached from the life of his brothers and lacking in spiritual value.

"Now I experience being 'simple and poor' as doing what needs to be done," he said.

Somehow the peacefulness on the other side of that sort of personal struggle pervades the abbey grounds, passing over monastery walls and filtering through to those who visit.

I wondered: Was it that mix of struggle and peace,

and not just the quiet bucolic setting, that lures 3,000 men and women—many of them not Catholic, some with no religious beliefs at all—to make overnight retreats at Gethsemani each year?

Is that what's behind the letters and calls that pour in from some 200 men a year eager to know more about the order?

My first night at the monastery, I met Ruth Peyton, a friendly woman from Charleston, W.V., who has made four retreats since the abbey opened its doors to women in June 1989. She told me how she signed up for two more next year.

We spoke in the dark on the stairs outside the church, between the newly renovated retreat house and the wall separating public from private parts of the abbey.

On one side of us, over the retreat house door, capital letters spelled out PAX, the Latin word for peace. On the other, above a gate opening into a court-yard of the monastery, there were two English words: GOD ALONE. Earlier that day, I watched a middle-aged man unceremoniously enter that monks-only gate, a duffel bag slung over his shoulder. Luke told me the fellow was coming to try out the life, one of four or five who end up entering out of the hundreds who inquire each year.

"It's so easy to become filled with awe at the trappings of the Trappists," Peyton said, smiling at her own turn of phrase. "But you quickly learn you have to pull back and say to yourself, 'That's not why I came.' And that's when you see the beauty of it."

My first visit had shattered so many preconceptions that, within minutes, I could hardly remember what I had originally expected. Had I really thought the monks—some ordained priests, most lay brothers—would somehow all look alike, cloaked and hooded and solemn and saintly and perhaps greeting me in sign language?

I quickly learned that, for years, some monks have worn street clothes at work, especially if flowing hems and sleeves could be a danger around farm equipment or other machines. And despite widespread beliefs to the contrary, Trappists never took a "vow of silence." Their vows are of chastity, poverty, obedience and stability— the latter being a promise to stay put at their abbey. Silence was and is considered a discipline, like not eating meat, a tradition still thriving at Gethsemani.

Most monks talk during the day, though there are times and places—during meals, for example, or in their rooms—where silence is strictly observed. Along with Latin Masses and heavy denim work robes, sign language went out in the '60s, and from all accounts nobody misses this powerful mode of non-verbal communication—nor the many aggressive uses of silence itself.

"There are many ways to tell someone to go to hell without saying a word," Father Michael, the vocations director, reminded me.

Father Abbot Timothy Kelly said he remembers coming back to the abbey in 1968 after three years of study in Rome to find life there radically changed.

"I left a Latin, silent community and found a talking, English one," he said.

Do not go to Gethsemani expecting to see what life was like in 1098, the year the Cistercian Order was established in Europe. Don't go looking for a glimpse of what it was like in 1848, when Gethsemani was founded by a band of French monks invited to Kentucky by Benedict Joseph Flaget, the first Catholic bishop of Kentucky. Don't even expect to see what Trappist life was like in Merton's time, when there were three times as many monks, most of them novices.

Unless, of course, you're willing to look below the surface.

The contemplative life of a Trappist monk—"a good system of taking you apart and letting you see inside yourself," as one monk described it to me—is the same as it was. The formula set down 1,500 years ago by St. Benedict, the Benedictines' founder, is still the basis of the life at Gethsemani: a balance of prayer, work and study.

Life in the abbey, the oldest monastery in North America, is punctuated by six daily prayer services, called "offices," which give form to the day, much the way well-placed commas lend rhythm and clarity to a long line of poetry. The first is at 3:45 in the morning, when the monks begin their day, and the last is at 7:30 in the evening. By 8, the men are in their rooms for the night.

All but a handful of the monks come to the abbey church for these services, taking their regular places in the rows of plain wooden prayer stalls that border the church walls. The others—mainly monks whose jobs leave less time for meditation during the day—pray in a quieter, simpler, less public way at the same time but in a room by themselves.

"My experience is monks don't find it any easier to pray than anyone else, but we have structure to support and encourage it," Ben said.

"God is teaching us who we are here, and that's mysterious. Faith is very important and trust and the willingness to be part of a community and to let others help us—and not to be so individualistic and independent, as North Americans always want to be."

Across Monks Road from the Abbey of Gethsemani, up a gently rising hillside framed by Nelson County knobs, there's a well-worn trail that begins in an open field and gradually leads to a place where the path splits and you must choose for yourself which way to go.

The only marker is a small sign to the left, pointing to where the trail moves up a slope into the woods. The sign says simply "To Statues."

If you choose that route, you eventually will come to two sculptures known collectively as "The Garden of Gethsemani." You will find the first one partly hidden among trees—three men in robes, resting one against the other on the ground, asleep.

If you move a few steps up the hillside, you will see a clearing with a second sculpture, a man alone.

He's on his knees, this larger-than-life bronze figure. His head is thrown back in what can only be agony or despair, arms upraised, palms pressed against his face.

On my first tour of Gethsemani, a Trappist brother took me to this clearing, which he said was a favorite spot for monks and guests alike. We rested there a few minutes on simple wooden seats. A circle of high trees surrounded us, blocking out the sound of traffic on the road below and forming a canopy of green lace over our heads.

"Every abbey has its flavor—that's ours," Brother Christian said, nodding at the statue. "Our main purpose here is to pray. But a part of our rule also is to have a place where people can come to fall apart."

I thought of the retreat house across the road and how some of the people who fill its 31 rooms week after week must surely arrive at the door in need of a place to fall apart—and perhaps a monk, like Luke, to counsel them or just listen.

I thought, too, of what Christian told me earlier in his broad Boston accent: how the contemplative life was not about escaping the world or running away from human relationships. "One of the aspects of our life people don't understand is that, as you get closer to God, you realize that he's not exclusive. He's all-inclusive."

He explained this as we rattled along in a dusty white pickup past cornfields and cattle barns and, tucked way back in the woods, a cabin with no electricity or running water where a monk, recently back from 20 years in Mexico, now is living as a hermit.

Christian's comment struck me as one of the many paradoxes of the simple life at Gethsemani—a life that encourages both solitude and community, that demands a personal withdrawal from the world at the same time that it warmly welcomes visitors from the outside.

"If you're praying to God, then yes, you're setting aside the noise and the nonsense—but not the people,"

Christian said, squinting through his dark-framed glasses as the truck bounced us over the rutted dirt roads.

"I really don't think you could stay here if you didn't believe what you were doing affected people."

Enter Brother Raphael, a monk who identified himself as "just a numbers-cruncher" over the phone when I arranged my first visit. Though he is, indeed, in charge of the abbey's promotion and sale of its Gethsemani Farms products, I had to laugh at the incongruity—the impossibility—of his self-description.

Raphael's intention, no doubt.

But later, in a room on the second floor of a converted cow barn on the "monastic" side of the wall, standing beside the computer at the high-tech heart of the abbey's mail-order business, I had to admit that Raphael did not fit anyone's romanticized image of a monk.

He was wearing tennis shoes and casual clothes, and when he stepped outside, he snuggled a baseball cap onto his head. At lunch, he talked about his stint as a World War II Navy flight instructor and confided that one of his fondest wishes was to ride in a United Parcel Service jet simulator he'd read about in The Courier-Journal. He bowed out of aviation well before the advent of jets.

Raphael came to Gethsemani in the mid-1950s, "disappointed in the culture's values" after World War II. He had never seen combat himself. He was on his way to the Pacific theater when the atomic bombing of Hiroshima and Nagasaki brought an abrupt end to the war. He remembers hearing news of "the bomb" while in St. Louis visiting his family before heading out. After the war, he returned home to work in a relative's heavy-construction business, which he liked well enough. But he wanted more.

At the abbey, in 1958, when he was assigned a job in the same converted barn where he now works, Raphael remembers thinking the "business" side of monastery life couldn't possibly be right for him.

"But I can see the providence of God in it now," he told me one day.

His assignment has made him one of the monks most in touch with people outside the abbey—from computer programmers and catalog designers to New York Times reporters and visiting politicians. Raphael is well-suited for the job, an easy man to talk to, whether the topic is God or FAX machines.

Though the abbey has no official media-relations monk ("We've had our PR man," says Michael, the vocations director, alluding to Merton), Raphael comes closest to filling that role. He has escorted a host of visitors from Phyllis George Brown to network-TV news folks.

On my first visit, Raphael took me to the bakery where—with amazingly little noise or commotion— hundreds of fruitcakes are baked six mornings a week (even on national holidays but never on Catholic feast days), from Jan. 3 till the first of December. He showed me the impressive machine, designed by a monk, that pumps bourbon into each cooled cake. He introduced me to the brothers who sort through California walnuts and Georgia pecans, looking for shell bits, and those who carefully and quickly place dyed cherries and nuts on the tops of the fresh cakes.

Brother Simeon, the chief of the bakery, begins work about 7:30 a.m., after Mass, and is finished with the entire process—including mixing ingredients for the next day's batter—by noon, in time for the next service at 12:15. Once a month, he takes a day off from fruit-cakes to bake bread for the abbey.

"Fruitcakes are our biggest item," Raphael told me. In the 1940s, when it became clear the monks could no longer depend on small farming to support them-selves, they decided to go all-out on cheese and fruitcakes. They sold their pigs and stopped selling sausage, bacon and ham. They sold their blue-ribbon herd of dairy cows and took to buying local farmers' milk to make cheese. They invested in beef cattle, a far less labor-intensive animal.

With help from a couple of local hired hands, just two monks now tend the 400 or so acres of cultivated land, including crops of soybeans and corn. Local farmers rent some land. A vegetable garden supplies eight tons of potatoes a year, plus other mealtime staples.

Today mail-order business brings in the major share of the $1 million a year it takes to run the abbey. That includes feeding and housing monks, providing routine medical care and running a 14-room infirmary. The retreat house has always paid for itself, though the abbey asks only a donation and doesn't even suggest an amount.

The monks offer, by mail order only, two sizes of fruitcake, three kinds of Trappist cheese, a variety of combination boxes and a new product—bourbon candy. "Americans love variety," Raphael said. Late fall is the time of year when orders pour in, down-to-the-wire requests for wheels and wedges of smoked, mild and strong cheeses and traditional red tins of bourbon-soaked fruitcake all to be sent out as Christmas presents. No one is likely to complain about the increased activity in the mail-order office.

As Luke likes to say, "It puts chow on our table."

Though I arrived at Gethsemani with an image of Merton as a warm, witty, well-read, spirited as well as spiritual man, I must have tucked him away in the "exception" category in my mental file on monks. I wasn't prepared for a jokester like Luke or the dry sense of humor of a monk like Gerlac, the novice master.

When I asked Gerlac about his name, he said he received it while the abbot at the time was away. When the abbot returned, another monk who was given a similarly exotic name in his absence asked to exchange it for something else, Gerlac recalled.

"The abbot said fine and renamed him Sylvester. I decided to stick with Gerlac."

Later, when I told Raphael I somehow hadn't expected the vividness of personalities I was encountering, he stuck up his thumb. "It's like this," he said. "From a distance, everybody's thumb print looks the same. But up close, each one is unique."

I was glad to be getting a close-up look—not just at personalities but at the life and the meaning it holds for people outside its walls.

On my first day at the abbey, Raphael drove me

into the woods for a glimpse of Merton's hermitage, a small cabin now used by monks desiring a quiet week alone to pray. We sat in the car, to avoid disturbing the monk staying there. But then he spotted us and invited us inside.

I'd seen photographs of the exterior of the hermitage many times, and I'd read so many passages about it in Merton's journals that I felt at home. The flat roof, the simple porch, the stand of trees. The Shaker porch furniture had been Merton's, I was told, again reminding me of "Simple Gifts." Inside, the smell of incense hovered sweet and thick. A visiting priest had just celebrated Mass.

At night, in the woods surrounding the hermitage, you can hear coyotes howl. Fox and deer come close to the house, a monk who stayed there told me. We walked through the front room with its fireplace and its shelves of Merton's books bearing his personal stamp inside the covers. We moved into the small kitchen for a look at the bedroom with its view of the woods and a peek at the room used for Mass. Then we said goodbye, leaving the monk to his prayers.

It had been a brief and accidental visit—an unforgettable side trip.

The day I talked to Brother Benjamin about how he got to Gethsemani, we sat outside in lawn chairs. "It's been a very difficult and profound experience," he said.

As a Catholic teen-ager in Canada, he stopped going to church and considered himself a non-believer. But touring Europe after high school, he found himself drawn to Catholic monasteries. He came home feeling "a strong need for God" and a renewed interest in prayer. He had read Merton; he knew about Gethsemani. He decided to visit. He remembers his first stay, during a long hot Kentucky summer, as a "lonely experience." That fall he enrolled in a Canadian university but could not shake Gethsemani from his mind.

"There was something a little attractive about it, and something a little frightening too," he said.

In 1974, at 22, he decided after all to become a monk. But after two years of trying it out, he felt he'd made a mistake. He left, earned a second degree, worked on a Quebec dairy farm, tried missionary work in Labrador—"but nothing felt comfortable."

Years passed, but his attraction to Gethsemani didn't. Eventually he decided to go back. He has taken his permanent vows.

"It's a challenging life. I don't get so frightened anymore when things fall apart. And things do come apart. Great changes take place," Ben said.

"When you enter, your hair is shaven, your name taken away and another given. Spiritually a lot of things happen out of that."

Benjamin said he has come to appreciate the "sense of continuity" in the monk's life—not just participation in rituals that have remained much the same for 900 years but also the chance to be part of a close-knit community. "We see men grow old and die here, and there's a sense of completion in that, which is very powerful," he said.

When a monk is close to death, his fellow monks

take turns sitting with him. When the time comes, bells toll and all monks gather at his bed.

"The starkness of the way death is handled—there's nothing cosmetic about it here—can be difficult for some people," Ben said. "We don't do a lot of embalming. There's no coffin. We just wrap the body and commend the spirit to God. The funeral's within 24 hours, especially if it's hot weather."

As novice master, the position Merton held from 1955 to 1963, Gerlac meets three times a week with the abbey's five novices—monks who've been there more than six months but have not made permanent vows. A novice can reaffirm his temporary commitment for up to nine years. After that, a decision must be made.

"Though it's not as hard as it was, it's still a hard life. But it's a healthy life for a healthy person," Gerlac said.

"Some people come to work out problems or to avoid them. But you can't forget your problems here. Some people try too hard to work them out through prayer. Have you ever read 'Franny and Zooey'?" he asked, referring to J.D. Salinger's story about a troubled young woman who unsuccessfully runs from her problems by constantly saying a traditional meditative prayer called The Jesus Prayer.

"It's not a life of having mystical experiences," Father Michael, the vocations director, said. "People tend to romanticize us, and that holds up for about three days."

To weed out weak candidates, all prospective monks are given psychological tests. Those under 22 or over 45, considered poor risks for adapting, are discouraged. The average age for new arrivals is 35.

The oldest monk at Gethsemani is now 90; the youngest, 28. Studies show that while novice classes go up and down in size, the number who stick with it remains fairly constant.

Michael said he looks for certain characteristics in candidates: good self-esteem, an ability to accept restrictions on movement.

"You can't just go out to a ballgame or watch TV or get a drink at a pub when you want to," he said. "We also look for men with some insight into what love is really about—not just an emotion but wanting to share your life with others and to suffer the consequences of that.

"And a person really has to have been touched by God enough to pursue his own spiritual destiny."

Carol Darst did not go to Gethsemani with the intention of falling apart. It just happened to happen that way.

I met Darst during my last visit to the monastery in early November. It was 8:30 at night, "late" by abbey standards. Darst was calling home on the one and only pay telephone in the retreat house; I was waiting to do the same.

Darst lives in Danville, just a 50-mile drive from the abbey. She, too, has stayed at the guesthouse four times since Gethsemani opened retreats to women. She is a Centre College graduate, but she had not known much about Gethsemani until she and her husband, an actor and writer, moved to California. There a fellow actor introduced them to Merton's writing.

At the time of her first two retreats, the Darsts were trying to adopt a child. Several times they thought a baby was on its way; then, at the last minute, adoption plans fell through.

"It always seemed to happen just before I was coming here, and I would get here and cry the whole time," Darst told me the morning after our phone-booth encounter, as we sat in a conference room on the first floor of the retreat house. The sun was just beginning to lighten up the sky and the room.

Darst said Luke, the guestmaster, helped her through those crises: "He was wonderful." Last January the Darsts finally got their baby, a Korean child they named William. They asked Luke to be the godfather. To their grateful surprise, he said yes. At William's baptism in Danville, Luke was represented by proxy. But the Darsts bring him to visit every month or so, and a framed photograph of William, now 15 months old, holds a prominent position in Luke's office.

"I guess what keeps me coming back is how welcome I feel. It's hard to explain. Everything I could say would sound trite," Darst said. "You grow to know the monks' faces, to look for them in choir. There's a feeling of peace here that I don't feel anywhere else."

Retreats at Gethsemani have never been promoted by the Trappists. People usually hear about the guesthouse from friends. Yet when the abbey quietly began setting aside the first week of each month for women last year, following the massive renovation of the guest house, Luke immediately found women's weeks were filling up months in advance. That pattern has continued.

The abbey's now considering giving women retreatants equal time.

Although many nuns and priests stay at the guest house, one out of four retreatants is not Catholic, Luke said. A Hebrew school from Lexington made a day retreat not long ago. And there's usually a mix of young and old during the two weekly retreat periods— Monday through Friday and weekends.

In the 1940s, before the community peaked at about 275 monks and a guest house was built, male visitors could stay overnight in one of 20 rooms in the front of the abbey. Sometimes in a pinch, Luke still can find such a room for a last-minute male retreatant.

"Lots of people come in crisis. In the middle of a divorce, say. I always have a room for someone like that," Luke said.

Retreatants come from all over the world; not surprisingly, most come with at least some desire to connect with the place that was home to Merton— Father Louis to his fellow Trappists. The first thing many do after arriving is find his grave. Merton, who died at a monastic conference in Bangkok, is buried in the cemetery behind the retreat house. His grave marker is like the 230 others in the plot, a small white cross in a line of other small white crosses. It's inscribed simply: Fr. Louis Merton and the dates of his birth and death.

Like retreatants, about half the men who inquire about becoming monks mention Merton too. "His spirit will never fade from here," Luke said.

A New York City native, Luke began his own

journey to Gethsemani by reading (and not liking) Merton's autobiography, "The Seven Storey Mountain." Later he reread it, made a retreat at the Trappist monastery and—echoing many of his brothers at the abbey—"just knew" right away it was home. He was 22, just out of college.

The first time I met him, he greeted me in the monk's customary robe and scapular, or apron—but with a camera swinging from a strap around his neck. His Tuesday night slide shows for retreatants tend to be lighthearted, full of puns and self-effacing jokes to put people at ease and quickly erase the romantic vision of monastic life that most monks find distasteful and distracting.

As a metaphor for what the monastic life is all about, Luke uses slides illustrating changes made to the church in 1966. The "before" slides show a cathedral-like interior with Gothic arches and vaulted ceilings made of plaster. The "after" slides picture a much simpler church, with plaster ripped away from the walls and ceiling and bare brick walls exposed.

Luke compares this transformation to a monk's goals for his own interior life: "Remove the bogus, reveal the authentic."

This line gets laughs, of course. But it also sets the tone for the simple, unadorned, do-it-yourself retreat that is encouraged at Gethsemani, where there is no gift shop and no bookstore (though plenty of Merton titles in the guest house library).

Though Luke and the abbey chaplain are available for conferences on request, how you spend your time is up to you—sleeping in your modern room with private bath, hiking on the 1,000 acres of Gethsemani land across the road from the abbey, sitting quietly in the church or guest chapel that are never locked, meditating in the meditation room, or chanting psalms with monks in church. The only "rule" is silence, which is kept in most inside areas, including the dining room. Luke said many people come simply for a quiet place to be alone.

"My guess is that the culture is so overstimulating that this offers refreshment without rival. There are no expectations here. No place to go and all day to get there."

Retreat meals consist of the simple food the monks eat, with a meat dish added. Everyone faces the same direction, looking out windows that open to the garden and the woods beyond the road.

The morning I was to leave for home, I sat looking out those windows, wondering how to explain what it is that brings people to this abbey from all over the world, particularly in times of pain or struggle. That's when I felt someone approach me and turned to see Carol Darst with a piece of paper. She had been pondering the same question.

The note she gave me said: "I think Psalm 130...sums it up: 'Truly I have set my soul in silence and peace. A weaned child on its mother's breast, even so is my soul.'"

When I think of Gethsemani now, it's no longer Merton I think of first, though he certainly led me there. It's not fruitcake or cheese. It's not any of the "trappings of the Trappists" that come to mind.

What I think of are the individual monks I met and the less-traveled path they have taken and how that path once seemed restrictive and rigid and now—for all its rules and regimens—seems refreshingly simple, genuinely free.

December 2, 1990

Beauty
In The
Branches

I discovered the beauty in bare branches this year. And the mystery. I found it in Cave Hill Cemetery in February and March on the nearly daily walks I took through that rambling 300-acre graveyard, which is a five-minute walk from my front porch.

It was a rediscovery, in some ways—both of the cemetery and of the significance of bare branches.

Years ago a friend from Louisville who went to college in Nashville and always thought of herself as a "Southern girl" looked up one day to find herself settled in, of all places, Chicago. From the start, the Windy City's long winters were hard on Gail. She missed spring, which is brief up there and never as spectacular as it is here. She missed summer, its green lushness. She missed autumn, especially the fireworks in the trees in late October.

Her aunt, who lived in Nashville, sympathized and sent her a book called "Bare Branches." I can still see it: a slim volume of black-and-white sketches, each one of a leafless tree in winter.

Leafless, mind you; but not lifeless. For all their barren bark, these trees seemed to be bursting with vitality. Not a bud on them or a blush of color, but still they were dramatically, mysteriously alive.

This was her aunt's message. The book was a reminder that sometimes we don't recognize life when it's smack in front of us, because it is not packaged the way we expect it to be.

If we keep looking, though, and watching and paying attention, even when we think it's deserted us, we may discover the pulse of spring in the least likely places.

In naked woods. In winter. In a cemetery.

I've thought of those "bare branches" off and on over the years—and of the message of hidden life they seemed to convey.

But it didn't really come home to me until this year in Cave Hill, during those two glorious months that overlap the gap between winter and spring.

Those Cave Hill walks quickly became a part of my weekday routine during a two-month leave from full-time newspapering that I took earlier this year.

I chose February and March because I associate them with grim weather and a dormant time of year unlikely to distract me from an indoor project I wanted to complete.

What I discovered day by day was a series of subtle but unceasing changes in trees and bushes and ground cover, starting in February, preparing the way for spring.

Wherever I looked closely at bare branches I found specks of green, nearly invisible, or tiny swellings in the bark that would gradually sprout into leaves or twigs.

It became an addiction—finding the secret bulges where life was beginning to burst out of what looked like dead wood.

And, of course, I had to laugh at my naivete. A botanist, an arborist or just a more outdoorsy person would have known better than to think these months would be bleak and spiritless.

Unlike my first-grader, I am not convinced of the existence of ghosts. But at times I came to appreciate that spirits were at work, playing with my imagination, sending me messages, if you will.

One day I passed an ironwood tree and then another called limber wood, and I thought of how those two, together, are what most of us long to be—strong but flexible and resilient. We want strength to bear our burdens but in a way that allows for bending, flexing, giving.

The very next tree I came across was a Turkish filbert, which made me laugh: What a nut to be reading so much into tree names!

The geese and ducks were out that day, perching on gravestones or honking at one another, and the swans were gliding effortlessly as ever on the lake, hardly ruffling the surface. It felt terrific to be alive, and I did not overlook the irony of this rush of life while traipsing through a cemetery.

On other walks, I made mental notes of epitaphs and last names.

"FELL ASLEEP," reads one small marker along the main road. "MAGGIE DIED," says another, followed simply by the date.

And the monument I always look for, like a signpost along a trail, is a simple rectangular stone with a family name carved in capital letters that I never fail to read as some kind of personal mandate:

"QUEST," it says.

The trees' names are just as wonderful, from the sublime to the down-home. Star magnolia. Forest pansy redbud. False cypress. Red buckeye.

My Cave Hill walks were hatched, I'll admit, for aerobic exercise, to keep my heart fit and healthy. And I usually kept a brisk pace as I wandered the roads, sometimes weaving up a grassy hill, hopscotching between the humblest grave markers and the grandest of monuments.

But gradually I began to lose that goal, or maybe it's better to say "let go" of that goal. Intentions had little to do with my walks, after a time. What was important was being quiet, being alone, being led.

Most people know Cave Hill as a Louisville landmark, dedicated in 1848, home of some of the most gorgeous monuments you will ever see and the biggest names in local history. They know it for its five spring-fed lakes or as a place to drive through on a pretty afternoon or on the morning of a funeral.

But if you like to walk, if you're willing to empty yourself of preconceptions, Cave Hill is a marvelous spot to let nature have its way with you.

The 13 miles of paved roads inside Cave Hill tend to

spiral off, winding back into one another—a lot like my thoughts on those walks.

Some days, I found my peripheral vision picking up certain lines of poetry or Scripture, a pleasing sculpture here, a first forsythia budding there. That would lead me to remember a person or a place or other memorable lines from books or bits of conversation.

One day it dawned on me that I was slowing down, taking time actually to *stop* and read the lines on the monuments, to examine the yellow buds pushing out of their bark wombs. It also dawned on me that this, too, was good for my heart—the one that pumps the blood as well as the one that fuels the spirit and fosters those rhythmic connections that nourish the soul.

That is the day I spotted another of my favorite tombstone names: TRUEHEART.

Gradually I mustered new respect for the four weeks of February. The poor month has often been maligned for being "bleak"—usually by those of us who've watched the passing of too many winters through sealed-up, smoke-filled windows in office buildings.

From what everyone tells me, this was a particularly long, gray winter—the kind that breeds "wintertime blues" and Florida vacations. I've had seasons like that, where day after day clouds kept the sun at bay, when I felt I'd go anywhere to get away from them. But this winter I never noticed a lack of light.

There also is wildlife in Cave Hill, enough to keep you guessing all the time. Years ago I saw a deer right outside the cemetery wall near Cherokee Road. I had been hitting tennis balls against the wall with a friend when the deer suddenly appeared, unnerving me with its grace.

Later I learned from a cemetery groundskeeper that deer sometimes swim across the Ohio River to Beargrass Creek and find their way into the cemetery. He told me he had never seen a deer there himself. But he'd found antlers many times, and that was enough to make a believer of him.

This year I've seen chipmunks scurrying down an embankment and turtles sunning on a tree fallen across the lake and Canada geese perched on monuments in such perfect stillness you would swear they were one with the stone.

Once at Cave Hill I was visited by a peacock.

It was officially the last day of my leave, the final Friday of March, a few days before Easter. I was sitting on a rock atop the hill that slopes down to the lake, half hidden by some weepy bushes.

I sensed a rustling below me. I hadn't realized I was sitting directly above the cave that gives the cemetery its name. I looked down and at its opening, in a sweep of turquoise and deep-green and plum-colored plumage, a peacock walked out. A friend told me later that peacocks are ancient religious symbols, first used by the Greeks to convey man's hope for immortality beyond the grave.

A few weeks ago, after returning to my job and a schedule that allows far fewer saunters through Cave Hill, I found a spare hour around lunchtime to walk.

Spring had taken an awesome hold on the grounds by then. Everywhere you looked the colors dazzled. Coral dogwoods. Lavender lilacs. Fuchsia azaleas. Scarlet peonies. And wild strawberries everywhere, like drops of red paint in the grass. The trees that didn't look splashy as Easter eggs were a luscious, ripe green.

But it was noisy inside. Wagonloads of men, pulled by tractors, rumbled along the roadways—ivy trimmers, lawn mowers, tree pruners. The hum of power tools drowned out some of the usual birdsong—though not the rowdy honking of geese.

A young woman worked hard to make a grave rubbing on one hillside I like to walk. A van full of Cub Scouts disembarked at the lake, cameras clicking. A carload of sightseers in a sleek white convertible stopped me to ask, "Where's Col. Sanders?"—one of the more celebrated citizens of this haven. As the convertible moved on, I had to fight off a self-righteous urge to shout to all these fair-weather friends, "And where were you in February?"

But I caught myself.

They were where I was, of course, for so many winters before this one.

May 16, 1991

Staying Put

My next-door neighbor was born in a house four blocks from the one where her husband was born.

And not much farther away from those two houses is the one where she now lives—and has for 44 years.

I call that stability.

If you're tempted to write off this retirement-age couple as unadventuresome, consider their travel itinerary over the past five years.

They've made trips—some on foot, some by train—through China, Britain, France, Italy, the Galapagos Islands and a number of U.S. cities, including San Francisco, Boston, New York and Los Angeles.

It's clearly not fear of the unknown or lack of curiosity that has kept them in the neighborhood they've known all their lives.

It's not an *absence* of anything, but the presence of something—a fierce affection and an abiding connection to the place where they were born. They are rooted to it, as stubbornly as the ivy growing up their porch wall.

My neighbors understand the paradox of staying put. They know that by anchoring yourself to one place, you can travel every bit as far as those who move from one spot to another.

I thought of my neighbors a couple of weeks ago when the Census Bureau broke the news that Kentucky had the fourth-highest percentage of natives still living in their home state.

For my friends, staying put is a calling. It's a lifelong commitment to better understanding the place where they live, the people who inhabit it, the trees and dirt and skies that nourish it.

The wife is a walker who knows the personal history of each house on the block. The husband, a runner, knows the hills and flat stretches of a nearby park by heart.

"He calls it his English countryside," she told me recently. "He says it's been a gift to be able to watch it all these years."

After hearing the new census figures, Kentucky historian Thomas Clark remarked, "There aren't many Americans who have a more emotional attachment to place than Kentuckians do." Perhaps that is why two of the country's best-known and most prolific writers on the topic of "stability" have been Kentuckians: Thomas Merton, a transplant, and Wendell Berry, a native.

Berry doesn't just write about the environmental benefits of staying put, he lives them out as a farmer in Henry County.

As a Trappist monk, Merton took a "vow of stability," a solemn promise to stay put in one community for life. But he wrestled hard with temptations to move on to monasteries beyond the one in Nelson County where he lived until his death in 1968.

It's difficult for many of us to imagine agreeing never to move. We can't conceive of putting down roots the way a tree does, with every intention of getting all our needs met from one humble plot of earth.

But we certainly can identify with the internal conflict, the choice between sticking with a problem or running from it.

A Zen master put it this way: "Where can you find the truth if not right where you are?"

I'm sure my neighbor thinks of the park as a "gift" because of the relationship he has shared with it. The land has taught him about survival. And about renewal.

He has seen it ravaged by a tornado, flooded by overflowing creeks, scorched brown in droughts. But he has also witnessed it bursting with wildflowers, swirling with autumn leaves, hidden in a blizzard.

All this has motivated him to protect the park and enhance it. It's his way of returning the favor.

But not all people who live where they were born behave as my neighbors do.

Provincialism, infatuation with the status quo and plain old unfriendliness can thrive when too many like-minded people of similar backgrounds gather in one place.

I think of a reader who called me to say she loved

Louisville but found it hard to "break in." She had lived here for decades, it turned out, but was still constantly reminded of her outsider status by the perennial question: "Where did you go to school?"—meaning, of course, high school.

As someone who spent the first half of her life virtually within one house, and the second half solidly within one neighborhood, I concede it took a long time for me to appreciate either the comfort or the challenge of staying put.

Today my feeling about it is best described in the opening of a poem by Berry called "Traveling at Home." It's about the art of walking a familiar path.

"Even in a country you know by heart," says the poet, "it's hard to go the same way twice."

March 28, 1993

Water, Water Everywhere

I remember one miserably hot week a few summers back when I lugged a lawn chair and beach bag and my little boy to the swimming pool every night after work, not caring what else might be going on or how many other people might have the same idea, just desperate to find a cool wet place to rest my body and let him unwind for the few hours until sunset.

I still can see the group of us, idling in the tepid water of one corner of the pool.

Children, retirees, husbands and wives. Some of us stood in water up to our shoulders in the four-foot area, barely moving. Some sat on the long wide steps that ease their way into the pool, water lapping at their waists.

Even the kids seemed to move in slow motion.

In my mind's eye, the scene is hazy with heat and slightly out of focus, like a Maurice Prendergast watercolor of a seaside resort.

I like this memory because it's so out of character. Most days the sprawling pool where I've spent the past 15 summers looks more like one of those hustle-bustle Pieter Brueghel paintings of a European village. You know the scene: boys spinning hoops in one corner, girls milking cows in another, and every inch of available space crowded with parades, outdoor suppers, farmers harvesting crops and people dancing, playing ball, splashing in a lake.

None of them are aware of the others, so obviously immersed in their own fun.

That's what I love about hanging out at the pool: the organized chaos of it, the personification of summer itself.

Maybe it is the perpetually adolescent atmosphere that pervades a pool in summer. Or maybe it's the smells we remember from childhood: the sting of chlorine; exotic lotions, sweet and sticky against damp skin; smoke from the concession-stand grill teasing tears from our eyes.

Whatever the reason, pools seduce adults into feeling like kids, and kids into thinking they're all grown-up.

Watch the first-time cannonballers crash from the high dive—the explosion of spewing water, a rite of passage not to be forgotten. See the grandmothers in their swim caps heading with purpose to the lap lanes, where they become as lithe and nimble as their memories. Like revelers in a Brueghel painting, the lane-lappers aren't aware of the high-divers or anyone else.

How could they be?

At any given moment, the landscape is in motion with toddlers testing the water in their "swimmies," sunbathers turning over their beach towels, guys shooting hoops on the basketball court, couples chilled out on matching floats in the raft area, kids juggling junk food from the concession stand and the token panicked parent surveying acres of water for a child who was smack under foot just a second ago and is now lost in the mass of latex and flesh.

I'm easy, I guess.

Just give me a sweaty Pepsi and a pair of shades, a chaise lounge in the sun and a solid stretch of, say, 10 minutes without someone calling, "Mom Mom Mom WATCH THIS!" and I can fill up with a sense of wonder at human nature in its infinite permutations.

I've often thought it could be the steady chant of children, like katydids on an August night, that lures me into this state.

One day I set out to really listen to those poolside sounds. Here's what I heard: a constant chorus of whoops, cries and laughter; a low drone of gossip; a symphony of splashes, squishes, drippings, spewings and whooshes of water, water, everywhere water.

And, oh yes, the *pop* of floats bursting in the hands of overzealous pumpers at the air-hose station. A lifeguard's piercing whistle and the stern shout that follows: "No running!" The raspy loudspeaker spitting out illegally parked license-plate numbers with the cool detachment of a Bingo caller.

It's a grand, goofy, guiltless world: a pool in summer.

What else would you expect at a place where the dress code is any colorful variation on an underwear theme, and the snacks du jour run the gourmet gamut from nachos to snow cones?

I asked a friend recently what she remembered most about growing up spending summers at a pool. She said it was the surprise each year when she'd meet up with the kids she'd hung out with the season before—only now they looked a year older.

I know what she means.

Some summers it seems all the women are pregnant. The next season they're dipping baby toes into shallow water. And after that, it's a progression from a perch at the edge of the wading pool to the top of the steps or to the bleachers by the lanes where swim lessons are given.

There's a swimming pool culture: a language of its own, a set of traditions and unspoken rules. Pool lingo is alliterative, rhythmically monosyllabic like swimming itself. Flip-flops. Swimsuits. Lap lanes. High dives. Water wings.

Our pool has no parking lot, so part of the ritual of going there is cruising the neighborhood for a place to parallel park. Sometimes, after I've circled the same streets two or three times and noticed in the rear-view mirror that the car behind me is making the same circles, I feel I'm part of a grand dance of summer.

The last waltz is this week: School starts, and the pool closes. Fall unofficially begins.

It's true, I could go to the pool when it reopens for winter, with a bubble pulled over part of it. But somehow it wouldn't be the same for me without the birds swooping down to clean up the leftover chips by my blanket, without the hovering bees moving in for their share, without the sweat and the sun.

Without summer.

August 29, 1993

A Week
Of One's
Own

"You take vacation time to come here?"

We are standing on a porch in Nelson County, Ky., surrounded by trees ablaze in autumn colors. Maples. Dogwoods. A ginkgo on the verge of yellow. In every direction, there are woods in the distance—first the low rolling hills and then, circling the earth as far as we can see, great wooded knobs rising up in a ring.

"What do your friends think of this? Spending your vacation here?"

My questioner is a Houston television reporter. He is making a documentary and this place is one of his stops.

"Do they think it's odd?"

If I were out here in God's country on a camping trip with my family or with coworkers sharing an office planning session or on a weekend getaway to finish a novel or on a rendezvous with a lover, perhaps no one would think it odd—my spending five days off the beaten track here in Central Kentucky, living out of a

10-by-12 room with no TV, no radio, no telephone.

But I'm here for nothing. I mean that literally. I have nothing planned. Nothing to accomplish.

Of course, being the human being I am, I *will* accomplish something. I will read the next chapter in the book I brought. I will explore the path beyond the meadow I've seen but never taken in the past. I will outline a story an editor expects to have soon after I return. I will catch up on sleep lost while my husband was out of town on business the week before.

I will make a friend, meet my first red fox, find a 300-million-year-old fossil to take home to my son.

But none of that is why I came.

I came for nothing.

If you dig deep into the word "vacation," you eventually reach its Latin root, *vacare*.

It means to be empty, to be free—as in words like vacuum, vacant or vacate. In Latin, in fact, "vacate" (VAH-KAH-TAY) is a one-word command meaning "Be empty" or "Be still."

Or "Be free."

Thus it is not so unorthodox, spending a vacation free of plans, empty of goals, still and alone.

I have been doing this twice a year for three years now. Same place; roughly same time. The Abbey of Gethsemani guesthouse—early spring and mid-autumn. I come with the budding wildflowers and the falling leaves.

I'm not alone in wanting to be alone. Rooms here are booked a year in advance. What's odd to me is not the choice I make in coming, but how quickly I adapt to the pace once I arrive. I don't miss the jangling phone, the humming computer, the mail delivery, the weather channel, the front page, "Morning Edition," driving, snacking, schmoozing or even sleeping in my own bed.

The truth is I'm so overstimulated and worn-out by the time I get away from the busy-ness of life, I am more than ready to surrender the amenities I tell myself I can't do without.

Dorothy was right: There's no place like home. But sometimes you have to get away from it. Being blessed with house and family and friends and work doesn't cancel out the need, now and then, for a room of one's own.

Of course, it's my choice. It's not a forced alone-ness.

"No doubt about it, solitude is improved by being voluntary," writes Barbara Holland, author of a book about living alone. "If you live with other people, their temporary absence can be refreshing."

But if I were honest, I would say that what I find refreshing has little to do with getting away from the people I live with, and much more to do with leaving behind my own spinning head.

I generally notice the absence of that spinning somewhere near the Brooks Road exit off I-65, not long before I give up the interstate for country roads.

The day I left home for this trip, I was gulping down a last cup of coffee in the kitchen when a newspaper advertisement caught my eye. It was an outdoor scene: a canyon, a tree on a ledge, a waterfall, and in the foreground, a woman in hiking boots and flannel shirt leaning against a tree, field glasses in hand, knapsack at her side.

I couldn't identify the place but it was remote. This woman was clearly trying to get herself some solitude.

But then my eyes turned to the message along the border and the sketch beneath it of a compact cellular phone, just the right size to tuck inside a fanny pack.

"NOW THAT YOUR CALLS CAN FIND YOU, IT SHOULD BE EASIER TO FIND YOURSELF."

I glanced back to the scene. Maybe those weren't field glasses but a portable phone in her hand. Is this what's meant by "getting away from it all" in the 1990s? I grabbed my bags, flung them into the car and headed for the highway as fast as possible.

I admit I call home every night from the lone pay phone here. It's true there's a number my family can call in emergencies—though the switchboard closes about 8:30 PM.

When I call, my husband is kind. He doesn't tell me the news I'm missing. Murders at Fort Knox. Copycat deaths of teen-agers imitating movie characters who lie down in front of traffic. I'm a news junkie, but I can survive without this.

He limits himself to our son's day at school, the Chinese dinner his parents brought in, the kitten's latest antics.

When I hang up, it's always bittersweet. They're there. I'm here. It takes a few minutes to wean myself from the comfort of their voices.

My last morning, walking on a familiar path, I look

down and see the fossil I will take home to my son. It's a crinoid, the stem of a sea lily that grew near here 3 million centuries ago. I roll it in the palm of my hand, then pocket it.

On the drive home, as my head starts spinning again with plans and appointments, I take comfort in having that lily stem with me—my portable piece of eternity, a souvenir of my vacation.

November 7, 1993

The Wind And The Willies

I grew up in a family whose women, my mother included, were fiercely afraid of storms.

At the first flicker of lightning or rumble of distant thunder, they might bolt for the basement, stopping only long enough to arm themselves with rosaries, blessed candles and kitchen matches, and, if there was time enough for luxuries, perhaps a flashlight, maybe a radio.

One aunt built a storm cellar and became the envy of her sisters. Even my grandmother, a strong woman who'd weathered so much in her life—a Depression, a flood, widowhood, the deaths of two infants and the rearing of nine others—had consented to be hypnotized more than once to get herself through a thunderstorm.

My mom was famous in her own right for calling my brothers and me home from wherever we happened to be playing on those summer afternoons when the sky turned a queasy pea-green and the clouds took to churning and bubbling like a sick stomach.

"Oh, Mom, do I *have* to?"

I was determined not to be afraid. I did some pretty dumb things along the way to prove I was not a prisoner of my genes.

Like planting myself on a river bank during a raging electrical storm. Black clouds, white lightning, ear-splitting thunder: no big deal. I defied them.

What can I say? I was 20-something.

There was, however, one small nagging shred of my inheritance I couldn't shake.

It was the wind. It spooked me.

Was I the victim of too many viewings of "The Wizard of Oz"? Could be. While most people remember the Yellow Brick Road scenes from that movie, I recall the farm being blown apart in black and white.

What made me most uneasy about wind was the sound of it.

Trees creaking and popping. The rattle of windows. A mournful breeze whistling through eaves. Ominous, mysterious sounds. Give me an honest lightning bolt and a straightforward thud of thunder anyday.

I never really understood why wind, of all things, made me so uncomfortable—until I met my first tornado. That's when I learned there's good reason to be wary.

Here's what I recall about the twister that hit Louisville on April 3, 1974:

Standing at a Courier-Journal window, watching a funnel cloud head for the Fairgrounds, where it peeled away the roof like a lid from a sardine can.

Trying one impassable route after another on the drive home from work that evening; finally ditching my car and hoofing it the rest of the way; arriving at Alta Avenue and not recognizing it; climbing over utility poles and broken trees and wind-scattered debris to get to my apartment; finding my door barred shut by one fallen tree, my living-room ceiling punctured by another, my cat trembling under a bed, afraid to come out.

My friend Gail lived a few houses away. I have a snapshot of her grimacing beside her orange Datsun B-210, smashed smack down the middle by a huge oak tree.

I took pictures of everything, immediately, an activity some of my neighbors considered tacky and heartless. Until I had prints made, and they all wanted copies. No one really wanted to forget.

I recall a few days later driving by an apartment in Crescent Hill that I'd almost rented the fall before. Now it was a pile of rubble. It could have been MY rubble.

A few streets away, on Kennedy Avenue, I helped a coworker sift through layers of black grit in what used to be rooms in her home. The house had no roof, walls were missing. Yet she stayed incredibly upbeat and, like so many of the wind's victims, had the guts to rebuild.

I remember interviewing a woman who lived in Rolling Fields whose family photo collection had been swept up in the wind and blown to another town altogether, where some thoughtful person found the pictures, tracked down the owners and—amazing but true—returned them almost as good as new.

What couldn't be returned or rebuilt were the trees.

Cherokee Park, for instance, was transformed by the

wind. There's no other word for what happened. One minute there were trees so thick you could barely see through them even in winter. The next, there were huge empty spaces. From the air, you could see trees lying flat, one on top of the other, like pickup sticks scattered for miles. You can still spot the misshapen bodies of those that were battered by the wind but survived.

If you moved here after that April, you can't imagine the glory of Eastern Parkway in spring and summer, the way the trees met in the middle, the leafy tunnels they formed, the safe feeling they created.

I've heard people say it sounded like a hundred freight trains roaring by when the tornado struck. A thousand chain saws seems more like it to me.

Recently I had a chance to think again about the awesome power of wind. A woods I love in another county was hit last fall by a brutal windstorm—a "mini-tornado," according to folks who live in the area. The wind toppled a silo, ripped off a roof, destroyed fences, crushed barns.

Most of the damaged property was quickly repaired or replaced. The woods, on the other hand, will never be the same.

I've tried to imagine what the wind sounded like whipping through the hills that day. Did birds squeal? Where did the frogs and lizards run? And the nests in the trees? Did they sail to another state like those family pictures 20 years ago?

A friend who's lived beside these woods for 40 years reminded me that such a wind can be nature's way of clearing out dead wood. "Like the fires out West," he said. Winds can heal the land, stir up new life, make way for fresh growth. He pointed to new vistas the wind had opened up.

After our talk, I hiked alone to a spot that used to be thick and shady with trees 100 feet tall. It's now a sunny, root-scarred clearing. When I looked down, though, I saw tender green shoots poking out of the ground where I could have sworn nothing but moss and lichen grew before.

And was that my imagination or was it the wind I heard humming a sweet song up the hillside?

April 3, 1994

Portraits

Whistler's Grandmother

My son is a whistler. Sometimes when he's doing his Spanish homework, I recognize his rendition of the "Puerto Rico" refrain from "West Side Story." At bedtime, I hear the cocky rhythms of the Alfred Hitchcock theme drifting down from his bedroom. Soon it will be "Jingle Bells."

Whatever the tune, his whistling makes my heart sing. You see, my mother was a whistler.

It's a link between these two people I love, who never had the good fortune to meet but somehow have so much in common.

She died on Halloween in 1978. He was born the day after April Fool's in 1984. Yet he's like her in quirky ways that no one else in my family seems to be.

For instance, there's the way he points out the animals and the people taking shape in the clouds when we're driving on the expressway. She did that too.

"Look at that!" she would call out as we rode on an

errand in my brother's car—me at the wheel, her right beside me close enough to touch, in the days before bucket seats.

"Do you see that big bear chasing a little girl with pigtails? And look at that—the witch's face with the big wart on the nose!"

I would always look and sometimes I'd see.

Now it's Josh who points out the dinosaurs and alligators that lurk in the sky on cloudy days. Together we stare at the shapes above us, waiting to be reminded of some thing or somebody.

One of the things that made me sad when my son was born was the thought that he would never know my mother. It was bad enough that my husband knew her only through my stories and snapshots. How would I ever make a memory into a grandmother?

But the sadness wore away with time. Life went on. I kept telling stories.

The time she fell and twisted her ankle running around the house to get a good look at Sputnik. How she got so nervous taking her driving tests, she flunked twice and then gave up.

The way she named my little brother for John Kennedy before the Massachusetts senator even had the presidential nomination of his party.

The times she read Wordsworth to me out of her English book from Atherton High, which was as far as she ever got in school.

I guess my son was listening because one day, in the middle of something we were doing or talking about, something I can't remember except that it made me think of my mother, he nonchalantly said to me, "I bet your mom would like that."

And he was right.

It's a gift really. These little ways he brings her back to life for me. At Thanksgiving, especially, I am grateful for it.

On holidays, my mother's whistling—like her kitchen—picked up steam. Cooking brought out the trilling bird in her. And the ham, as well.

Can you "belt out" a whistled tune? I swear that's what she did. She liked the popular classics of the '40s and '50s. She'd whistle "St. Louis Blues" and "Summertime." "Stormy Weather." "Night and Day"—literally.

I thought of this a few weeks ago, when I saw New Yorker Marga Gomez perform her powerful one-woman show "Memory Tricks" at Actors Theatre of Louisville. The one-act is about her relationship with her mother, a flamboyant and complicated woman. One of her mother's most memorable habits was to sing about the house—only she never knew more than the first few words of a lyric.

Undaunted, she would begin: "Embrace me, you..." and without losing the melody, she'd gloss over the missing words with: "LA-LA-LA-LA-LA-LA-LA."

My mother used her whistling that way. If she forgot the words to a song, she would whistle it until she got to the spot where she could pick up the lyric again. Though I tried to mimic her, my whistle was always too squeaky, too flat, no lilt to it.

They say some traits skip generations. There's probably a sound scientific reason for this. But to me it's just a pure, plain comfort.

A few days after Halloween this year, my son dreamed of my mother.

The three of us were going somewhere together, he said. We were in a car, and she was driving—something she couldn't do when I knew her.

That's the beauty of the relationship they have—my son and my mom. It's alive, unlimited, growing. What I know about her is all memory now. If I'm honest, she stopped changing for me the morning she died. She's no older, no different.

But for him, there's always more to learn about her.

"You mean, she liked the Beatles?" he asked once, astounded.

"She had a cat too?"

"She really played basketball?"

In his dream, my mother was going back to college. In reality, she never had the chance to start.

"She said to us, 'You're going to see me doing a lot of studying,'" my son told me over cinnamon toast at the breakfast table the morning after his dream.

"Really?" I said, and found myself wondering—is it art she's studying or political science or literature?

Obviously the regret I once felt about my son not getting to know my mom was unfounded. He knows her; she knows him.

And for that, I give thanks.

November 28, 1993

Healing
The Healer

Marj Graves doesn't remember many details from her tour of Vietnam as an Army nurse, but she can't forget the incident that made her decide at the age of 25 never to work in a hospital again.

It happened just before she was due to fly home after a year at the 24th Evacuation Hospital at Long Binh.

"There was a big Chinook helicopter taking about 60 soldiers out of one of the fire bases, one of the places on the front lines. The guys hadn't had any time off for three months, and they were taking them to a beach resort within Vietnam to have what was called a three-day in-country R & R.

"The helicopter got right outside of our hospital and exploded."

The bodies were brought back to the hospital for "identifying and recovery." Marj, a senior nurse, was asked to help.

"I remember one fellow had a broken neck and his

whole body was almost squashed like a major birth defect I'd seen. Another fellow had one of his leg bones sticking out through the bottom of his boot. The rest of the bodies they brought in would be maybe a burned trunk of a body with maybe tags hanging from it. There might be an arm. It was hard to understand those were human forms because they looked like charcoal briquettes. You'd see a wedding band on a hand. The army corpsmen would be trying to match body pieces, trying to get forms ready to put in body bags."

She tells this story without wincing, in an unwavering voice adept at keeping emotions at bay. She sounds calm, cool, controlled, all the qualities she was trained to maintain in such situations, defenses she says sometimes get in her way now when she *wants* to feel emotion.

When she finishes, she detects a lingering question in her listener's eyes and answers it: "Nobody survived."

When the young captain from Fern Creek returned to the U.S. in May of 1972, she asked to finish out her four months in the service working in a pediatrics ward in a military hospital.

"I told them I did not want to be assigned where I would be taking care of soldiers." She got her request.

For three years before volunteering to go to Vietnam, she had been head nurse on orthopedic units at U.S. military hospitals. All her experience was hospital-based. But she chose to forfeit it when she returned to civilian life.

"I wanted no more of death and destruction," she says today.

She also knew civilian hospitals had a "kind of class system" that divided doctors from nurses, nurses from aides—unlike Vietnam, where "we were all in it together."

"Your coworkers were your friends, family, people you depended on, off-duty and on-duty, in order to survive."

I first met Marj in January, 1972. She was 24, on a trip home midway through her Vietnam stint, and I was 22, a cub reporter for The Louisville Times.

I interviewed her about life as an Army nurse and wrote a story that ended with a quote from her: "I enjoy Army nursing and want to do more traveling, but I also want to settle down someday and raise a family. The two don't mix."

What I didn't know until recently was this: Bob Graves, a Vietnam vet in law school at the University of Louisville at the time, read my story, showed Marj's picture to his mother and said, "That's the girl I'm going to marry."

He wrote Marj a letter, she wrote back and, as Marj tells it, they "fell in love through the mail." Seven months after she got home, they married.

Marj Graves worked for 18 months as an industrial nurse before her first daughter was born, then 6 months for an oral surgeon before her second.

Then she got out of nursing entirely. She worked as a teacher's aide at a preschool. Her husband, perhaps sensing the Vietnam connection and understanding it, supported her through it all.

"I was trying to figure out where I fit in," she says.

"There are some empty places in my soul I don't know will ever come back again."

Four years ago, Dr. Janice Yusk encouraged Marj to try nursing again. Yusk hired her as part of her office team. Marj felt a reawakening, a "longing to be a healer again."

In 1991 she left Yusk's office for a job at United Parcel Service, where today she is a medical services supervisor, serving 6,000 package sorters at the airport hub. As an employee-assistance program coordinator, she often finds herself counseling young Gulf War vets.

"I'm where I need to be," she says, "where I ought to be."

Last Sunday, 21 years after I first interviewed Marj, I sat down with her again at the St. Regis Park home where she and Bob live with their daughters Kristin, 19, and Ashley, 15.

It was the day after she returned from the Veterans Day dedication of the Vietnam Women's Memorial in Washington, D.C. The bronze sculpture of three women helping a wounded GI honors the 11,500 women who served in Vietnam as well as 265,000 other women who served in that era but not in Vietnam.

The goal of the memorial is to make clear that while women were not in combat, they faced similar traumas—and deserved to be recognized.

Graves went to the dedication with an old friend, Donna Williams, a Vietnam-era Air Force nurse who served in the Philippines.

"I realized there that many things I've struggled with

for 21 years, that I thought were just a part of my personality, were the same things most other women who served in Vietnam were going through," she said.

Graves had written me in October to fill me in on the romance my story had hatched and let me know she was planning the trip to D.C. She hoped to find the women she'd worked with there.

"I long to know how they are, if they are still in nursing—to laugh, recall, hug and cry together."

Marj Graves did find old friends in D.C. Medics, doctors, nurses. She found faces she didn't know she was looking for. She laughed, remembered, marched, hugged and, Lord, did she cry.

"My nose is still scabbed over I cried so much," she laughed.

"I never in my life felt as respected and as thanked as I did there. Every one of the soldiers who saw you grabbed a hold of you and put his arms around you and whispered—'Welcome home.'"

November 21, 1993

Sisterhood

When Lucy M. Freibert started teaching English at the University of Louisville in 1971, there were no women's studies courses to be taken.

I know, because I left the campus with my B.A. in English just a few months before Freibert arrived. The only classes that focused on women when I was there were offered through a spunky alternative student-run program known as the Free University. They were usually taught off-the-hip, by other students, and were strictly non-credit.

But Freibert wanted to legitimize the study of women.

Armed with a doctorate from the University of Wisconsin and energized by the "radicalizing" five-year stint she'd spent at the Madison campus in the late '60s, she created and taught U of L's first women's studies class, an English course called Women in Literature.

The year was 1973. Freibert remembers it took only 40 minutes for the course to fill up on registration day.

In a short time, similar classes were popping up in sociology, political science, history, law. Soon Freibert was adding new women's lit classes, including minority women writers, as well.

By 1976, when I first interviewed Freibert for a story on her innovative and sometimes controversial work at U of L, the university had set up a committee on women's studies (which Freibert chaired) and a campus feminist organization was thriving (with her as its adviser).

She shrugs when given credit for the major role she played in all this.

"The time had come," she says.

And now Freibert's time has come.

On March 24 The Center for Women & Families will honor her as one of five Women of Distinction at its annual fund-raising dinner at The Galt House.

And in June Freibert will retire from U of L, with 22 action-packed years to her credit.

When she looks back at her career over the past two decades, she says she sees change—lots and lots of dramatic change.

"It's been incredible, and it happened so fast," she says.

For me and for many of those who've known her over the years, Freibert has been a refreshing reminder that women can break the rules, live outside of traditional roles, speak loud and clearly against the status quo, and not just survive the flak that follows but thrive—

and in the process nourish the dreams of others.

Freibert is quick to express gratitude to other women faculty members for the support they've given her. But it's safe to say few women anywhere have focused their lives so totally on women's issues.

She has not stopped at teaching neglected women writers, for example. She goes out of her way in her classes today to help women and minority students speak up.

Sometimes, for example, she starts a class by asking three questions and telling her students to jot down their ideas about each one. Then, when the discussion begins, women feel confident enough about their ideas to speak up and share them.

"Men, on the other hand, will always speak up, spontaneously, whether they know the subject or have thought about it before or not," says Freibert. "I really feel we have to give women and minorities a sense that we want them to participate, that people want to hear them."

Her efforts have earned her the respect of colleagues and students, who keep up with her from all over the country—including some who have gone on to become published writers.

She was named University of Louisville Distinguished Teaching Professor in 1987 and won the prestigious Trustees Award for her "extraordinary contribution to undergraduate life" in 1991.

At the time of my first interview with Freibert, part of what set her apart from other faculty was that she was a member of a Catholic religious order—a Sister of Charity of Nazareth, who first started teaching in Louisville parochial schools in 1947, gradually moving through the faculties of Presentation Academy and Spalding College.

It was "very unusual," even in the early '70s, for sisters to teach at secular institutions, Freibert says.

"My community was very supportive. They gave me the opportunity to become who I am."

Living alone, as she has throughout her career at U of L, and going to a large liberal school like Wisconsin for graduate work, also were unconventional choices for sisters.

"Now sisters all over the country are doing it," she says.

Though Freibert still expresses a "strong, unfailing commitment" to her religious community, she says "most people don't even know I'm a sister. Or they knew it, and they've forgotten."

She says, "That's as it should be. Why should a teacher's personal life matter in the classroom?"

But *she* hasn't forgotten. Nor has she been any less single-minded about working for women's issues in her church than at her university.

Last fall, soon after returning from a sabbatical in Massachusetts where she was researching American humor, Freibert delivered an invited homily at Mass at her home parish.

In it, she criticized what she saw as a lapse in the congregation's efforts to use inclusive language and images when talking about God and questioned whether it was appropriate for a parish that's committed to non-violence to read Biblical "passages about wars and battles," as were read that day.

Freibert says she learned long ago that you can "survive" the criticism that inevitably results from taking an unpopular stand.

It takes time, she says. And patience.

"Eventually, people will understand."

March 14, 1993

One Great Story Leads To Another

If you've ever put down a book and said to yourself, "That's me! That's my life!" you know just how Tyonda and Mary Ann and Jessica and Tamika and Tina and Anna and Taryn and all the other girls at Maryhurst felt when they finished reading Toni Morrison's short story "Recitatif."

It's a scary feeling, like someone's taking notes on your life.

It's also a comfort: being understood, knowing you're not alone.

It makes you see your life in a new light. Your problems look different. Possibilities open up.

That click that comes when you recognize yourself in a made-up plot or an imaginary character is what makes great stories great.

"I like it because it tells the facts about life," Tina said about this tough and touching story, the chronicle of a fragile 25-year friendship that begins in a girls' shelter when two 8-year-olds (one white, one black) share a room for four months.

"You can't change what's happened to you," someone chimed in. "It shows you have to work with what you got."

On a sunny spring day not long ago, I spent four hours sitting at a long table in a conference room at Maryhurst, a treatment center for troubled teen-age girls, located in eastern Jefferson County.

With me were 15 young women who live there and five adults, most of them teachers from Maryhurst and the University of Louisville.

The girls looked like any group of teens you might spot hanging out at a mall food court. They were black and white, in braces and mascara, their boom box blaring. The youngest was 13, the oldest 17.

Like most girls at Maryhurst, their histories call to mind a line from the Paul Simon song about the girl who calls herself a "human trampoline… falling…tumbling…bouncing."

The typical Maryhurst resident has ricocheted from one "placement" to the next, 10 times on the average: foster homes, hospitals, adopted homes, shelters, detention centers, halfway houses.

"Since I was 9, I've been on my own," Mary Ann said.

Many Maryhurst girls were runaways or truants, sexually or physically abused or severely neglected. The good news is eight out of 10 who complete the program never return to juvenile court. Most earn their diplomas or their GED.

I visited Maryhurst to observe a U of L–sponsored seminar called "Great Stories and Young Women." In February a similar group discussed Joyce Carol Oates' "How I Contemplated My Life From The Detroit House of Correction and Began My Life Over Again."

"Great Stories" is a 7-year-old project of U of L's Center for Humanities and Civic Leadership. Joe Slavin and Bob Schulman, its directors, have worked with lawyers, doctors, businessmen and school administrators. Stories are always tailored to the group discussing them.

It would be hard to find a tale more appropriate for the girls at Maryhurst than "Recitatif."

"My mother danced all night and Roberta's was sick," the story begins. "That's why we were taken to St. Bonny's."

You couldn't call what happened that day group therapy. There were no therapists in the room. It wasn't exactly literature class either. The discussion was too personal for that.

It was something in between: a conversation that allowed real life and fiction to merge. If there is a healing power to literature, it comes in that miracle moment when reader and character become one.

Anna, for example, identified with the way Twyla and Roberta feared the older teen-age girls.

"The first shelter I went to, the big girls picked on me," she said.

Mary Ann related to the scene where Twyla gets queasy as soon as she meets her roommate: "I remember being sick to my stomach my first day in a shelter."

Tina reacted strongly to the girls' feelings of being "dumped" by their mothers. "Sometimes children can be taken away, no matter how much their parents love them….My parents didn't want me to be given away. Sure sometimes they don't come see me, but it doesn't mean they don't love me."

The conversations veered to discussions of what they want in a mother ("a good friend…someone to talk to") and how they felt about their dads ("he buys me things when he's feeling guilty…he hates me because I'm a girl") and what they regret ("if I had a time machine, I'd go back and not do any of this stuff").

In the story, Twyla and Roberta run into each other four times after leaving St. Bonny's. One reunion comes during an anti-busing demonstration, when they're both mothers but on different sides. Twyla is in her car, alone, when angry protesters begin rocking it back and forth. Roberta's in the crowd—but when Twyla reaches out for help, no one takes her hand.

That was the first scene mentioned by Tyonda, who was 3 when her mother left her to go to prison.

At 13, Tyonda, who was eventually adopted, said she knew well how it feels to reach for help and not get it. Sometimes, she said, "I feel nobody trusts me."

At the end of the day, Slavin asked what had bonded the two characters. What happened at the shelter? What allowed their friendship to withstand years of neglect and huge differences in lifestyles?

"Love," Tyonda said, sounding exasperated that anyone should have to ask.

In the shelter, she explained, Twyla and Roberta

learned to care for one another, "like sisters and brothers." Nothing could change that.

Listening to her, it struck me that the girls had created for each other what they lacked individually—a family.

And that, by anybody's standards, is a great story.

June 13, 1993

In God's Name

Elizabeth A. Johnson, Ph.D.

Sister Elizabeth.

Professor Johnson.

Beth.

These are some of the names people use when they talk about the winner of the 1993 Grawemeyer Award in Religion.

Each calls up a different image of the same 51-year-old, Brooklyn-born Fordham University theologian, whose 1992 book, "She Who Is: The Mystery of God in Feminist Theological Discourse," earned her the $150,000 prize.

There's the "deep, deep thinker," as she's described by Charles Grawemeyer, the man behind the prestigious award. "Her work was head and shoulders above the other finalists," he said. "Anyone who hears her will be entranced."

And there's "the extraordinarily good classroom

teacher" remembered by Bellarmine College theology professor Michael Downey, who was in the doctoral program at Catholic University with her.

There's the Roman Catholic sister of the Congregation of St. Joseph, who spent 12 years teaching science to elementary, high school and college students on Long Island before pursuing degrees in theology.

And there's the gregarious feminist with a shrewd sense of humor, whose writings challenge her church's traditionally masculine ways of speaking about God and call for equal time for feminist imagery.

"A lot of feminist literature has been necessarily strident because it's so hard to get people to consider change," said David Hester, a professor at the Louisville Presbyterian Theological Seminary, which sponsors the award jointly with the University of Louisville.

"It's like shoving off from shore—it takes a lot of momentum to get going.

"Maybe with Beth's book, we've reached a point in the journey where we can be a bit more considered and reflective. She doesn't pull any punches but there's no tone of hostility."

The book has drawn support from feminists in the pew, so to speak, as well as from theologians inside and outside the Catholic Church.

The book lends itself to discussions. Louisville family therapist Maddie Reno found herself so excited about the book that she called a group of friends and began meeting every other week with them to "explore ideas" from it.

I'm one of the friends she called. Halfway through the book, I telephoned Johnson at her New York home to ask her how she explains the support she's received from both sides of what some would call the battlefield.

She laughed the kind of laugh that makes you feel instantly comfortable with a stranger—one of her trademarks I came to learn.

"I wrote the book carefully," she said. "It wasn't written with a lot of angry rhetoric—angry though I feel sometimes about those issues. I was functioning as teacher, trying to teach the church, the academy. If you're trying to teach, you don't get anywhere getting angry with your students."

Rather than being denounced by church leaders, Johnson said, she's received letters praising her book—even from Catholic bishops.

"No attacks, so far. But the other shoe could still drop."

Some observers of the Catholic ordination debate point to one irony in the church's ban on women priests: It's resulted in many women becoming theologians, a potentially far more influential position than parish pastor.

In Louisville last April to accept the award, Johnson drew some good-natured chuckles with her reply to a comment that spoke to that point.

"If male authority had been smarter," she said that day, "they would have ordained us early, and we would be out ministering, and we would not have time to think these thoughts."

It's fitting—and a bit humorous—that Johnson

should be known by all those different names. It goes to the heart of her case for "naming God."

In her book, Johnson makes clear that God has many names too. And they are not just the traditional masculine ones evoking images of power and control.

To speak of the Divine in exclusively male terms limits our understanding, she says—just as surely as we would limit our understanding of Johnson if we thought of her only as scholar, only as sister or only as a New Yorker.

Female images of God as wise, merciful, suffering and creative are deeply rooted in Judeo-Christian tradition, she says. But it's as if they've been "forgotten"—buried under centuries of patriarchal teachings, blotted out by male images.

Asked why she decided to write a book about a potentially explosive issue within her church, she says it was something she had to do to "put the two halves of my brain together."

Johnson was trained in the classical theological tradition at Catholic University and is also well-grounded in feminist theology. "So much was going on in both worlds, and yet they were not talking to each other," she said.

In her book, she tackles head-on the common complaint that female images of God suggest that God is a woman.

"God is spirit and so beyond identification with either male or female sex," she says. "Yet the daily language of preaching, worship…and instruction conveys a different message: God is male, or at least more like a man than a woman, or at least more fittingly addressed as male than as female."

It might not matter so much, she says, if images of God were simply decorations for the opening of prayers. But these symbols are much more powerful than that. They "function" in our lives, she says. Think of it this way:

If the names we give God are King, Ruler, Lord or Master, the image of God as "dominator" will not stop with the way we think of God. It will affect our relationships with ourselves, other people and the land we live on.

Her science background has drawn her to the efforts of eco-feminists and their discussion of the linkages between the "rape of the earth and oppression of women and our forgetting that God is our Mother, through creation."

Johnson dates her "conversion" to feminism to the years at Catholic University, where in 1981 she was the first woman to earn a doctorate from the theology department. She was also the first to teach in that department and the first to get tenure.

"This was supposed to be the center of Catholic theology in America," she said—and yet there had been no woman doctoral student or faculty member before her.

In 1988, when she was eligible for tenure, the board of trustees—largely comprised of bishops—"had some discussion about whether I should get it, since one, I was a woman, and two, I'd written feminist theology." A special panel interviewed her, a process not required of men candidates.

"After that, I began to see much more clearly how the

absence of women in theology and church leadership was a real injustice," she said. "That was my moment of conversion to feminism."

The tenure vote was unanimous in her favor.

In 1991, however, Johnson left Catholic U., in Washington, D.C., for Fordham, in the Bronx. Her decision was prompted by the Vatican's controversial decision to ban Catholic priest Charles Curran from continuing to teach theology at Catholic University. The Vatican had censured Curran for his dissenting teachings on divorce and contraception, and several academic-freedom groups had criticized the university for going along with the ban.

"I was vastly disheartened by that incident and not willing to spend my professional life in an institution that would do those kinds of things."

Johnson was recently voted president-elect of the Catholic Theological Society of America, some of whose members shared her disappointment in the Curran case. Women make up only about 10 percent of the group.

"Here I am, very clearly on record of wanting to do feminist theology, and I receive affirmation of a largely male body. It was extremely heartwarming."

You can add to the other images of Johnson that of an eldest daughter who dedicated her award-winning book "with love, delight and gratitude" to her mother, godmother and grandmother.

When she gives her free public lecture this week at the Presbyterian Seminary, Johnson will have her mother and godmother with her, as well as her editor, a colleague and a representative of her religious community.

"I was told spouses are invited," Johnson joked. "I'm bringing my circle instead."

The audience is sure to be full of fans, like Reno, who think her book is a breakthrough for Christian women searching for ways to feel at home again in churches where the lack of women clergy and the dominance of male talk about God has made them feel isolated and angry.

"If a woman with her training and tools can say, 'Yes, it's possible to retrieve the positive,' then that's very encouraging to me," says Reno.

U of L's Lucy Freibert, a Sister of Charity of Nazareth, says she's arranging for Johnson's work to be read by all members of her community. And Bellarmine theology professor George Kilcourse says "She Who Is" will be discussed on campus next spring as a "book of the month."

Despite the far-reaching effects of her work, Johnson doesn't see smooth sailing ahead for her ideas. She quotes feminist theologian Anne Carr, saying that while "the women's movement comes as a transforming grace for the whole church...terrifyingly, grace may always be refused."

Her trademark laughter disappears when she adds: "I predict tension and conflict ahead. I don't see it being resolved in the near future, because sociologically we haven't changed."

October 24, 1993

Getting To Know Amy

The moment I laid eyes on Amy McNeely, I knew we'd be friends.

Her hair, so yellow and bright, caught my attention first—and that smile of hers, as natural as the grassy wind-blown spot where we met.

But it was the look of teen-age mischief around her eyes that invited me to come closer.

I crouched beside the gravestone with her name carved into it:

AMY JOANN MCNEELY
JUNE 11, 1975–OCTOBER 23, 1990
DAUGHTER SISTER FRIEND.

I moved as near as I could get to the yellow hair and big smile in the photograph attached to that stone. It was a school portrait someone had wrapped in plastic for protection from weather and time.

Scattered about, on the flat part of the stone, were trinkets and mementos, the kind of keepsakes girls keep in boxes under their beds.

Butterflies made of wire and cloth. Yellow ribbons. Hand-scribbled notes. A miniature hockey stick. Plastic cats. A rock. A bracelet. A poem.

All signs and symbols, I was later to learn, of the high-spirited life Amy led.

Like anyone who had heard news reports of this pretty 15-year-old's sudden death in a traffic accident on her way to Atherton High School, I had tried at the time, in a safely distant manner, to find some solace in Amy's story.

The car she was riding in was hit, broadside, at a Bardstown Road intersection not far from her home. Drivers of both cars escaped without serious injuries.

Amy was dead before her first class ended.

After I encountered Amy face-to-face that day in the cemetery where I often walk, things changed. She was no longer a name in the newspaper. She was a smile. I began to hear her name come up frequently.

Unexpected places: along a path in the woods far from Louisville; in a doctor's office; across a table in a restaurant.

I heard stories for two years about the connection her friends still felt with Amy and their devotion to her memory and spirit.

Spontaneously, the morning she died, her classmates in Greg Hemesath's English course poured out their anger and frustration in messages scrawled on the wall of his portable classroom.

In two days there were 200 messages.

"They were stunned. Amy brought the whole class together as a family. Her energy vibrated through the whole school," says Hemesath.

The portable burned down the next year, taking the students' messages—but not their memories.

"A year and a half later, when many of her classmates were applying to be Governor's Scholars, they were mentioning Amy in their essays," Hemesath says.

"Since Amy died, every morning I am just glad to be alive," one of her friends wrote in a school-application essay, in response to a question about attitude-changing experiences in her life. "Death has made me see...how very precious life is," the friend wrote.

Laurie Dobbins is a Sacred Heart Academy student who met Amy on a Crescent Hill Baptist Church trip to Kings Island.

"I definitely hear Amy laugh every day," Laurie told me recently.

It was Laurie Dobbins who pulled Wanda McNeely aside in the days preceding the funeral and told her that Amy had specifically asked that a big party be thrown in her honor when she died.

So that's exactly what Wanda and her husband, psychiatrist J. David McNeely, did. They opened up their home to Amy's many friends and celebrated her life.

"The house was filled with flowers and children from top to bottom. I didn't know half the kids there," says Wanda.

"Both sides of the stairs, going up and down and into the living room, were filled with flowers. Later I put a sheet on the floor and gathered all the petals up. I saved every single one and made them into potpourri."

She keeps the potpourri—what she hasn't given away to friends—in a big brass vase in Amy's third-floor bedroom. The room is still decidedly Amy's, filled with reminders of her love of animals and sports and all things slightly wacky.

"When you're sad sometimes, you hear what Amy would say, her wit, the little comebacks," Laurie says. "My brother and I say these things to each other and we laugh. She definitely lives on."

There is a Navajo song that says the dead are lonely for the living and they tug at them from time to time, trying to draw them away from this life.

Like Laurie who hears Amy's laugh every day and like the Atherton field hockey player who heard her cheering the team during a game, I felt Amy tugging at me too—gently, like a new friend.

A few months ago I decided to find out more about her continuing effect on people's lives.

I sat with her parents in their home and talked to her sister Sara, who is five years older and Amy's role model.

I read some of the many letters from classmates and parents that have come to the family, tucked in the back door or left at the gravesite, where Wanda McNeely stops every day to visit.

I listened to friends and teachers and neighbors.

"There was no one who disliked her. She was a friend to everyone, very much like her sister," says Steve Lin, Atherton's choir director and director of the Chamber Singers, a group Sara and Amy both sang with.

On a family vacation to Hawaii a few years ago, her

mother recalls, "Amy ran with the kids she met on Maui like she knew them forever."

"She loved people, and she didn't have a lot of fears," Sara says.

"I know it sounds corny, but she was so full of life. If you were in a bad mood, you couldn't stay in it around her."

She had pals across the country, friends made at summer church programs in North Carolina, field hockey camps at Northwestern University and Ohio State, on a vacation cruise she took with a classmate and her mother, on family and school trips.

"She did everything," says her mother.

Besides being a member of the Chamber Singers, she was goalie for the varsity hockey team, an "almost-straight-A" student in the Advance Program, an active member of her church's youth group, a member of the choir. She performed in school plays, babysat, dated.

"I used to say, 'Amy, what are you going to save for old age?' And she'd say, 'Oh, Mom, don't worry about it!'"

What Wanda McNeely hears her daughter telling her now is advice that's difficult for her to follow.

"I hear her say, 'Forget it, Mom. It's over. Move on.'"

The death of someone so young and vibrant raises questions that test even the strongest faith and deepest courage.

Amy's parents find comfort in the fact that their daughter did live life to the max, as if she somehow knew she had only a short time here.

Her mother showed me a story Amy wrote in

middle school, called "A Cry In The Night," about a boy dying of AIDS.

The last line, written in a cramped eighth-grade penmanship, reads: "Robbie would go on living forever, in our hearts."

Not long before she died, Amy happened to read Raymond Moody's book "Life After Life," and discussed it with her father and some friends at her church youth group.

When I asked Amy's parents what meaning they drew from these stories, her mother shook her head and smiled.

Her father said, "Sometimes the soul knows what the mind doesn't."

The mementos continue to show up at Amy's gravesite.

At Halloween, tiny pumpkins arrive. Christmas brings pine cones and holly. For Valentine's, there are hearts and flowers. Bunnies no doubt will be there for Easter.

But there are other tangible reminders of Amy's ongoing relationships.

For example, the nearly daily tooting of horns in Amy's memory as old friends drive past the family's home near Cherokee Park.

"Twice this week I heard the horns—at 7:18 and 7:30," her mother told me recently. "You don't ever want them to stop."

Hemesath says "you can still feel her presence" at Atherton, especially now, in the months before she would have graduated.

A Bradford pear grows in the school's courtyard and a red oak on the side of the building, both planted in Amy's memory. There's also a tulip poplar in the park, an evergreen at a church camp near Asheville, N.C., and "a forest" of trees in Israel.

Choir director Lin says Amy is the inspiration behind the successes of this year's Chamber Singers, a group he describes as "very very close, like a family."

With donations made in Amy's name, the singers have built a new set for their Madrigal Dinner fundraiser and have bought dinnerware and outfits. "Though it's been three winters now, we still get donations in her name," Lin says.

Members of the family also set up scholarships for promising hockey players at Highland Middle and Atherton to attend summer training camps, and an annual "Spirit Award" for team members.

Last week snow drops blossomed amid the ivy by Amy's grave.

A handmade sign that read "Beloved" lay against the stone, near the laminated photograph taken by her father that's replaced the school picture that introduced me to Amy two years ago.

I see less mischief in her eyes in this portrait, more affection in her smile.

But maybe that's just the way it seems, now that we've come to be friends.

March 21, 1993

Meeting
Merton

When Martin Luther King died in Memphis, the news came to me on the car radio as I was driving a dark highway back to Kentucky after spring break.

Bobby Kennedy's assassination in Los Angeles came during finals at the end of that semester.

In that chaotic year of 1968, I distinctly remember protesting the Vietnam War. I remember the papal encyclical on artificial contraception, the Prague spring, the Paris student uprisings.

But I can't recall Thomas Merton dying.

I have no memory of Dec. 10, 1968, the day he was electrocuted by a fan in a room where he was staying in Bangkok, Thailand. He was 53, a Trappist monk and well-known writer, hermit, poet and pacifist taking part in an international meeting on monasticism at the time of his death.

I'm sure I read about it, maybe even talked about it. But it took two decades to matter to me.

One day, in a bookstore, a title popped out from a shelf: "A Vow of Conversation." It was one of Merton's journals. I bought it, took it home. A year later, I read it.

Looking at that book today, I find this paragraph underlined:

"My ideas are always changing, always moving around one center, and I am always seeing that center from somewhere else. Hence, I will always be accused of inconsistency. But I will no longer be there to hear the accusation."

After "A Vow," I read everything by Merton I could get my hands on.

It was a little like finding a soul mate in your next-door neighbor, the one you thought you had nothing in common with and so put off getting to know.

He was there all along, waiting for the conversation to begin.

Though I'd grown up Catholic in Louisville, an hour's drive from the Abbey of Gethsemani, Merton's Nelson County home, I'd never read "Seven Storey Mountain," the 1948 autobiography that made Merton a household name in the postwar years.

But Rosemary Haughton, a British theological writer, "was a fan from the beginning." She knew Merton's work well by the day in 1967 when she got the chance to walk and talk and picnic with Father Louis, as he was called at the abbey. She was in the States on a lecture tour when a friend proposed the meeting.

Merton, the loner who lived his last years in a cabin in the monastery woods, was known for his remarkable hospitality. He was a friend to farmers, folk singers, photographers, whole families.

Haughton's visit was brief but unforgettable. Today she lives in Gloucester, Mass., where she runs a family shelter she set up 13 years ago that has evolved into an education and economic-development center.

Homelessness, sex discrimination, street violence, pollution, changing gender roles, AIDS: These were not Merton's concerns in the '60s. He wrote about the cold war, civil rights, peace, ecumenism.

Yet Haughton says today she finds Merton's insights more relevant than ever. Certainly he was talking about our overemphasis on individualism and our naively optimistic faith in progress long before environmentalists, communitarians and post-modernists took these as theme songs.

"We have more of a vantage point now," says Haughton, "for understanding his prophetic voice."

It is that distinctive voice—growing fresher and more immediate as time passes—that is the heart of a three-day conference on Merton at Bellarmine College this week. The conference is part of The Merton Year, a series of events planned in memory of the 25th anniversary of his death.

If you read over the conference topics, you find attempts to tie his work to the "eco-feminist theology of earth healing" and to "contemporary American women writers on natural religion." You find the jargon of inner-child recovery programs in a paper titled, "…Thomas Merton's Own Healing Journey from his Childhood Woundedness."

Bellarmine theology professor George Kilcourse, a conference organizer, said there's a feeling among some religious scholars that the time has come for a "second reception" of Merton's writings.

The line-up of speakers suggests he's right: two dozen women and men from the U.S., Canada, London and Taiwan, including a Quaker, a Zen scholar and an Illinois state representative.

While some in the past have studied Merton "as an object of curiosity," Kilcourse sees a shift toward "the wider concerns of contemporary culture that Merton himself would have shared and explored."

In an essay in the just-published "Merton Annual," Haughton imagines Father Louis greeting efforts of this kind with a "wry, half-startled amusement."

But she also believes he would be vitally engaged and at home with the conflicts of American life in the '90s—particularly the struggle to celebrate individual differences while still seeking connection and common identity.

"This was a man who had trouble all his life with identity, trying on one and then another, passionately believing that each one was the real one, until it let him down and something else showed through," says Haughton.

Jim Walsh, a Bellarmine graduate student, says he studied Merton's correspondence with Catholic feminist Rosemary Ruether for signs of the monk coming around to her views.

"He could be obstinate," says Walsh, an environmentalist and founder of Louisville's Project Warm. "He was hard on Ruether at first, but if you follow the letters, you can see a progression, a movement toward what she was saying."

Friendship was one of the ways Merton came to know himself, says Paul Wadell, an ethics professor at Catholic Theological Union in Chicago and a conference speaker.

"Merton knew the art of friendship. At its best, friendship is a commitment to bring out the best in each other. It requires mutuality," says Wadell.

"It's a kind of ongoing conversation."

For Merton's readers—both long-timers like Haughton and newcomers like me—the conversation grows.

Anyone who reads him knows he can be, as Walsh put it, obstinate. Also infuriating, inspiring, empowering, challenging, a comfort, a paradox, a joy.

So what else are friends for?

Yet there is one difference. Take it from me: The beauty of a friendship with a writer like Merton is it's never too late to be introduced.

March 13, 1994

The Dead Woman's Story

Except perhaps to her two daughters, Corrisa, 4, and Alaina, 8, Elaine Lismon-Brown was not a celebrity. Neither was her estranged husband, Curtis Brown. At least not before May 11, when he shot her, spewing six bullets into her body from head to buttocks as she collapsed in a corridor at Norton Hospital, where she worked.

A second-shift operating-room technician, Elaine was on duty at the time of the attack. Her coworkers, accustomed to trauma and death, watched in horror as their friend lay dying.

Brown escaped, briefly took a hostage at a nearby hotel and then died in a volley of gunfire with police—from a bullet wound it's believed he delivered to his own head.

At that point, both Elaine and Curtis achieved an infamous but very real celebrity status.

That is also the point when the grisly story of O.J.

Simpson's dead ex-wife, Nicole Brown Simpson, and that of Elaine Lismon-Brown begin to sound alike to me.

The way, at some level, all spouse-abuse stories sound alike. The way all notorious murder cases sound alike.

It's important to remember that O.J. Simpson has not been tried yet for the murder charges filed against him last week. He pleaded not guilty and is presumed innocent until shown to be otherwise in a court of law.

But what's indisputable is that Nicole and Elaine are both dead, victims of brutal attacks.

In both cases, the tragedy of their deaths has taken a back seat in our cultural consciousness to the more powerful urge to *understand* (and in some cases, *sympathize with*) the known or alleged killers.

That's what is triggering a lot of anger now, and not just among women.

Mark Kraemer, one of Elaine's coworkers, wrote a letter to the editor of The Courier-Journal that appeared a week after her death.

Feeling that coverage of the murder failed to "represent Elaine above all as the victim," Kraemer said he felt "the implications of the article draw us away from the tragedy of a violent act perpetrated against a defenseless woman."

Other coworkers circulated a eulogy of sorts that criticized the media for leading readers to "believe Elaine was as guilty a party to the violent act as the person who cold-bloodedly murdered her."

Media coverage of Elaine's death seemed desperate to find someone to blame, to find a reason for what happened. Relatives and friends of Elaine and Curtis were interviewed on TV and in the paper, arguing the guilt of one or the other party.

Elaine's hot temper and toughness were noted by her father. Her mother-in-law claimed Elaine "created the monster, if that's what (Curtis) was in the end."

I suppose there is some relief in finding circumstances in a murderer's past or present that explain how an ordinary human being could turn into a killer. Certainly there is no comfort in the investigation of the randomness of death.

In Simpson's case, every detail of the story—from funeral procession to freeway chase to pitiful surrender—has been videotaped, psychoanalyzed, lamented. Friends, experts and news anchors have shaken their heads at the sad sight of a Fallen Hero.

But I have to wonder in both cases:

What about the Story of the Dead Woman?

Is there no lesson for us there? No need to understand the tragedy of the children left behind by Nicole? Or by Elaine, whose girls first heard of their mother's death on a morning newscast?

Like the rape victim who is made to look responsible because she was wearing a short skirt or too much eye shadow, some friends of Elaine Brown felt her "toughness" was used as evidence that she only got what she had coming. She asked for it.

Elaine, we seemed to be told, was to blame for her own death.

And that, precisely, is the reason why three of Elaine's coworkers called me one day not long after her death and invited me to hear about the Elaine *they* knew.

It's true that Elaine's marriage was rocky, they said. It's true that it was increasingly violent, sometimes on both sides.

But it's also true that Elaine was in the process of breaking away from that when she died.

Anyone who knows anything about domestic violence can tell you that the most dangerous time for an abused woman is when she attempts to leave. That's when the jealousy and violence are most likely to escalate to murderous proportions.

What Elaine's friends wanted to do was tell me the stories that make Elaine more than a crime statistic. The stories that provide the wrinkles and laugh lines that give life to a flat police mug shot.

The three of them—physician, administrator and a technician who shared Elaine's shift for three years—painted a portrait in which the word "tough" takes a different meaning.

Elaine was tough when she enrolled in vocational school after having her children, when she stayed off welfare, when she worked hard to gain a good reputation at the hospital, when she shared child-care duties with a coworker so they could work their respective shifts without worrying about their children.

But she was also soft, they told me.

She won the Miss Congeniality award when she graduated from vocational school. A neurosurgeon who worked closely with her remembered her for knowing when to be light in surgery and when to be serious. On the Monday after Mother's Day, just a few days before her death, she brought small gifts to all the moms working that day.

One doctor told me Elaine "haunts" her, especially whenever she hears a reference to motherhood. She remembers how Elaine liked to dress up the girls, who now live with their grandfather, and take them out for manicures and shopping trips.

Myself, I am haunted by the words of Pat Lage, the coworker who shared the 2:30-to-11 shift with Elaine. Each time I get a glimpse of O.J. Simpson on the news, and each time I look again at the news photo of Curtis Brown, I think of Lage's comment.

"This is really not about finding someone to blame," she told me as we parted company.

I knew she meant what she said. And I knew she was right.

What this is really about is not forgetting who is the victim in the rush to understand the crime.

June 26, 1994

Family Photos

Animal House

Surely you've heard by now that the northern leopard frog is disappearing throughout Kentucky. Some experts claim it's a sign of just how out of control the environment's become, that these critters can no longer be found in their usual habitats.

Some worry it's a harbinger of impending ecological doom.

But not me.

I figure some naturalist will eventually discover the frogs are not gone at all, they're just vacationing at our house.

Every other form of wildlife seems to be dropping by—why not them?

Some species have found the environment here in our humble bungalow so comfy they've set up housekeeping—like the two brown squirrels who briefly occupied the territory beneath our back-porch roof.

They might have gone undetected if they hadn't kept throwing those noisy parties right over our heads.

Rustle, rustle, tip-tap, chomp, chomp, CHOMP.

They were easy enough to lure out from the eaves, though, once we decided to take the eviction route. All it took was a Have-A-Heart live trap stocked with a ball of rolled oats and peanut butter—a trick we'd learned from a professional live-trapper in the past.

Sure enough, the temptation was too great for our bushy-tailed intruders. First one succumbed; then a few days later, the other. We drove each of our squatters to a lovely wooded spot, far from our house, and set them free.

Proud of the non-violent way we'd handled our territorial dispute, we consoled ourselves with the fact that the squirrels would surely prefer nesting *al fresco* to making their home in the deep dark recesses of our house's infrastructure.

Back home, peace was restored.

At least, until the bat arrived.

In the hallowed tradition of his horror-movie counterparts, our bat showed up on a dreary night when my husband was out of town, our son was sound asleep in his room on the third floor and the family cat was (most likely) dozing under a chair somewhere, making like Garfield.

I was reading in bed when I thought I noticed something hovering over the dresser. *Eye strain*, I told myself. *New contact lenses.*

But then the little devil moved into my direct line

of sight. He circled the room, spooking me with that soundless, eerie swooping act bats perform.

All I really remember is that before you could say Nosferatu, I was out of there.

In the bright light of the next day, with my husband back home, we searched under beds and behind curtains but couldn't find the bat.

Come nightfall, though, he was back.

I'll spare you the details of his eventual departure, other than to say it involved a broom, a tennis racquet, my husband's deft backhand and a great deal of lurching and tripping and shrieking before it was all over.

At one point, as I stood sentinel at the open front door, I heard a shout from upstairs where father and son were tackling the job in their best Laurel-and-Hardy fashion.

"JOSH!" (Angry.)

"What?" (Defensive.)

"Swing the broom at the bat!" (Frustrated.) "Not my head!" (Pain.)

After that incident, still recovering from the squirrels and remembering the sewer rat we'd trapped last year, the three of us hit bottom.

We admitted we were powerless against wildlife invasions.

We stopped denying the inescapable truth about our house:

It's a jungle in here.

But rumor has it we are not alone. Word on our city street is that raccoons and opossums have been paying nocturnal visits to other homes in our area, chewing up wood, poaching food, planting the seeds of chronic insomnia.

Maybe the experts are right: Something's out of whack, imbalanced, in nature these days.

While deer and raccoons multiply at an alarming rate and move into areas where they've never lived before, certain songbirds and other animals are squeezed out.

I haven't heard of any neighborhood sightings of these missing creatures.

But from where I sit as I type this sentence, I DO see a squirrel—big as life—systematically defoliating a branch of my neighbor's maple tree that stretches gracefully past my corner window.

Leafy twig by leafy twig, the squirrel is stripping the green away. A quick nibble, a scurry down the limb to a "V" in the tree formed by a fork in the trunk, a frantic stuffing of leaves, then the scurry back for more.

So it goes.

I try bullying. I toss water out the open window. I rattle the storms. I pound on the glass. I shake my fist.

All I get in return is a quizzical stare that reminds me of the look a 2-year-old gives you right after you tell her "NO!" and just before she resumes whatever she was doing when you interrupted her.

All at once I know how the northern leopard frog feels: I give up.

July 11, 1993

The Sleeping Game

An experienced mother I know says a sleep-over is like childbirth.

When you're in the middle of it, you start to think it will never end. But the next morning, gazing at that sweet little bundle asleep so peacefully, you forget the details of what you endured. And before you know it, you're thinking of doing it again.

A father I know complains that the very name, "sleep-over," is a misnomer. It sounds so benign with its subtle stress on the word "sleep."

Don't kid yourself, he says. What the phrase really means is, all sleep is over for the duration.

Me? I don't know what I think. I'm too tired to analyze.

You see, I'm suffering from PSSD—Post Sleep-over Stress Disorder.

I admit I should've known what we were getting into when we invited a half-dozen boys to our house for our 9-year-old son's first group sleep-over.

There were warning signs. Like the responses we got when we shared our happy plans with certain parents:

"You're going to do *what*?"

"You're having HOW MANY?"

"You two are really...um, uh...brave."

Or most ominous of all: "Have you mailed the invitations yet?"

In our blissful state of innocence, we didn't pick up the cues.

To be honest, my husband—having once been a 9-year-old boy—wasn't as high on the idea as I was.

I was determined.

"Look," I said, "nothing could be worse than last year when we took all those boys to the pizza place for the birthday party."

He winced at the memory and staggered off to take an Advil: "Whatever you say."

So in the end we had a sleep-over—first, though, we took them to the pizza place for dinner. But that's another story....

I can't help it: I'm an optimist. I believe in progress. People change. I mean, they are all one year older, right?

Also, I kept seeing the faces of other parents when we picked up Josh after recent sleep-overs. Calm. Composed. Big smiles. What I didn't know then is they were dazed, sleep-deprived and close to hysteria.

But what most fueled my denial were my memories of slumber parties. Sure, we girls stayed up all night. But we whispered. We talked about boys (shhhh) and related topics (SHHH!). We listened to our favorite

45s, leafed through movie magazines, and sometimes we called boys on the phone, anonymously, and asked them about the colors of their toothbrushes.

To the best of my recollection we never had pillow fights at one in the morning or McLaughlin Group-style shouting matches about basketball teams.

Now here comes the moment you were warned about—the secret carefully guarded for so long.

It's this: the big people at a sleep-over—the grown-ups who you assume have greater stamina and patience—turn out to be the wimps. They're the ones who can't handle a little sleep deficit, a little noise, a little exuberance.

And the kids? They turn out to be masters of diplomacy and endurance.

I can't tell you how many times, when my husband and I trudged to the third floor to present them with this threat or that ultimatum, they graciously heard us out and politely waited until we were, oh, at least halfway down the stairs before bursting into bedlam again.

Just imagine a grown man and woman, bleary-eyed and cranky at some wee hour of the morning, inside their bedroom with the door closed, arguing about whose bright idea it was in the first place to huddle six boys and their sleeping bags into one room?

Be forewarned: It's a scene that will challenge your most cherished beliefs about relationships.

So how—and, more importantly, when—did sleep finally come?

Along about 1:45 a.m., the five boys who were still awake asked, please, to be separated and saved from themselves. Sleeping bags were dragged to all corners of the house on three different floors.

By 2, not a creature was stirring. By 7, they were up again, awaking in shifts, starting with our son.

On my way to make coffee, I passed the rest of them, one by one, bundled in their sleeping bags on the floor in the guest room, the hallway, the living room, the den.

As the mom of an only child, and one of three siblings so spread out in age that we felt like only children growing up, I loved the feeling of all those kids in all those rooms, asleep under my roof.

After breakfast, they played hide-and-seek with walkie-talkies all over the house. They watched Saturday morning cartoons. They built Legos. They chased the cat.

By the time their parents arrived, I could feel the details of the night before fading.

A friend calls this phenomenon "parental amnesia" and claims it's the first law of child-rearing.

Perhaps.

All I know is that *next time* I'll remember to split them up earlier. And I'll rent a different kind of movie. And maybe we'll skip the pizza place and order in.

What do you think?

April 18, 1993

So This
Is Love?

I've never seen a study on this but my guess is women receive more Valentines from the men in their lives than men get from the women in theirs.

All's unfair in love and war.

When I decided to check out my hunch with Mary Pat Mooney, owner of The Cardware Store downtown, she laughed and told me that the last few days before Valentine's Day, her shop is packed with men in a "feeding frenzy."

"I see men buying cards who I don't see the rest of the year," she said.

"Valentine's is the guilt holiday."

If it's true that men send more Valentines to the women they're close to than women deliver to their guys, it is certainly not the only lopsided tradition still flourishing in our male-female relationships.

Last week the Justice Department reminded us

of another:

Women are the recipients of 10 times as many physical attacks from the men in their lives—husbands, ex-husbands, boyfriends, brothers, sons and fathers—than men receive from either the men or the women in their lives.

This is nobody's hunch.

This is the conclusion drawn from 400,000 interviews conducted for the Bureau of Justice Statistics between 1987 and 1991.

The study found more than two-thirds of all violent attacks against women were committed by men they knew. Random attacks by strangers were not the big problem. Violence from "intimates" was.

"The most dangerous place in a woman's life is in her home," says Reba S. Cobb, executive director of the Center for Women and Families.

Dark alleys, the proverbial bugaboo when I was growing up, pose far less of a threat to women today than their own back yards or bedrooms.

"This is a reality we all need to come to terms with," Cobb says.

Sadly, these outrageous numbers no longer shock a lot of us. As a journalist, I've known some of the women these cold, hard scientific data represent.

Educated women. Working-class women. Homeless women. Wealthy women.

It is their real-life faces and their sobering stories—some that have ended surprisingly happy—that haunt me on Valentine's Day.

"What women really need on Valentine's Day is behavior that demonstrates love," Cobb suggests.

Actions. Not roses. Respect. Not bonbons. Nurturing. Not negligees.

Cobb rattles off a sorrowful litany of statistics: One out of two wives is beaten by a spouse in the course of a marriage; one in four women treated in emergency rooms is a victim of partner abuse; the No. 1 cause of injury to ALL women is a beating by a male "intimate."

In the last General Assembly, laws were beefed up to protect women from attacks by ex-husbands and boyfriends as well as spouses.

Yet one thing people who work with abused women know is this:

Whether in dating relationships or in marriage, violence doesn't begin with a beating or even a shove or a pinch. It's more likely to start with "jokes" at the expense of the woman, put-downs, fits of jealousy and nagging about how stupid, ugly, worthless or evil she is.

"We're in an epidemic stage of male violence right now," says Cobb. "There's a corporate rage against women because men are no longer able to control them. A lot of anger and defensiveness."

Granted, not all men are enraged to violence. And not all women are victims.

Yet the facts are daunting: In a typical year, about 2½ million females 12 and over are raped, robbed or assaulted by men, or suffer attempts or threats of such crimes.

Part of the problem is our faulty image of romantic

love. It's a sad fact that most women in shelters are in continuing relationships with their abusers.

Tonya Harding is an obvious example of a woman who returned to her abusive partner repeatedly, even after divorce.

There is a stage in such relationships called "the honeymoon phase." It's the kiss-and-make-up time, following an attack, when the man expresses remorse, promises to change and showers the woman with tokens of affection.

Cobb says we must educate young women and men to know that love is not defined by the romantic feelings accompanying it or the fancy trappings attached to it.

"I can see these (abusers) thinking they really love these women," says Cobb. "But what it's really all about for them is power and control."

When I read about the study last week, I thought of Carol Haub, a Southern Indiana wife and mother who—like Tonya Harding—got herself out of a long-term abusive marriage.

But unlike Harding, Haub did not return to her abuser. When he terrorized her for years, wanting her back, she sought police help. When he tracked her down in a restaurant and ripped a knife through her arm as she sat with a friend, she cooperated with prosecutors and joined a support group.

Her ex is now in prison serving a 50-year sentence for attempted murder.

I met Haub long after the trial, when she decided to let other women know how she escaped the cycle of abuse. She is still speaking out, most recently at an

FBI seminar on violence.

Telling her story is one thing she can do for abused women, she said.

On Valentine's Day, think about what you can do. Maybe it's giving a friend the Spouse Abuse Center crisis line number: (502) 581-7222.

Or if you happen to be one of the women the study is about, celebrate the holiday by doing something sweet for yourself.

Call the number.

February 13, 1994

Rites Of Spring

This is the week I love.

And what's not to love about it?

It will begin tomorrow night around a noisy, crowded family table, at a seder, the traditional Jewish meal celebrating Passover.

This springtime ritual brings us together—children and adults, family and friends—to share foods that symbolize the events and emotions of the Passover story. We'll join in prayers of thanksgiving and hope. We'll remember those who no longer sit at the table with us.

It's a ritual I married into: a wedding gift that grows in value each year.

The week will end Saturday night, in the dark, in an open field in rural Kentucky, celebrating the Catholic "fire rite."

Under the stars, surrounded by hills and woods and the sprawling Abbey of Gethsemani, my friend Kate and I will take part in this ancient Easter-vigil ritual known as "the striking of the new fire."

It starts with cold flint and rock, struck together by a monk until sparks ignite, then fanned into flame, kindled into a blazing bonfire and finally passed from one taper to another until the crowd itself becomes a ribbon of light.

It's an austere ritual, compared to the affectionate, family-style chaos of a seder. But I've never felt closer to my friend Kate, my companion at this ritual for two years now, than when we've stood around that fire on the grounds of the monastery near Bardstown.

There is song and movement to it, and a powerful, almost tangible, pull from the hills surrounding the abbey and the fields of wildflowers awakening along nearby paths.

A third-century hymn describes this ritual as the first step in "the mystic dance through the year."

"New is this feast and all-embracing; all creation assembles at it."

Though we grew up Catholic, this ceremony was totally new to Kate and me two years ago when we decided to forget about sleep and trekked to Nelson County for the ritual, which doesn't end till well past midnight.

Now, like the seder, it's something I can't imagine missing.

The reasons I look forward to this special week in the year are as simple and as complex as the rituals themselves.

For me, it's a time of mingling the symbols of my faith and my husband's faith.

We come from two strong spiritual traditions, and this week, in mysterious and visible ways, their paths cross.

I like what I learn each time I take part in both rituals—the seder with family, the fire rite with my friend.

What I learn is how much deeper our connections to other people grow—and how much greater our compassion and faith and love becomes—when we share our rituals.

Some people believe you water down the meaning of religious rites unless you limit yourself to the ones within your own tradition.

It hasn't worked that way for me.

In "The Magic of Ritual," theologian Tom F. Driver describes how he was bored with ritual until he studied the rites and ceremonies of people far removed, denominationally and geographically, from his own cultural background.

As he traveled through Japan, Haiti, New Guinea and back to New Haven, Driver began to appreciate the power of the religious rituals in his own life and was drawn back to them.

Like legends and myths, rituals do not belong exclusively to the people who create them. They become common property, common inspiration.

"The people who best know life is difficult are the ones most likely to cleave to ritual and make it work for them," Driver writes.

He points to the major role women's groups and minority movements have played in reviving interest in rituals in recent years.

This came home to me, in a fresh way, two weeks ago at a gathering that included men and women, American Indians and African-Americans.

We came together to celebrate the spring equinox with an American Indian ritual.

Sponsored by a local group called Project Rediscovery, the 40 or so of us who met at Fourth Avenue United Methodist Church were introduced to American-Indian beliefs about the unity and sacredness of all life.

But not through a lecture.

No, we learned through our own actions, as we wove a web of different colored fabric into a giant circle—a re-creation of the "sacred hoop" of Black Elk's famous vision.

The woven hoop held us together and allowed us to move, peacefully, as if we were one person.

I found myself wishing more people had been there.

But I had to smile when I realized what was keeping some of them away.

It was because another rite of spring that focuses on the "sacred hoop" was going on at the same time.

I'm sure you've heard of it. It's called NCAA basketball.

April 4, 1993

A Singular
Holiday

It's Derby Day, sometime in the mid-'50s.

A girl, 8 years old or so, takes a walk to a cemetery with her aunt, a single woman just the other side of 40—"an old maid," as she calls herself.

"Let's feed the ducks at Cave Hill," the aunt had suggested.

Carrying bags of soft white bread, they head out from the house where the aunt lives with her bachelor brother and their mother, a widow.

These two are old hands at making their own fun. They regularly explore the shops at the corner where Bardstown Road becomes Baxter Avenue. One favorite haunt is Walgreen's soda fountain, where they slurp butterscotch sundaes on high counter stools or in booths way in the back.

But this day, inside the cemetery, they pass hills of daffodils before reaching the lake where mallards and Canada geese waddle up to them to eat from their hands.

When the bread runs out, the girl and the woman walk home, hand in hand, as loving and connected a couple as you might find at any festive party that day.

I know Derby Day is about horses, but it always makes me think of my aunt and me at Cave Hill.

I also know Valentine's Day is officially about romantic love.

But the approach of this holiday never fails to send me searching for tokens of love to send my aunt — who for as long as I have known her has never been part of a couple in the conventional sense.

Today we accept that "families" can be something other than Mom, Dad and the kids.

And we are loosening up our definition of "couples." We're beginning to see the value in non-romantic relationships. The strong bonds between coworkers. The love shared by longtime best friends. The affection that flows from mentor to student. The emotional ties between brothers and sisters.

It's about time we redefined "couples" to mean more than husbands and wives. Americans are increasingly opting to postpone or forego marriage. And more adult children are choosing to live in their parents' homes, as my aunt and uncle did.

I feel lucky to have grown up in a family where singles—male and female—were an integral part of extended-family life.

But something happened between generations to make us view living with parents as some kind of failure on the part of both parties.

Was it that financial autonomy became more highly valued than the interdependence and comfort of extended-family life?

Flush times also made it easier for young adults to move out and live on their own.

Clearly today's harsher economics are fueling the trend to return home.

Though it's not for every family, it is not an all-bad choice, says therapist Caroline Bissmeyer, coordinator of family life education at Family & Children's Agency in Louisville.

"I think there can be some very good things about grown children living at home," she says, although she understands why we have negative reactions to such arrangements.

"They go against what we teach in our society now. We teach, 'Separate! Separate! Separate!'"

She speaks not just from professional observations but personal experience. Her son, who is 23, moved back home with Bissmeyer and her husband last fall.

"Connections with the extended family get stronger. A young person's understanding about what happens to parents as they age is strengthened. They learn how an older generation lives, the problems they struggle with."

I'm sure the mantel over my aunt's fireplace is covered with Valentines today.

She's never truly been a single person, if that word means "unattached." She's been coupled all her life with friends, with siblings, with neighbors, with coworkers, with nieces and nephews.

At 77, she still walks to neighborhood stores—only now it's often hand-in-hand with my son, who's about the age I was when we trekked to Cave Hill.

I have watched them some days in her back yard, ghosts playing all around them. There's my grandmother, shaking out clothes before hanging them on the line. My uncle sits on a stoop cleaning fish by a pond. My mother, in a halter top, trims weeds by the fence.

My aunt took care of all three of them when they were dying.

I asked her once how she felt about this role. She looked at me like I was 8 years old again and said, "It's what you do for the people you love."

That's the heart of Valentine's Day: honoring the people we love, whoever they are.

And that's why, instead of roses and chocolate, I find myself thinking of daffodil hills and soft white bread on this day that is dedicated to lovers.

February 14, 1993

What's In
A First
Name?

I know a schoolteacher whose 6-year-old daughter one day—"out of the blue"—began to call her Susan.

"I tried waiting to see if it would go away on its own, but it didn't," says the teacher.

When Susan asked her daughter why she never called her Mom anymore, this is the answer she got:

"Well, if I'm in a store and I yell out, 'Mom,' everybody turns around. If I yell 'Susan,' only you turn around."

Unable to fight that kind of logic, my friend turned to another revered instructional method.

"Bribery is what it was. I started paying her a penny every time she called me 'Mom.' So then it was 'Mom Mom Mom Mom Mom,' all day long. I gave up on that."

At some point, my friend says, she realized her uneasiness with her daughter's unorthodox habit had more to do with other people's reactions than her own.

"I realized I kind of *liked* it when she called me Susan. She was addressing me as a real person."

But Susan admits she requires her students to call her by her married title, Mrs. Johnson. And she expects her daughter to address her own teachers the same way.

Let's face it: Many of us are not consistent or logical when it comes to the issue of name-calling.

There's plenty of disagreement about what the use of first names indicates, when it's children addressing adults.

For some it's a clear sign of disrespect. For others it signifies mutual respect.

Susan sees a difference when the first names are all in the family.

"It's a matter of letting your children do what they want some of the time and not drawing the line at symbolic things," she says.

But Linda Wilson, director of the University of Louisville's Multicultural Center, notes that some ethnic and cultural traditions are "very, very strict" about how children refer to adults.

"I know in most African-American families, you call adults Mr. or Mrs. Such-and-Such. It's much more formal. In my growing-up years, you knew you did not call people your parents' age by their first names," says Wilson.

It was not just a respect issue, but an "authority" issue: "Calling adults Mr. or Mrs. meant they had the authority to act as parents to you."

The tradition continues in Wilson's family, but not without a little inconsistency for good measure.

"We don't allow my 8-year-old niece to call people

our age by their first names," she says. "Well, except for the next-door neighbors who've known her all her life."

In Jefferson County public schools, this difference in traditions can create dilemmas. Some schools, like The Brown School, encourage students to call their teachers by their first names. Most don't, however.

Margaret Lehocky, a teacher at Bloom Elementary who thinks of herself as "a pretty traditional person," remembers that it was "an adjustment" when her daughter began calling her teachers at The Brown by their first names.

"We ended up making jokes about it at the dinner table," says Lehocky. "I'm finding that there's a change toward the more casual approach."

Though my son still calls me Mom, I tend to have a laissez-faire response to what people of any age call me.

In most cases, I prefer they keep it simple. Dianne will do. No last name, no title, no confusion.

I admit that my relaxed attitude may be borne of necessity: I have one of those last names that people tend to remember as a first. They meet me, and the next thing I know they are calling me "April," a female first name I don't identify with at all.

In my early days as a reporter, there were times when I thoroughly enjoyed being mistaken for this April-woman. I recall interviewing a few men in positions of power who expected strangers to address them as Mr. So-and-So but who felt quite comfy calling me "April" right off the bat. I always found it amusing that, unbeknownst to them, they were talking to me as an "equal," in the casual last-name-only mode they usually reserved for chums on the racquetball court.

After I married, the name-calling became even more confusing.

Instead of legally adopting my husband's last name, I kept the byline that had been mine since the day it was matched up with my footprint on a Commonwealth of Kentucky birth certificate.

As a result, today people not only address me by my last name, thinking it's my first—but they call me a slew of other mistaken titles. For example, there are "Mrs. Shapero" and "Mrs. Aprile," neither of whom legally exist in our household. There's also "Miss" Aprile, the name used by people who knew me when I was single and assume I still am, since my last name hasn't changed.

Given a choice, I prefer to be called Dianne. That's what I tell my son's friends and the kids in the neighborhood.

But I answer to all the names above, as well as to my sentimental favorite, a title my son's friends bestowed on me when they were too young to know mothers had identities apart from their children.

I always knew it was me they wanted whenever I heard the name called out across a playground or through a back-yard fence: "Josh's Mom! Josh's Mom!"

March 7, 1993

Dads And
Daughters

I was talking to David Senn about what it's like to raise five daughters when he decided to tell me the story of his back-yard fence.

When his older girls were still toddlers, he erected a 3-foot-high chain-link fence to keep them safe.

Senn remembers telling his wife, Catherine, that when the girls got a little older, he planned to add another 3 feet to the height; and when they turned 16, he'd put up barbed wire; and at 18, he planned to get the "whole thing electrified."

Years later, when his oldest daughter was getting married, he remembers "sitting on the steps and shedding a tear or two" as he looked at the fence and muttered to himself: "The darn thing didn't work!"

When I finished laughing at the image he'd conjured, he added: "Even if you like the guy, it's hard walking your daughter down the aisle."

Senn, a planning analyst at the University of

Louisville for 25 years, said he and his wife always told their daughters there was nothing they couldn't do because they were girls. Today they're all professional women, doing well in their fields.

"It's not been all perfect and all smooth," he is quick to add.

But he also says, "I learned a lot from them. They made me more appreciative of the abilities of women."

Senn's comments go right to the heart of what researchers are finding out as they begin to look more closely at the father-daughter relationship.

We've heard plenty in the past decades about the powerful role dads play in shaping their daughters' self-esteem, career ambitions and future relationships with men.

But the equally powerful role daughters play in shaping their fathers' attitudes and actions is something the experts are just beginning to investigate.

And what they're discovering is something dads like Senn have known all along: When a man allows himself to become close to his daughter, he reaps all sorts of personal benefits—from greater self-esteem to smoother and more satisfying relationships with women, particularly his wife and his female co-workers.

When men have strong relationships with their daughters, they "soften" up, as psychologist Clark Clipson, of San Diego's Alzarado Institute, puts it.

They become more empathetic to women's concerns. They learn to nurture and listen. They grow more comfortable expressing their feelings.

"It's a transformational experience," says psychologist

Michael Horowitz, founder of The Fatherhood Project at the Illinois School of Professional Psychology and, more importantly perhaps, the father of a daughter.

It's intriguing, this idea that having a daughter can transform a man—if he lets it—in ways that having a son can't.

Raising sons can help men redeem their own boyhoods.

Raising daughters may be the way they make peace with the opposite sex and balance the male and female aspects of their own personalities.

Setting out to learn more, I talked to leading researchers who've studied hundreds of dads, and I talked to a few fathers themselves.

Senn told me he's been amazed over the years that so many people "made such a big deal" out of his having no sons.

"I've never thought of it that way," he said. "The most wonderful thing that can happen to a man is having a daughter, and I've been five times blessed."

Talking to him made me think of "Father of the Bride," a movie I barely remember with Spencer Tracy but find irresistible in its Steve Martin reincarnation.

It's Senn's enthusiasm and unabashed love for his daughters that remind me of Martin. The movie, after all, is not really about the "bride"—but about what she brings out in Martin, her father.

He mellows when he's with her. His whole demeanor turns softer. He can't hide his feelings when she's around; doesn't want to. At the thought of losing her, he commits the unpardonable male sin. He gets wildly irrational, overwhelmed not by anger but by plain unaffected affection.

And the audience, because this is a comedy and not real life, loves him for it.

Harvard medical school psychologist William Pollack, who has a new book on men coming out this month, says he finds many fathers are "positively surprised" to learn they can feel that close to their daughters. But once they open up, their daughters' response to them makes them feel "more complete."

Pollack speaks from personal as well as clinical experience: Besides being part of a Boston University five-year study of fathers, he is the dad of a 6-year-old daughter.

Having a daughter forces a man to concede "there's a lot about a woman's perspective we males don't understand, and there's a lot we can grow to understand by being in tune with our own daughters," he said.

It can also have repercussions in the workplace.

Consider this: In hundreds of interviews with men, Pollack found those who had daughters had "dramatically expanded their view of women's roles" on the job, compared to men who had sons.

But one question kept nagging me: Why were daughters, in particular, so powerful? Why didn't wives wield the same influence?

What was so special about the father–daughter relationship that it could beget such change in men?

Pollack had an answer for me:

When men deal with adult women, including wives,

they often are battling subconscious fears. As little boys, they were raised by women. They worried they might lose them. As a result, they still can feel vulnerable around them and defensive.

But daughters are a different story. They are female, but vulnerable, too, and in need of their fathers' care.

"With daughters, fathers can put down their shields of defendedness," Pollack said, "and be empathetic in a way not as easy for them to be with their wives."

Sometimes men with the best intentions run into trouble when their daughters approach puberty.

Clipson said "the job of a father is to appreciate his daughter's growing sexuality, without being seduced by it one way or another or too charmed by it."

But many men become "quite frightened" of their own reactions at this time and retreat from their daughters' lives.

"Just as fathers and sons have to find ways to talk about baseball or whatever, fathers have to find ways to relate to their daughters," he said. "It may mean having to abandon the usual role of mentor that's so comfortable with a son."

We know what can happen to daughters whose fathers withdraw from them. Their self-esteem suffers. They lose confidence. They feel like failures.

But what happens to the fathers?

The same thing, says Pollack. Many older men he's interviewed feel a "sense of terrible loss" from not being as close to their daughters as they now wish.

David Krauss, a Cleveland psychologist who helped start The Men's Council there, works with older men in nursing homes. He says many of them, as they grow older, sense "they've missed something....They often don't know what it is."

But how can the father-child relationship be repaired at such a late date?

"It is up to us as adult children, in a gentle and sensitive way, to take opportunities to tell our fathers we love them, to feel more connected to them. This is probably easier for daughters," Clipson said.

It's not an easy task, rebuilding such a relationship, but Pollack says it's worth the effort:

"When this turns out to be satisfying and reinforcing, fathers often say, 'Well, my God, I never knew she felt that way.' And from the daughter's point of view, it's an opening for…intimacy that didn't exist before."

One day, in the midst of my research, I realized there was one expert whose knowledge I hadn't yet tapped. I went to see my father and asked him the questions I was asking everyone else.

How had he changed because of being father to a girl? Did having a daughter, after having a son first, make him think differently about himself?

I sent him the questions ahead of time, so he could think about them. Sitting at the table in his kitchen, he read me his written answers, word for word. Like a good reporter, I taped our conversation on a mini-recorder that sat spinning between us on the table.

"Yes, I did feel different about myself," he said, reading from his own hand, "in that I saw in you the fulfillment of a dream to have a daughter to love and be loved by forever."

There's a pause on the tape after that statement. I noticed it later, on the way home in the car, playing back the conversation: A gap of time, passing.

Then his voice breaks the silence and I can hear him whisper:

"I didn't put down anything I didn't mean."

June 20, 1993

Call Me Coach

The first "live birth" I witnessed was not really live. It was on tape. I was a medical reporter, writing a story. It was part of my research to watch it.

I was amazed. When the baby's head crowned, I cried. I can't tell you why. I just did.

Not being a farm girl, I didn't grow up watching cows or horses give birth. Not even cats, for that matter. Under my mother's rules, all pets either had to be male or "fixed" as soon as possible. No surprise litters in her house!

So it was unfamiliar territory to me: seeing new life enter the world.

Years passed, and the next birth I witnessed was an altogether different experience. It was the birth of my son.

In all honestly, I didn't see it. It took place behind a draped wall erected at my waist. But I heard it, and I more or less felt it. He was a C-section baby who, as I remember, started crying before he was out of the womb. I can't be sure. Behind the green drape, I missed most of the details.

My husband filled me in on them though—countless times, at my request. The slice into my abdomen. My organs pushed this way and that. The sudden glimpse of baby. The lifting out and up for me to see. The first caress of father to son.

(Some people are squeamish about such details, I learned. The funny thing is, they are often the same folks who have no trouble digesting gruesome front-page descriptions of dismemberment and mayhem in war-torn lands.)

In any event, during the decade that followed, I became the happy recipient each year of wonderful Mother's Day gifts.

But no amount of cut flowers or homemade cards could quell my old yearning. Like my friend who stares at her garden twice a day in early spring, I wanted to see life blossom.

Then last summer my sister-in-law Cathy called with a question: "Would you be my birth coach?"

I don't think I've ever said "yes" so quickly or with more conviction.

Cathy was already enrolled in prepared-childbirth classes. In fact, she was halfway through them when she called. Her husband, a pediatrician who specializes in treating newborns, would be at the hospital during her first delivery. That was a given.

But Cathy wanted me at her side as well.

She'd read that childbirth sometimes goes more

smoothly when the prospective mom is coached by a female friend who has "practical experience" giving birth.

I was psyched. Look out, Denny. Move over, Rick. The coach was on the court.

As Cathy's due date approached, I remembered what a photographer friend once told me. No matter how many times she shoots a delivery — and she has snapped scores of them in the course of her career — she's always caught off guard by the same sudden realization:

"One moment you're standing in a room with three people, and the next moment you're in the same room but now there are four of you. Everything changes in that one moment."

I wanted to share that moment with Cathy and her baby.

There are, of course, as many ways to become a mother as there are women in the world.

It can happen by plan. Or by surprise. By adoption. Or by a surrogate's pregnancy. In a hospital. At home. With drugs. Or "naturally."

Cathy wanted to try unmedicated childbirth—a delivery without use of painkillers. We would use deep breathing and other "natural" techniques to help her cope with backaches and cramping, hallmarks of childbirth. If that wasn't enough, she would take whatever pain relief her doctor deemed best.

For weeks, we synchronized our inhaling and exhaling. *In 2, 3, 4, 5.* We went to childbirth classes. *Out, 2, 3, 4, 5.* We discussed what to take to the hospital. *Take a deeeeeep cleansing breath.* We practiced what to do if Cathy panicked and started pushing at the wrong time. *Look at me! Watch my face! Blow!*

A book bag packed with pens and notebooks sat by my front door, awaiting the big day. I was ready: Gentlemen, start your pitocin drip!

Cathy switched from reading pregnancy books to baby books. She was ready too.

The night before the birth, I craved a kind of ice-cream cone I hadn't tasted in years. Vanilla dipped in caramel coating, the kind that's crunchy on the outside.

A friend had mentioned having such a treat at a Dairy Queen. My husband and I tried two locations that night, but were informed no such concoction existed. I settled for something lesser and fell asleep still hungering for a caramel cone.

Perhaps you've heard of *couvade*—the condition in which expectant fathers seem to experience sympathetic contractions as their wives go into labor. I may have suffered the only documented case of sympathetic craving: I dubbed it *caramelade*.

The next morning on the way to the hospital where Cathy was already starting to labor, I stopped my car in front of a coffeeshop on Bardstown Road for a quick fix of caffeine. I couldn't believe what I saw when I walked inside, chalked onto the big board above the counter:

"Karmal Latte" was the flavor of the day. Caramel coffee!

I gulped down a mug of it and took the coincidence as a sign: While I might have to be patient in this birthing enterprise, the payoff would be better than expected.

At the hospital, in a room with a generous view of trees and sky, nurses and family popped in and out. But we were alone most of the morning. Cathy catnapped between contractions. I watched, took notes. We played no TV, no music, no games.

If I had to compare the experience of the early part of that long day, I'd compare it to meditation. It had a similar rhythm and intensity, the same deep peace.

Of course, the rhythm changed.

In the end, Cathy had an epidural to ease the pain.

In the end, I changed from a pink sundress to drab scrubs when a dropping pulse rate made a C-section a possibility.

In the end, when push came to shove, the room was filled with women—coach, obstetrician, pediatrician, nurses, aides—all gathered around the bed, encouraging Cathy. The only men present were her husband and the anesthesiologist.

In the end, Sara was born.

I was inches away when she made her grand arrival. *Push, Cathy! Push! Just one more time!* I was holding her mother's head, pushing her chin into her chest, squeezing her hand, when my niece—a ball of baby— made her entrance.

In the end, this is what I remember. A snip of cord. A squirt of blood. A new mother. A new life.

In the end, Cathy and I cried. I can't tell you why. We just did.

May 8, 1994

Women's
Work

A few weeks ago, as we were putting away groceries, I asked my 9-year-old if he thought there were any differences between women's work and men's work. Without looking up from the microwaveable Lunch Bucket he was stacking on a pantry shelf, he answered my question with one of his own:

"Do you want to know if there *actually* are differences, or if there *should* be differences?"

Having grown up around reporters, he knows how to handle the press. But on the eve of Labor Day, as I consider the status of "women's work," I find myself wondering about those same distinctions between what is and what ought to be.

Of course, my son said, there should be no differences. Women can fly jets. Men can teach first grade.

But women pilots are the exception. And male elementary-school teachers are rare. The same goes for the home front. Men can pick up kids when they get sick at day care or stay home for six months when a baby is born, but those who do are the exceptions.

Even the country's top women executives feel greater stress and higher levels of burnout than their male counterparts, according to a report released in July by Catalyst, a New York firm that tracks women's workplace progress.

Why? The report says it's the result of women juggling demanding roles both at work and home and bearing a disproportionate share of family duties.

"They've made it," said UCLA professor Carol Scott, who conducted the study. "But there's blood on the floor."

There's sweat there too.

Listen to Hillary Rodham Clinton, a woman few would mistake for an old-fashioned gal. In an interview with a New York Times reporter, she compared herself to the typical American Mom who: "gets up in the morning and gets breakfast for her family and goes off to a job…who runs out at lunch to buy material for a costume for her daughter or to buy invitations for a party that she's going to have and after work…picks up her children and maybe goes out with her husband."

Now don't forget this is also the Lady who's spent the first half of 1993 tackling one of the toughest issues we face, health-care reform. But, of course, it's a volunteer job.

Last month you heard voices everywhere urging the president to take his long overdue vacation. Did you hear anyone worrying about Hillary?

Change comes slowly, but it comes. Meanwhile, we cope in our own resourceful ways.

Have you noticed, for example, how much more likely it is these days to enter an office where you wouldn't expect to see a child in the middle of the day and find one there anyway—perhaps sprawled on the floor reading a book or hunched over a table scribbling?

We're not talking on-site day-care programs. This is far less official than that. Somewhere nearby there's usually a working mother, either feeling terribly guilty for committing the social *faux pas* of mixing work and family or feeling energized by not being forced to draw arbitrary lines between the two.

The first few times I stumbled on this scene, I wondered what was going on. Probably the child woke up too sick for day-care or school but not sick enough to be confined to bed. Most likely Mom couldn't afford to miss a day at the job. Or at the very least, she felt compelled—child in tow—to pick up work to take home.

I've seen this scene in all sorts of workplaces. At hospitals. In newsrooms. At gourmet shops, beauty salons, bakeries, libraries and law offices.

Eventually it dawned on me: These were the guerrilla tactics of working mothers. In a society that had a difficult time throwing its support behind a rather innocuous family-leave law, this grassroots improvisation of workplace "flexibility" is one way of fighting back.

What employed parents most want is to be late without censure if a child-care problem arises, to be able to attend a school play or teacher's conference or take an elderly parent to the doctor, to have the options of job-sharing or part-time work during "family-intensive" times of life, according to a recent report by Ellen Galinsky, of New York's Families and Work Institute.

Today the definition of "women's work" has broadened to include taking on the role of the parent and the employee most likely to push for and take advantage of these options. Perhaps as more men get more involved in parenting and feeling the frustration of family-unfriendly policies, this, too, will change.

A few weeks ago I interviewed someone in my home. My son was working in another room on his hobby, origami, the Japanese art of paper folding.

When we finished the interview, he showed the two of us a box he had made. Intrigued, our visitor asked him to teach her how to make one.

Watching him demonstrate how to bend and crease the paper and then gently open up the folds to create new spaces and shapes and forms, it struck me that perhaps there's a new metaphor for the balancing act that women today perform.

I'm tired of talking about juggling, with its dire implications of risk and danger and any-moment-now collisions. I'm sick of glass ceilings. Super Moms. Mommy tracks. The imagery of women's work today is cold and hard, stressing the struggle but hardly ever suggesting the satisfaction when it all comes together.

I propose origami might be a better image. Unlike juggling, it's not about going round and round in circles. And it doesn't, by its nature, end in failure.

It's about flexing and folding and bending. It's about working with what you've got, using your imagination, being creative and ultimately making something better than what you started out with.

My son showed our visitor the "nesting crane" he had made, a bird that seems—at first glance—on the verge of flying out of a box, her nest. But if you look from another angle, the bird appears to be settling into the box, her home.

Clearly you could see it either way. In fact, you could see it *both ways at once* if you let yourself—a bird hovering in the delicate balance between nest and sky.

I suspect there's something quite familiar about that position for most working women. It's the place where many of us spend most of our days.

September 5, 1993

Burying
The Past

When she called, I'll be honest, I wasn't sure what to think.

Anne Maron was inviting me, a stranger, to take part in a ceremony at her home. It would be a ritual, she said, to say goodbye to her childbearing years and to honor her body for a job well done.

Maron, a counselor at St. Frances School in Goshen, Ky., had a hysterectomy last July. At the time, she persuaded her gynecologist ("God bless him") to save a piece of her uterus and ovary for her to take home.

"I did not want it thrown in the trash," she said.

Now, in spring, she planned to bury it in her perennial garden where, "in a symbolic sense, it could continue to bring life into the world."

When she mentioned her plans for the ritual and the burial to a few women friends, she said they told her— *after* they stopped snickering or groaning—"Do it! I wish I'd done something to commemorate my menopause."

So now the time had arrived.

"I'd like other women to know about it," she said. "Will you come?"

This is not your traditional Mother's Day story. It's not about babies or breast-feeding or child-rearing.

It's about the end of the motherhood cycle, and how one woman—with a lot of help from her friends— decided to make the most of it.

"Women are good at supporting each other when we're pregnant," says one of Maron's friends who attended the ritual, Marcelle Gianelloni, curator of education at the Louisville Zoo.

"But we're not so good at other times, like divorces or menopause. We need to take time from hectic schedules and talk to each other."

There's plenty of talk these days about menopause, as Boomer Women head into it in droves and popular authors like Gail Sheehy write books about it.

But most of the talk is medical and impersonal. The emphasis is on "symptoms" and "warning signs" and ways to mask the changes that age brings on.

There's a countertrend out there, however. Anne Maron seemed to be tapping into it. It's a movement to embrace "the change" as a natural rite of passage to be celebrated, not ignored—openly saluted in song and prayer, dance and art, rather than discussed clinically, like an illness, at hospital workshops.

With all this in mind, I accepted Maron's invitation. And that's how on the first day of spring, which also happened to be Maron's birthday, I joined a circle of women in the living room of her home in eastern Jefferson County.

We sat on chairs and on the floor—teen-agers, grandmothers, housewives, professionals, women of many faiths, friends, family and, for good measure, a few skeptics like me.

Maron's husband, Mel, a University of Louisville professor, manned the video camera. Their children, Melanie, 19, and Danny, 21, hovered on the perimeter of the circle.

"My children are my great joy," she says.

Mel Maron, who calls it a "privilege" to have been included, supported the idea from the start. The two women Maron calls her "spiritual guides"—her mother, Florence Ross, and good friend Rabbi Shoni Labowitz—flew in from Fort Lauderdale for the ritual.

Labowitz opened the ceremony by lighting the Shabbat candles, a Jewish Sabbath ritual.

"I think celebrating motherhood is very important," Labowitz said. "But there is a creativity beyond motherhood as well. As our bodies change, we change too."

And that was part of the ritual's purpose: to mark Maron's transition to the next stage of life, a time for applying what's been learned. Whatever discomfort I felt when I arrived was quickly replaced by a feeling of sharing a sense of history and humor with the others.

"This may sound strange," one woman told Labowitz, "but I want to celebrate my father." The rabbi shot back: "What could be stranger than what we're already doing?"

Two small boxes, containing a portion of Maron's

uterus and ovary, rested on the coffee table in front of Labowitz. Because it was raining, the burial had to be postponed for another day.

I look at it this way: Most people, when they retire from a job they've held 20 years, mark the event with a party.

Why shouldn't Maron do the same?

"Being a mother has been my favorite job," she says.

And she's held down plenty of them: She has been a hospice worker in Harlem; a Long Island social worker; a film librarian for the British Broadcasting Corporation in Glasgow, Scotland; and a school librarian and counselor at St. Frances.

Some people save mementos from the jobs they leave. Maron saved the parts of her body that made her favorite job possible. Her doctor, gynecologist Ron Levine, says her request was "a first" in 30 years of practice.

"But I had no problem with it," he says. "I thought it was very interesting."

Two weeks ago, alone in their perennial garden, Ann and Mel Maron completed the ritual. Among the spring flowers, they buried the past and moved on.

May 9, 1993

No Place
Like Home

If you listen, you can hear spring in the air. It sounds like…chain saws whining against plywood. Hammers banging on two-by-fours. Roofers shouting. Power mowers howling. Tillers trilling. It's the season when homeowners look around and see that everything needs work.

Sitting on my back porch on the day not long ago when it seemed that every dogwood in town burst into bloom on cue, I could barely hear bird song above repair noise.

It's easy sometimes to forget the motivation behind this springtime frenzy of refurbishment:

Home is our haven.

Laverne Cunningham, a 53-year-old housekeeper who grew up in Louisville's Russell neighborhood, has learned not to take such things for granted.

She owns a Habitat for Humanity home, a two-story blue frame with a back yard and patio on a spruced-up block of South 20th Street between Chestnut and Madison, not far from where she grew up.

Habitat for Humanity is a program designed to provide decent, affordable housing for low-income families at a zero-interest mortgage rate. Mortgage money is then reinvested to build more houses.

One of the requirements for owning a Habitat house is a commitment to donate 500 "sweat-equity" hours to building other people's homes.

When I asked Cunningham to describe the home she, her daughter Lisa and 4-year-old grandson Phillip have lived in for two years now, she didn't mention its three bedrooms or the upstairs utility room or the tomatoes she grew last summer.

Not at first. At first, she just said: "It's fabulous."

Cunningham moved out of public housing when she moved into her new home. Though she lived in a house when she was married, this is the first she's owned on her own.

"I just feel like I'm living in paradise," she said. "Not that there's anything wrong with other avenues, like public housing. It's just so much better when it's yours. When you have your own little yard and privacy, and the kids aren't always clustered together."

Cunningham's two other daughters, who are older, and their friends shared the 500 hours of required hands-on labor.

"Sometimes I would move dirt from one place to another. There was a lot of that to do," Cunningham laughs. She also hung dry wall, cleared trash, hammered nails.

As a mother and a grandmother, she said she'd do almost anything to get a house for her family.

"When I heard about the program, that's exactly what I thought of—my daughter had a kid, a boy at that, and I thought it would be just great if I could get him out of the projects. Maybe they would take more pride in their own home," she said. "And I do think that's what happened."

Most of the Habitat homes built in Louisville are owned now by single mothers, like Cunningham and like Jeanette Johnson, a Brown School office secretary. Johnson and her teen-age daughter, Sara, lived for a time in public housing at Cotter Homes. Eventually they ended up living with friends because she had nowhere else to go.

"This is a blessing to women who are really trying," Johnson said. "It doesn't always seem like the system is designed for women who are trying."

She believes the Habitat homes going up in Russell are "a blessing" to the neighborhood too, encouraging more renovation.

"And my daughter is able to have friends over now," says Johnson. "She's become part of the community."

To date, Habitat has built 24 homes in Louisville and plans 14 more. It's not surprising that single mothers and their children are the biggest beneficiaries.

Women make up two-thirds of all low-income adults, and they are more likely to live in substandard housing than men. When they are homeless, their plight is often hidden because they are more apt to live like nomads, moving from friend's house to friend's house.

Because they often have children with them, they are less likely to do what men do—sleep on the streets, where they're noticed.

But now Habitat of Louisville is asking the more fortunate sisters of these women to notice.

Executive director Diane Kirkpatrick and board member Linda Harris are calling on Louisville women to raise $16,000 to sponsor a house *specifically* for a single mother and her children. Matching funds are available if the $16,000 goal is met.

"We do not want 16 wealthy women to give $1,000 each," says Harris, who is general manager of the Jefferson Club. "We prefer to get many, many women to contribute gifts of all sizes"—and to do so in honor of significant women in their own lives. Moms, bosses, friends, teachers, aunts, sisters.

If successful, Harris hopes next year to have a house not just financed exclusively by women—but *built* by them too.

So far the donations are trickling into Habitat's new office at 801 Vine St. at a steady rate.

"It seems like there are a lot of women around who can imagine how hard it is, raising a family without a home," Harris says.

One of those who imagined it and then did something about it is the woman who sent a Habitat donation in lieu of the flowers she usually buys a friend on Mother's Day.

"In honor of Eunice," she wrote, "because we've always been blessed with a roof over our heads even when times were rough."

Back on my porch, listening to the sounds of noisy home construction, I watch birds building nests in my trees. Like Cunningham and Johnson and you and me, birds weave whatever materials they find into the fabric of their homes.

Grass, sticks, string. The stuff of a bird nest.

Self-respect, hard work, love. The ingredients of a Habitat home.

Birds know, as we do, that a home is much more than a symbol of success or productivity. Home is where young lives begin, where wings learn to spread and ultimately fly right.

Every family deserves a decent one.

May 1, 1994

A Father's Days

There's another new book out on the subject of what happens to women when their mothers die. Its title is blunt: "Motherless Daughters: The Legacy of Loss."

Those of us who are motherless daughters don't need books to explain the legacy. We live it. But a few weeks ago, a long-distance call from a stranger got me thinking about it from a new perspective.

The caller was a widower who wanted to talk about what happens to a father when his daughters lose their mother.

How, for example, does a man handle being the sole parent when his wife was the heart of the family?

How does he make up for his daughters' loss of a female confidante and best friend, when he's stuck in his own grief?

It depends, of course, on the man.

If he is Ken Dean—my caller from Madisonville, Ky.—his legacy of loss will inspire a personal journey from despair to a closer relationship with his daughters. It also will inspire an urge to tell others to wise up while there's time.

"It makes you hug your family all the tighter."

Those words were close to the first ones out of Dean's mouth the day we met in the two-story building in Madisonville where he and his wife, Dorothy Jean, built a comfortable law practice. He handled cases. She handled business.

In 1984 Dorothy Jean found a pea-sized lump in her breast and was diagnosed with cancer. She had a radical mastectomy, chemotherapy and radiation treatment. The couple's two daughters, now both physicians, were still in school: Jacque was a junior at Ole Miss; Donna was 14.

Not long after their mom came back to work, the cancer came back too. And kept coming back. A spot on her spine, a place in her ribs, her neck. More chemo. More radiation. Slowly her body deteriorated. She used a walker, then a wheelchair. In the end, she was bedridden.

Eventually the Deans sold their house, and Ken turned the second floor of the office into an apartment.

"She had this little bell," he said, taking it out of a drawer to show me. "I'd leave my office door open downstairs and she would ring it when she needed me."

She lived there until the last 41 days of her life, when she moved to a hospital. She died on Feb. 21, 1989, at age 47. Dean buried his wife in the family plot in

Gillette, Ark., the couple's hometown, following a funeral she helped plan.

A big man whose passions are hunting and fishing and practical jokes, he is surprisingly candid about how rough those first 18 months were.

"I couldn't function. I cried every day. I had some very dark times," he said.

"When I looked back, I felt guilty for not being the husband I should have been. For taking my wife for granted, as a lot of men do. For taking my whole family for granted, as if they'd always be there."

Yet the scrapbooks he showed me on a tour of the apartment were filled with mementos of family outings and parties.

"Sure, I was there as a father figure. I took my daughters fishing. We traveled a lot. But their mother really raised them," he said.

"I had feelings of remorse and guilt, despair. There were times I should have seen a therapist, but friends got me through. And my daughters. And my wife's words to me—to take care of her girls."

Today both daughters are engaged to be married. Jacque, an internist, is a rheumatology fellow at the University of Louisville. Donna, a recent graduate of the University of Kentucky School of Medicine, starts a combined internship in internal medicine and pediatrics there this month.

"I think probably the second hardest thing for us to deal with when mother died was watching my father," Jacque says.

"His productivity at work fell off precipitously. He

would make any excuse to drop everything and go back to Arkansas. He'd say it was for business but it was because he wanted to be with her."

Dorothy Jean and Ken were high school sweethearts. He was all-state quarterback. She was valedictorian and homecoming queen. A storybook romance from Day One.

"We met in the lunchroom," Dean said. "I had a job washing dishes."

Though they both came from Gillette, a small town on the lower edge of the Grand Prairie, their backgrounds were different.

Her family owned land they farmed. His were sharecroppers.

The couple dated through high school, married in college, had children early.

"We grew up with our kids," Dean said.

Law is his second career. He was on the education faculty at Murray State University when, desiring a new challenge, he entered Chase Law School at age 36. In two years, he was graduated. Though she recalls being embarrassed by his "student" status, Jacque now sees it as a family lesson in the value of education.

"We have 10 degrees among us. My parents didn't push us for good grades, but when you brought them home and you got such praise, who wouldn't want to do it again?"

Both women also credit him with their academic and career success.

"He always said he wanted us to have our own

careers," Jacque said, "and never have to rely on a man to support us."

When their mom was dying, Jacque took a leave of absence from medical school to stay with her. Donna was at Ole Miss, where she dropped back to part-time. Her father says she drove the 650-mile round trip home for six consecutive weekends at the end of her mom's life.

"Sometimes," Donna says, "I'd be halfway there and not remember the first half of the trip."

Dean never asked his daughters to work to pay for their schooling. It was a gift.

"I said, you do your part and I'll do mine. I got the easy end of the deal. All I had to do was pay. I didn't have to go to class, cut up cadavers. They amaze me."

He also gave them a love of the outdoors. This spring both women went on separate fishing trips with their dad.

"He's gone above and beyond where my mother left off. We joke that he has to do the hand-wringing now," Donna says.

She recalls a time not long ago when she was disappointed about something. She called her dad and "he was ready to drop everything and come to Lexington."

Dean says, "I guess I've done enough worrying for both of us."

Most importantly, he's provided a model for not giving up when life gets painful. The summer after his wife's death, despite his own simmering depression, Dean packed up the family and took a Virginia vacation.

"I guess I redoubled my efforts to stay close to my

children," he says.

On my drive back home, I thought about my last exchange with Dean as we paged through photo albums in the apartment that bears reminders of his wife in every room.

"It was pretty scary at first, being the only parent of daughters," he said.

"But we've all adjusted. We talk about Dorothy Jean every time we're together. Funny stories. Like the way she would get in such a stew over things."

Standing over the album, he leaned closer to the photos that tell his family's story, from baby poses to funeral shots.

"We remember the good things," he said.

There's a lot of peace and healing in that comment. If loss must have its legacy, surely those five simple words represent the best a mother could hope for her daughters and their dad.

June 19, 1994

Close-ups

I Get
Exercised

If you had asked me a month ago what Tipper Gore, Demi Moore and Madonna had in common, I probably would have said, "First names that make me glad I'm a Dianne."

But that was before I read a blurb in Time magazine entitled "Toning Tips of the Pop Icons."

It was in that penetrating 2-inch analysis of exercise and diet habits of the rich and famous that I learned what these three busy women (two of them wives and mothers) have in common.

Each of them works out for three hours every day.

Three hours.

Now I'm a working mother and a wife. Maybe you are too. But even if you're not, can you imagine finding three spare hours to carve out of your daily schedule to dedicate to running, biking, power-walking, weight training, swimming or even trudging in place on a treadmill in the privacy of your own home?

Most working women I know would trade almost anything—maybe even their next pay raise—for the luxury of three hours a day to use as needed.

These women are eking out exercise time a half-hour here and there, at the crack of dawn before the rest of the family wakes, at lunch, after dark when the kids are asleep or at one of the rare gyms that provide baby-sitting.

My sister-in-law, who's about to have her first child, is the only working woman I know who exercises three hours a day and is likely to keep up the pace postpartum.

But she owns an aerobics studio, so it's in her job description.

You could argue that staying in shape is the top priority for Madonna, Gore and Moore. (Sounds like a Halloween costume shop, doesn't it? Or maybe a girl group that specializes in hymns and heavy metal.)

But I must admit that I am disappointed in Tipper Gore.

In an interview with New York Times food writer Marion Burros, she said that when she was looking for ways to trim down after her husband became the vice president, it was Al Gore who urged her to fit an exercise routine into her busy schedule.

"I said I didn't have enough time. And he said, 'You never have time. Make time.'"

The Veep is right, of course. We all find excuses for exercising too little. A quarter of our adult population is clinically "sedentary," a recent study showed. Another third is "barely active."

But three hours?

In People magazine, Tipper Gore confessed that chiseling out those 180 extra minutes a day wasn't easy: "I had to give myself permission to free myself from wanting to do everything perfectly."

I bet there are lots of you who would have no problem giving yourselves such permission. That's not really the issue.

For Tipper, "permission" meant she could let go of some of some household chores, like laundry, and give up her desire to serve "perfectly cooked meals."

But for most working moms, it would mean something a bit different—like the laundry would stay dirty and the family would starve.

Reading between the lines, we know *somebody* is doing the wash for the Gores, and there's a good chance the kitchen help is serving tasty, low-calorie family meals.

All I can say is, I hope Hillary Rodham Clinton comes up with a more practical health plan than her sidekick has.

Face it, these are not the kind of tips that arouse hope in the average working woman trying to shed a few pounds.

They're more likely to inspire guilt, despair or the kind of anger that does nobody's heart any good.

A few weeks after the "toning tips" appeared, Time ran a letter from Dr. Kerry Swindle of Tucson, Ariz., proving, among other things, that some physicians actually read the magazines in their waiting rooms.

She wrote: "Here I have been wasting my time being a part-time physician and full-time wife and mother and trying to squeak out 30 to 60 minutes of exercise a few days a week. Forget the laundry, groceries, cleaning, sports lessons, church functions and trips to school and the doctor, dentist and vet, I'm going to head off to the health club! Thank you for straightening out my priorities."

Way to go, Doc!

To be fair, I suppose if I were pregnant and planning to model nude for the cover of a national magazine, as Demi did, I would rely on more than my sporadic neighborhood walks to tone up my body.

Or if my husband were working at the White House and I couldn't escape the paparazzi, I guess I would make the sacrifice, give up cooking, cleaning, chauffeuring and spend that time getting fit for photo ops.

Or if I were in the business of making music videos in skimpy undergarments, a la Madonna, I would get myself a personal trainer and go all out.

But, luckily, I'm not rich or famous, so I can afford to spend those three hours driving my son to and from day camp, pinching back basil leaves between bouts at the computer, buying my own groceries and cooking my own less-than-perfect meals while listening to a 9-year-old and his dad recount their never-dull days.

"Priorities," as the doctor said.

It makes me wonder though: What's the purpose in touting the high-life habits of celebrities to the lowly masses?

Is it to make us feel weak, flabby, lazy and deserving

of all the health woes we end up suffering?

No question, it shifts the focus from more significant inequities. Earlier this year, the government reported that the gulf between health care for the rich and poor is widening. Illness and death rates are quite different depending on income, family status and education.

Now this is something to get exercised about.

August 22, 1993

"Is Grits Groceries?"

I know it was summer, though I recall little else about the day.

I remember rushing into the house, hot and sweaty from playing outdoors, not expecting to hear what I heard coming out of my mother's mouth.

Poetry.

She was in the living room, alone, reading out loud from a book.

Her voice stunned me.

Proud and passionate, almost electric, it surged from room to room.

It made me think of the gutsy heroines in the old black-and-white movies she and I liked to watch in the afternoons, stretched out on the carpet in front of the TV.

It was the first time I remember being thrilled by the human voice.

When she caught sight of me, she was embarrassed.

So was I. As far back as I can remember, she read me poems in a familiar, affectionate way. Me and the book, together on her lap.

But this was different. It was the out-loud excitement in her breath, the rising-falling drama in her voice, that stopped me in my tracks and made her cheeks redden.

I don't remember the poem now—only the way she sounded reading it.

That unforgettable voice: proud and strong and complete.

Then, a few weeks ago, out of the blue, I heard it again, live and in color, at the Macauley Theatre.

This time it came out of Maya Angelou's mouth.

Angelou is the woman who brought poetry back to prime time with her fiery delivery at the Clinton inauguration. Her poem, "In the Pulse of the Morning," commissioned by Clinton, has been translated into 40 languages. The popularity of the poem boosted Angelou's fan mail from a hefty 500 letters a week to a phenomenal 1,500.

Her appearance here, a benefit for the Bingham Child Guidance Center, must have made converts of many who had dismissed poetry as stuffy stuff, required reading in school but hardly a night's entertainment.

Angelou's definition of poetry is as diverse as the audience that filled the theater that night.

To her, it is as much about Negro spirituals and rap songs as Shakespearian sonnets or Homerian epics. It's about movement as much as sound.

It's about what we know but can't prove—"Sometimes facts can obscure the truth," she told the SRO crowd as she wrapped it around her finger.

Later I met Angelou backstage and asked her what it was like to look out at a sea of strangers and to tell them up front, as she had, that she intended to talk about "love in all its forms"—and, what's more, she was going to do so in the language of African-American poetry!

She laughed and grabbed one of my hands and said, "I know! I know! You should see what I see from up there. Their faces! They're kind of thinking, What am I gonna do with *this*?"

But inevitably, she said, the faces relax and the minds open.

Angelou said she's part of "an avalanche" of renewed interest in poetry—on stages and in cafes.

"There's a resurgence," she said.

Just six weeks earlier, I had heard a legendary poet of the Beat Generation, Lawrence Ferlinghetti, read at the University of Louisville.

Even without a presidential endorsement, Ferlinghetti attracted so many more people than expected, U of L had to move him to a larger room.

Like Angelou's crowd, this one was un-categorizable: Middle-aged suburban housewives sat beside grungy teen-agers young enough to be the poet's great-grand-children.

This would probably not have surprised an English-teacher friend of mine, who says "something's changed" about young people's reaction to poetry, particularly when it's read aloud.

She says that today when she asks seventh-graders to read a poem in class, even the boys shoot up their hands to volunteer.

Is it, my friend asks, that elementary teachers are doing a better job of preparing children for poetry?

Or is it the impact of books like the "The Outsiders"? In that still-popular teen saga, which was made into a movie, Robert Frost's classic "Nothing Gold Can Last" plays a pivotal role—helping to "popularize poetry," she says.

One of her male students ultimately was turned on to poetry through an obsession with Jim Morrison's rock lyrics. She wonders: Is the awkward imagery of a suicidal pop idol a worthy pathway to poetry?

I think of a line Angelou tossed out to her Macauley crowd:

"Is grits groceries?"

Poetry—especially read aloud—may be "resurging" simply because it represents the shortest distance between a writer's heart and a reader's.

Stop by Twice-Told Coffeehouse on Bardstown Road some "open-mike" night and ask the folks there why they come to hear amateurs read. My guess is they're hoping to experience what I did when I stumbled on my mother's voice in the living room that summer day.

It's all one voice really; all connected.

Angelou at the Macauley. The teen-age boys in my friend's classroom. The cafe readers. Even Rita Dove, the nation's new poet laureate and the first African-American woman in that post.

It's an unforgettable voice, once you've heard it: strong and proud and complete.

June 27, 1993

My Left Breast

The night before I saw Susan Miller's one-woman show at the 18th annual Humana Festival of New American Plays, I dreamed I had breast cancer.

It wasn't a terrifying dream. I was watching my husband talk on the phone with a doctor. I felt sad, already missing my left breast, the one with the lump in my dream. But I also felt stoic.

The inevitable had finally arrived.

For many women today, particularly those whose mothers or sisters or aunts or grandmothers have been diagnosed with breast cancer, this once-whispered-about disease has—rightly or wrongly—taken on an air of inevitability.

Breast cancer takes the lives of 46,000 women each year. But to some women, it's come to represent more than that.

What AIDS has been to a generation of gay men, breast cancer is to these women—a powerful metaphor

269

for personal loss and a rallying cry against injustice. Survivors of breast cancer, like those of AIDS, have lobbied—tirelessly and wisely—for all-important research funds and equally crucial media attention.

And they have used the popular arts—theater, in particular—to awaken the public to their plight.

Which leads me back to my dream.

When I awoke, it didn't take long to figure out why I dreamed of breast cancer that particular night. It surely was prompted by anticipation of the Susan Miller play I was to see the next day at Actors Theatre.

I didn't know much about its "plot" when I fell asleep—but I did know the subject was breast cancer. And (oh, what a plagiarizer the sleeping mind is!) I knew the play's title was "My Left Breast."

When my mother was diagnosed with breast cancer in 1973, I knew no one who'd been through the same experience.

It seemed that we were the first and only family, anywhere ever, to grapple with this disease. We choked on the words—*breast* and *cancer*—or we avoided them altogether. There was no body of popular literature to draw on for comfort and education. There was no easily accessible network of support. There was no Hospice.

From the start, I talked to my friends about my fear of losing my mother. But I never told her. We had an unspoken pact of silence. I remember sitting with her on the living room sofa, our arms around each other, knowing we shared the same feelings but lacked the vocabulary, perhaps the courage, to express them.

About the time my mother died in 1978, my friend Melissa died. She too had breast cancer. The average age of the crowd that gathered at her funeral was probably 30.

Happily, in the years since Melissa and my mother died, the women I've known with breast cancer have been survivors. They've beaten the odds for as many as 25 years. My husband's mother. My aunt. My colleagues. My good friends and their mothers and sisters and daughters and neighbors.

Happily, too, we no longer whisper. Quite the opposite: We demand attention.

Witness the angry reaction to recent news reports of falsified data in breast-cancer treatment studies and intentional cover-ups of serious side effects from experimental drug therapies.

For years women were left out of large-scale medical studies. Now disturbing questions arise about lax attitudes and unconscionable neglect.

In researching a recent front-page story on the controversial tamoxifen drug trials, Courier-Journal staff writer Leslie Scanlon found some of the 150 women in the Kentucky portion of the study were angry about this cavalier approach to women's health care.

But the overriding spirit of the women was an altruistic, almost crusading desire to help in the search for an effective treatment for breast cancer and possibly a preventive therapy for those at high risk.

Skeptics may claim that's rationalization. How else can one live with the dangers involved in taking an experimental drug, they ask. Putting an idealistic spin on the risk gives it transcendent meaning.

I don't buy that. Not entirely.

I think breast cancer has come to stand for more than the individuals who suffer it. It is no longer the "silent epidemic" Miller refers to in her play.

"I care about my sisters out there, and what they can learn from me being in this," said one woman Scanlon interviewed.

I don't think women talk that way about lung cancer, though it's the No. 1 cancer killer of women. Breast cancer is No. 2.

Of course, fear plays a part too.

"I might come up with another cancer," one woman told Scanlon, "but I'm probably going to get this (breast) cancer anyway—so what's the big deal?"

Her sense of predetermined fate and the fear accompanying it "outweighed everything else," she said.

Accepting the inevitable.

Maybe it's just a mind game some of us play: this focus on breast cancer. After all, its survival rates are better than, say, ovarian cancer. Singling it out eliminates the need to obsess about other fates we love to fear—heart attacks, Alzheimers, strokes. The list goes on.

A friend, whose mother also died young of breast cancer, asks me: "Why target one disease? You could be killed at a crosswalk this afternoon."

That's when I remember the play that started me dreaming in the beginning.

"My Left Breast" is not really about cancer. It's about loss. Loss of breast, loss of love, loss of a sense of security, loss of children who grow up and leave home, loss of partners, loss, loss.

But it is also about surviving.

The best thing to come out of all this may be our willingness to talk to each other. Women with breast cancer now write poems about it, and essays and songs and, yes, even plays for highly visible stages like the Humana Festival.

ATL's Elizabeth Clarke says the themes that emerge from plays in the festival tend to "project what's *really* going on out there in people's lives."

"My Left Breast" is no exception.

At one point in the play, Miller lifts her shirt and shows the scar where her breast used to be.

She prepares her audience. She tells them what's coming. She gives them ample time to decide how they wish to deal with this baring of flesh, this moment of guts and vulnerability.

They can choose to keep their eyes open or to hide them.

Me? I looked.

And as I did, the stage suddenly flooded with memories of another day, 20 years ago, a day spent with my mother, a day I believe was a turning point for both of us—the day she presented me with the same choice Miller offers her audience at each performance:

To be a witness or to turn away.

I looked that time too. I've never regretted it.

April 10, 1994

Full
House

After a recent night at the theater, a young man asked his mother why there's always a line of women snaking out the door and into the hallways in front of ladies' rooms—but never a line in front of the men's room?

He'd noticed it at concert intermissions and half-times at football games.

"How come, Mom?"

"Elementary, my dear son," his mother said. "Because the bathrooms for women aren't big enough."

"But why not?" he wanted to know. "Men's rooms are the right size for men."

"Well, that's because men design the buildings, and they know how big a bathroom THEY need. When women design the buildings, the bathrooms will be big enough for women."

This last statement led to a brief reminder of certain anatomical differences between the genders, followed by a quick comparison of men's and women's fashions,

274

including a digression on long skirts and pantyhose, items of feminine apparel that, the woman noted, contributed mightily to those long lines outside ladies' rooms.

"You see," she said, "what women need isn't always the same as what men need."

I was reminded of that story on a cold, windy Wednesday night last month when 200 people—mostly women—were turned away from the chapel of Louisville Presbyterian Theological Seminary.

There wasn't room for them inside. Those who arrived early enough were crammed into pews, crouched in aisles, leaning against walls, even sitting on "stage" beside the podium.

The speaker who attracted this overflow crowd was Elizabeth Johnson, a woman who had won a Grawemeyer award in religion. Her topic was feminist theology.

Surely no one could have predicted that 700 people would create a traffic jam on Lexington Road, a bottleneck in the seminary parking lot and a crowd around the chapel door just to hear a woman talk about female images of God.

But wait a minute! Why couldn't they predict it?

A year ago, at the lecture given by Carol Gilligan—last year's Grawemeyer winner in education—the same thing happened. About 500 people, mostly women, filled a University of Louisville auditorium, leaving the leftovers in the lobby, straining to hear what the Harvard psychologist had to say. Hundreds were turned away when the lobby crowd exceeded fire marshal limits.

It happened again a few months later at a public lecture by Molly Ivins, the strong-minded political commentator. It took no time for Ivins fans to fill the 150-seat basement auditorium of the campus library, where she was to speak.

"We scrambled to set up extra chairs and still had to turn away hundreds of people, men and women," says university Women's Center director Judi Jennings.

And it happened—again—at the J.B. Speed Museum, when hundreds of men and women were turned away from a lecture that opened last year's exhibition of the work of Audrey Flack, an artist whose name is hardly a household word.

Speed director Peter Morrin says he was "pleasantly surprised at the huge turnout" that far exceeded the capacity of the museum's 600-seat auditorium.

"I think it showed there was a kind of hunger to hear from a woman, much of whose career has been devoted to fashioning images of women," Morrin said.

It's true these events were free. But Morrin says standing-room-only crowds for any lecture are rare. He could think of only two others at the Speed, one focusing on male architects, the other on Native American dancers.

He thinks the phenomenon is more complicated than women simply turning out to hear women: "I think this institution and others in this community are coming to terms with the fact there is a hunger out there for visual information and other information *for the heart*, for one's emotional sense of self—I don't know how to say it exactly—for a sense of spirituality at some level."

It so happens the hunger seems deepest among women. Maybe it's like the mother said to her son: What women need isn't always what men need.

How many overflow crowds does it take to make a point?

"There's not much stuff about women out there, so when someone gives us a chance, we turn out," says Jennings.

But, like Morrin, she thinks it's more than a women's issue. She points to the SRO crowd at a recent campus forum on racism: "There's a hunger for discussions of difficult topics. People want to talk about tough issues."

People aren't just "showing up," she says. They come not out of duty but out of a desire to engage and connect.

If you were there for Gilligan or Johnson, you know what Jennings means. There was an electricity in those crowded rooms, a connection not just between speaker and audience but between strangers sharing pews.

Think of it in terms of the atmosphere at a football stadium when the home team is on a roll.

Certainly private fund-raisers for U of L's multi-million-dollar football stadium remind us how *it* would be a place where fans could come together to connect in support of their heroes and teams.

As a U of L alumna, I would also like to see a place on campus suited for the big, eager crowds turning out for speakers like Gilligan, Ivins and Johnson.

I'd like to see the Women's Center, for example, become a true meeting place as its name implies and not just office space in the basement of a building.

Meanwhile, the new stadium should have room for everyone, from pricey corporate "suites" going for $20,000 a year to $25 seats in the "crunch zone."

I just hope somebody remembers the room with the best seats in the house and makes it big enough—for all of us.

November 14, 1993

Is The
Party
Over?

A few weeks ago, when I heard the news about the 22nd Annual Derby Bacchanalia, I called my friend Gail who lives in a suburb of Chicago.

"Do you think it's true?" I asked. "Could this be the last Bacchanalia?"

Back in 1972, when Gail Harris-Schmidt (Harris period, then) was finishing up at Vanderbilt, she and two friends from Waggener High School concocted the First Annual.

They drove home for Derby: Gail from Nashville; Rick Blum from Washington University in St. Louis; Chris Harmer from Cornell in Ithaca, N.Y.

They each brought a carload of friends, and they all spent Derby Day in the infield.

After graduation, the trio moved back to Louisville and the infield get-together expanded to a week of activities, including tennis and basketball tournaments and Friday night dancing at the Do Drop Inn. Most everybody camped out in one house, cooked together and spent nights on the floor in sleeping bags (as many as 50 crammed in one house some years).

Some, like Gail and I, scaled back or dropped out when we married and had kids. Newcomers picked up the slack. At its peak, the event attracted as many as 80 people—from both coasts, Canada and, one year, even Thailand.

Formal invitations were sent out, poking fun at more pretentious Derby parties with a discreet note at bottom left: *Reception before, during and following the Kentucky Derby.*

For a long time, Bacchanalia seemed like a suitable (if tongue-in-cheek) name for these annual reunions. Today, though, there's general agreement that the name is more about wishful thinking than reality. Although the sleeping-bag and infield traditions live on and younger people join the ranks each year, the average age of the revelers is 40-something—with one old-timer soon to turn 50.

A typical job description is "parent."

"It gets mellower every year," Rick Blum, now a Richmond, Ky., pediatrician, said. This year he and his wife brought their 3-year-old son, Nathan.

"What's kept it going all this time is the combination of good friendship and fun. Not many people do things that are just plain old fun," Rick said.

Harmer says it's mostly about relationships. He points to long-term friendships among people "whose only connection is the Derby" and to numerous romances that blossomed. One couple who met at

Derby and later married still show up each year.

Harmer, who is single, has missed only two Bacchanalias—1983 and 1984, years he was in Thailand as a Peace Corps volunteer. An engineer, he now lives in Dayton, Ohio, but his family—like Harris-Schmidt's and Blum's—is still here.

In fact, one of the quirkier traits of the Bacchanalia is the way it spans generations. Beverly Harmer, Chris's Mom, hosts Friday supper every year, featuring her famous bourbon brownies. Rick's mother, Emma, starts cooking 10 days ahead to prepare what's known officially as "Ma Blum's Burgoo Breakfast" the Sunday after Derby.

"These kids," Mrs. Blum still calls them, though some now have offspring the same age Rick was back in '72. "We really think of them as family."

For years, Chris's rambling house in Old Louisville served as "Derby Central." When he left for Thailand, the baton passed to Nan Campbell and her three-story house nearby.

But last month Nan, a teacher, moved to Lanesville, Ind.

"I didn't want the tradition to die, but I also can't stay in one place my whole life because of one week every spring," Nan said.

Though she opened up her new house for a party and sleep-in last night, the handwriting's on the wall: The Party's over. There's nobody left in the group with a lifestyle conducive to hosting four-day sleep-overs.

That's why this year's invitation proclaimed: "The Last Roundup!"

But 22 years is a respectable lifespan. Did anybody ever really expect it to last that long?

"Sure!" Chris said. "I didn't see any reason why we wouldn't be doing it forever."

With 12 Bacchanalias under her belt, Trish Crawford—a social worker from Kingston, Canada—feels a "responsibility" to carry on the tradition. I talked to her by phone, a week before Derby, from Queens University campus where she manages a campus pub for grad students. (The maze of relationships that led to her first trip down for Derby would drive an experienced genealogist mad.)

I asked how she describes her yearly reunion to friends in Canada.

"I call it a combination of 'Same Time Next Year' and 'The Big Chill,'" she said. Trish is getting married this summer, and Chris and his mother will be there.

"Did you know Trish got her ring here at the track?" Mrs. Harmer asked me. "Did she tell you that?"

No, she didn't. But she did tell me how cold it still was in Kingston, and she did say the half-dozen diehards in the Canadian contingent are seriously considering buying rental property in Louisville.

"We could each put up $2,000 for a down payment, and ask the tenant to leave one week a year," she said.

"That's not too much to ask, you think?"

May 2, 1993

Behind
The Masks

If you're like me, you found it almost too painful to look at the recent front-page photograph of "Baby Jessica," crying her heart out, on the day of her big move.

Strapped in a car seat, surrounded by familiar toys, she made no effort to mask her misery.

The caption explained: Jessica DeBoers was being taken from Ann Arbor, Mich., where she's lived with her adoptive parents since shortly after her birth, to a new home, new name and new life with her natural parents in Blairstown, Iowa.

The battle for custody of Jessica was fought relentlessly by two sets of parents professing a fierce love for her. It ended when the Supreme Court refused to prolong the 2½-year custody war, which the adults in the case appeared ready to continue at any cost—even to Jessica.

In his dissent, Justice Harry Blackmun described Jessica's plight as one that "touched the raw nerves of life's relationships."

I thought of Blackmun's phrase and Jessica's tears one day last week at the Water Tower, as I took in an exhibition called "Becoming Real: Removing the Mask of Shame."

The show, a collection of 30 disturbing ceramic masks, is about the abuse of children by adults.

The masks are mostly faces. Some split into two or three parts. Some ferocious. Some zombie-like. Some sickeningly cheerful.

At their core, most appear sad and lonely. They are all based on childhood memories.

The masks were designed and created by men and women who, as children, were abused sexually— sometimes emotionally and physically, as well.

They were made in workshops with Louisville potter Lisa Payne Austin.

Looking at them, you feel the jangle of the "raw nerves of life's relationships" that Blackmun spoke of— the betrayal and confusion of children hurt by adults who should have been protecting them but were thinking of themselves instead.

Only a few masks show tears like Jessica's. Yet each conveys the same poignant pain and vulnerability.

Austin's mask, which she says represents the effects of her own abuse, is a stark, shield-like image, steely blue and wrapped in coils of real barbed wire.

"I started thinking about how barbed wire's used to keep people away, keep them out," said Austin, 45. "But as I worked with it, I realized it's also used to keep prisoners inside prison walls."

She made her mask in the form of a shield—"big and imposing and hard to get around"—to represent the intimidating sarcasm she's used to keep people away in the past.

Primitive masks, like the ones Austin studied in Africa and with Navajo artists in New Mexico, were her artistic obsession for years before she made one inspired by memories of sexual abuse.

"All survivors put on a face to the world....As children it was a survival mechanism," she said. As adults, survivors need to find out what's behind the masks, she said.

Making her mask accelerated Austin's work with a therapist and motivated her artistically. In 1990 she decided to share these benefits. She asked arts groups to underwrite mask-making workshops for survivors and to support a show of their work.

She got nowhere fast: "They would say it's either too controversial or too much like therapy, not art."

After three years, she found moral and financial support from the Norton Foundation and the Louisville Visual Arts Association. She conducted three regional workshops, always with a therapist present.

Though none of the participants were experienced artists, their images are intense and imaginative.

"Someone I know came to the opening and was crying at the end," Austin said. "She told me it made her feel so terribly sad. I said, 'Don't be sad. We're putting this behind us. We're letting it go. That's what the title of the show is about.'"

The mask-makers also wrote something to display with their work.

One face mask, which sports an alarming pompadour of red hair bursting into flames, is accompanied by a poem that ends:

"I can almost breathe; I can almost smile; I can almost live."

Looking at that flaming mask, it's easy to leap backwards to another infamous front-page photo from 20 years ago.

Remember the little girl running down a dirt road in Southeast Asia, her naked body on fire with napalm? The war that ravaged her land was intended to save children, not burn them up. But burn they did.

In those days, none of us wanted to see the picture of the girl on fire. If we'd never been forced to witness that mouth of hers stretched open in a silent scream, most of us would have lived our lives without thinking such scenes possible.

But we did see it, and there was no going back once we did. Like Jessica's photo and these masks on display, such images can't be denied.

Wars, bloody custody battles, abuse. Why is it so hard for us to see the damage done to children in the name of peace, justice, even love?

Austin, who has shown the "masks of shame" at several national conferences and has been interviewed about it in arts publications, hopes to keep the exhibit traveling.

"We believe the public needs to know the total effect of childhood sexual abuse," she said.

"These are our faces."

August 15, 1993

Connoisseur Of Fine Lines

I keep a coffee mug on a glass shelf by my kitchen sink. It's not there to drink from, but to read.

It's surprising how many times the lines inscribed on it catch my eye as I'm peeling carrots or scrubbing skillets or even, in the predawn hours, filling a measuring cup with water for the day's first dose of caffeine.

"Words are sacred," the mug says. "They deserve respect. If you get the right ones, in the right order, you can nudge the world a little."

I never tire of these lines from Tom Stoppard's play "The Real Thing." I'm a believer in the sacredness of words and their power to move us. That's why I surround myself with sentences like his that nudge me in the right direction.

Lines from poetry, fragments of essays, pieces of prayers. Even fortune-cookie prophecies. These favorite phrases have a way of ending up on my office walls or tucked discreetly inside a plastic sleeve in my wallet.

Occasionally they work their way into my writing. It was this route that led to my acquaintance with Sally Thomas. The week after my first Sunday column showed up, Thomas, a Louisville lawyer, sent me a note. I had referred to a quotation I keep over my desk to remind me that facing the unknown is not necessarily a bad thing. Thomas wanted to know where I got it.

The quotation "is wonderful," she wrote. "I cut it out and put it on my refrigerator."

Now here is a woman after my own heart. A connoisseur of fine lines. And a refrigerator anthologist, to boot.

I was happy to ring her up and tell her that French writer and Nobel Prize winner Andre Gide wrote that reassuring line. In return, she shared a few of her keepers with me.

Now the rest of you do not have to raise your hands or send me a postcard, but I wonder how many of you, like Sally and me, can't resist a good aphorism.

Who among you has a favorite line (or two or three or four) attached by magnets to a file cabinet or scribbled on a checkbook cover? Maybe some of you own whole books of these things. There are certainly plenty on the market.

Leah Dickstein, a University of Louisville medical school professor, tells a funny story about addressing a national group of professional women. She was suggesting they carry with them, at all times, "affirmations"—lines they found encouraging. The idea was that when they felt overwhelmed by the negative messages they were hearing about themselves as women, they could boost their spirits by reading the more positive phrases.

As she spoke, the women began rooting in their briefcases and purses, pulling out examples of exactly what she was talking about.

Call them affirmations, axioms, maxims or plain old "sayings," in their collected form they are becoming the '90s replacement for those books of "lists" that became best sellers in the '80s.

It's tempting to write off the popularity of these collections as a low-brow literary spin-off of our sound-bite culture. Have we come to prefer quick-hit sum-ups of our beliefs to the complexity of a full-length credo?

Maybe. But I'm not so sure that this is a peculiarly modern phenomenon. Think of the Bible—Proverbs and Ecclesiastes, in particular. It seems there is and always has been a time to be long-winded and a time to be terse.

Wearing a lapel pin is another version of hanging on to favorite lines. Recently, at Just Creations on Frankfort Avenue, I was digging through the huge supply of pins they sell there. Each one proclaimed a philosophical position in the fewest possible words:

Live simply that others may simply live.

Every mother is a working mother.

Consume less.

Peace.

Phrases on pins and store-bought quotes can certainly nudge the world, but I don't think they are what Tom

Stoppard had in mind when he said words are sacred.

More to his point, I think, is the mysterious feeling that comes when you stumble on a passage in the middle of a book that reads like a personal message with your name all over it.

I've never been entirely sold on the idea that you are what you eat. But I can see some merit to the theory that you resemble what you read.

The other night I saw a commercial on TV for Time-Life books. The subject of the series being hawked is mass murderers. One book is about serial killers; another tells all about rapists.

It's hard to imagine reading these books and finding a line worth a moment's meditation. But the spiel of the salesman, accompanied by a toll-free number for fast ordering, went something like this: "Understand how their minds work!"

Sorry. I think I know how they work. One cannot live in the 1990s and miss out on that lesson. I doubt many of us need or want tutoring on the topic.

I would rather spend my spare moments trying to understand the minds of people who nudged the world a little in a positive direction. Someone like novelist Edith Wharton, who took the time years ago to remind us:

There are two ways of spreading light: to be a candle or the mirror that reflects it.

February 7, 1993

Letting Go

Sitting in the coffee shop with my recently retired friend, on the day he is packing up the remains of his teaching career and making the big move from office to home, I keep hearing the refrain of a pop song from my adolescence:

"So we gotta say goodbye for the summer..."

My friend reminds me that in each successive stage of our development as individuals—each season of our lives—there comes a time when we must let go.

I smile behind my coffee mug as another old song drifts into mind: "That's life."

Back home, a week earlier, another friend called late one night to say she'd just cried through her daughter's last high school concert. Her only child is a college-bound senior, headed for a school on the East Coast this fall. This will be their last summer together before everything begins to change for both of them.

She'll be home, of course, for holidays and summers,

but it will never be the same.

Another friend on another day tells me when we meet to talk about our work that before her son took off for a week-long, Outward-Boundish, school-sponsored adventure, one of his teachers warned:

"When your child returns, he won't be the same child who said goodbye to you."

She's not sure she likes the ring of that. She likes her son as he is. What could possibly happen to him, in a place where she won't be, to transform him?

And then there's the call from my brother, telling me he is moving this month from the small town in Ohio where he and his family have lived for years. He's leaving his job, moving to a big city, even farther from here, his hometown.

I sense his anxiety about letting go of the security and comfort of a familiar place. Or is it *my* uneasiness I sense?

I have my own minor letting-go to do this summer, a subtle variation on an eternal theme. This time around the spiral, it's camp. My 10-year-old is headed for a week at Piomingo. To sleep in bunks and tents and commune with nature on his own terms—he can't wait!

I can't imagine.

My friends and I, like the song says, gotta say goodbye for the summer. To jobs. To homes. To concerts and offices. To our children as we've known them. To the past.

I watch closely the ones who do it well, making mental notes of how to let go gracefully. Someday, I suspect, there will be a final exam on this material.

It was just last month, as a nation, that we said farewell to the Queen of Letting Go, the Goodbye Girl for a generation of Americans.

If you think about it, one of Jackie Kennedy Onassis's great talents was her ability to leave the past behind.

While others were still endlessly analyzing the Camelot White House, she started a new life with a new husband and, after his death, started over again as a book editor. When some were shocked and others scandalized by her audacity in choosing to go on living, she ignored them as she had ignored the paparazzi.

Since her death, there has been a litany of meditations on what exactly Jackie bequeathed us. Certainly she showed us how to grieve with taste, grace and courage.

But that in itself is neither good nor bad. Noisy grief may unsettle us, but it's hardly a sign of weak character.

I think it was more than Jackie's much-heralded "class act" as a public mourner that impressed us. In her poised detachment throughout Dallas, D.C. and Arlington, and in the years that followed, I believe we sensed her understanding that you cannot cling to what is over.

Everyone has an unforgettable image of her from that era. The bloody pink suit. The swollen eyes behind the black scrim.

But mine is a vocal memory: her voice the night she appeared on TV with her brother-in-law Robert F. Kennedy, shortly after the funeral. A soft voice, but strong, expressing thanks for the many cards and letters. Then, in an impromptu digression of raw sorrow and disbelief, she spoke a line I've never forgotten:

"All his bright light gone from the world."

When I heard those words replayed on the radio after her death last month, it struck me how letting go does not have to mean turning our backs to any person or part of our past. It is simply our acknowledgment that the deepest meaning in life must always be found in the present.

The other public figure whose death recently triggered a spate of recollections is Richard Nixon. Unlike Jackie, Nixon suffered a chronic inability to let go. He was a pro at nursing old wounds, brooding endlessly over his past in memoirs and speeches.

In his many eulogies, friends and foes alike singled out as his signature trait his "tenacity": his refusal to let go, no matter the cost to himself or the nation.

As we drained our mugs at the coffee shop, my retired friend told me a story he'd read in a review of a new book by the Southern writer Reynolds Price.

After being diagnosed with terminal cancer, Price told a friend he'd found an unexpected benefit from the discovery of this bad news. In the face of incurable illness, he said, there's no alternative but to say goodbye to life as you've known it and embrace the new life you're given.

Of course, he's right. My friend with the graduating daughter is spending this spring cherishing their time together. But she has also discovered a newfound enthusiasm for flower gardening, particularly perennials, which always come back.

For my part, I am slowly assembling items on the official camp list. Trunks, slicker, flashlight. I can begin to imagine it: him there, me here.

To cling to the past is to miss what the present and future may offer.

The Friday after Jackie died, I heard a local religious-show host make a gratuitous slam against the current first lady. "I knew Jackie Kennedy," he said, "and Hillary Clinton is no Jackie Kennedy."

Nor, one can assume, would she want to be. That was then, this is now.

To honor the past is wise. From all reports, Jackie Onassis did so to her dying day. But to live in it is something else again.

June 5, 1994

The Long View

Learning The Language Of Loss

"Do you like pasta?"

The question is asked by a 96-year-old woman in a wheelchair. It is addressed to an 8-year-old boy sitting across a table from her in a nursing-home activities room.

The boy flashes a big smile and a thumbs-up sign that leaves no room for doubt: He likes pasta all right.

The old woman, my grandmother, beams approval at the boy, my son.

And I have to laugh at myself. Growing up, I used to snicker at her name for spaghetti. *Pasta!* Where did she come up with such a word?

At Grandma's house, the Parmesan never showed up on the table in the round green-cardboard shaker we used at home. It arrived in a bowl—a mound of white shavings, grated from a hard chunk of cheese by Grandma herself. We sprinkled it with a spoon. How odd, I thought. How old-fashioned!

Today the joke is on me. Grandma's way of serving

up spaghetti is the way of the Yuppie. Her native tongue, Italian, is not only OK, but *au courant.*

It was not always so. When she was not much younger than my son, fresh off the boat from Sicily, newly transplanted to Louisville, her language was—in the truest sense—politically incorrect.

To become an American was to melt into the pot. A part of the process was to give up old ways of communicating and learn the majority voice.

In my Grandma's case, the tradeoff was not so simple or painless as memorizing new nouns and verbs.

She was the youngest of 13 children. Her father worked for years to earn money enough to send his family to the United States, a few at a time. My grandmother, Victoria Giacalone, and her mother, Marie Antoinette, were the last to arrive.

Her older brothers, by then familiar with the facts of life in this new world, urged their mother to teach Victoria to speak English as quickly as possible. They suggested she stay for a while at one of the Catholic orphanages in town. There she would have no reason to speak Italian and every opportunity to learn English.

Her mother—God knows what feelings crossed her heart in making the decision—agreed to her sons' plan.

"I wasn't there very long," my grandmother says today.

But long enough.

When her English classes were complete and she returned to her family, she could speak "American" with no trace of her native tongue sneaking into her pronunciation or tripping up her syntax.

There was, however, one little problem.

She could no longer speak Italian. She could not understand her mother. Or her father. And they could not understand her.

"It made my mother feel bad," my grandmother told me recently, when I wanted to hear the story again.

I asked how *she* felt about it, and she gave me one of those empty looks people wear when there's too much going on inside to express.

"Good old mother," she finally answered. "I still call her in my sleep."

Naturally, my Grandma relearned Italian, as a second language. But it was pigeon-Italian. I grew up hearing this odd patois she and her cousins and in-laws fell into, especially when emotions ran high. It was a hodgepodge tongue they fashioned—a pinch of Italian sprinkled here and there, spicing up an otherwise bland English sentence.

I'm not sure when I first heard the story of how Grandma learned English.

But I know exactly when it became real to me, when I stopped thinking of it as just another bit of family lore and, for a split second, *felt* the isolation— and anger—she must have felt at the moment she realized she'd lost an essential bond with the people she loved.

The moment she spoke and could not be heard.

It happened one night when I was flipping TV channels and caught the start of a documentary on American Indians. An old man was recalling his childhood. He talked about being taken from the reservation where his family lived and enrolled in a boarding school as part of a government movement to "Americanize" children like him.

He was taught not only the language of the majority there, but its social customs, religious rituals and cultural expectations. Discipline was strict, goals clear.

The scene from this documentary that I will never forget begins at a railway station, as a passenger train pulls in. The old man's voice, in the background, describes the excitement of arriving at the station for his long-awaited first trip home. He tells how he ran out to the platform to greet his beloved grandfather, and how the two embraced in a rush of words.

It might as well have been a silent reunion. Like my Grandma and her mother, the narrator and his grandfather understood not a word the other said.

The old man wept that day, he said, bitter with the knowledge that "they had beaten my language out of me." And he vowed to preserve what remained of his native identity.

This is the dark side of the melting pot of American Culture—the culture of assimilation.

The exchange of one language for another or one tradition for another is rarely a balanced transaction, even when it results in greater acceptance. It is more than a symbolic surrendering of ethnic or cultural uniqueness. It can be a crushing disconnection from family, home, history—one's own deepest spirit.

On a visit to Miami last year, my son the pasta-lover was fascinated by signs we met everywhere that spoke to him in two languages: English and Spanish.

While it may have been nothing more than a grudging resignation to political pressure that got the bilingual ball rolling in Miami, it still offers the possibility that children there will grow up with more confidence in themselves—and with greater affection for a culture that gave them a new language without making them give up the one they had.

This appreciation for what makes us different as well as what binds us together is, of course, the challenge of current efforts to celebrate diversity in America. I think of Maya Angelou's words to a reporter the day after Bill Clinton asked her to compose a poem to read at his swearing-in ceremony.

Yes, she's African-American. Yes, she's Arkansas-born. Yes, she's a woman.

But she insists it's the common theme that runs through her writing—and not her ability to represent several interest groups at once—that won her the honor.

"In all my work," she pointed out, "I stress that human beings are more alike than we are unalike."

This is where our hope hides out. It lurks in these deeper connections that exist within us all: the shared human impulse to know ourselves better, to dig for meaning in our personal and cultural pasts.

We can learn from each other's experience, Angelou is saying: "This is one country, and our differences and uniquenesses make us stronger, rather than divide us."

There's a happy paradox at the heart of what she's saying, and if you've ever sat with a friend whose problems seemed worlds apart from your own, you know

what I'm talking about. It's in the struggle to understand and accept another person's story that we gain the
greatest insight into our own.

And so I'm not surprised that in the childhood
memory of a Native American man, I discovered something significant, perhaps defining, about my Sicilian
immigrant grandmother and the family she raised.

January 10, 1993

The Pause
That Refreshes

When he was in Louisville this spring, the poet Lawrence Ferlinghetti repeated something his mom used to tell him when he was growing up.

"Lawrence," she would say, "don't be so open-minded that your brains fall out."

Good advice, especially if your son is a beatnik.

But I don't think it's a big cause for worry in the United States these days. If anything, we are living in an era that's noticeably short on open minds—and long on open mouths.

No one listens very closely. It's just not done. We're all too busy formulating our replies. Consequently, few of us are swayed by anything we hear that doesn't already fit our way of thinking.

If you're unconvinced, tune in to what's euphemistically called a TV "talk show" and see what I mean. It doesn't matter if it's "The McLaughlin Group" or "Oprah." Everybody's interrupting everybody else.

We kvetch about network news and the "instant analyses" that typically follow a presidential appointment or campaign debate. But we do the same thing in our conversations, whether at a staff meeting or around the kitchen table.

What we've come to call "listening" has little to do with hearing what another person has to say. More often, the time is spent figuring out the response we'll deliver as soon as the other person shuts up.

So it was with more than mild interest that I heard a different definition of listening recently. The emphasis in this one is on *receiving* what another is saying—not responding to it.

I heard an explanation of this gentler "talking style" during a two-day meeting sponsored by the University of Louisville Women's Center. It was held at Nerinx, Ky., in a retreat house on the grounds of the Sisters of Loretto motherhouse.

Fifteen women, many of us meeting for the first time, attended the overnight "retreat." The group included women of different races, generations, religious traditions, family situations and professions.

We gathered with a specific purpose in mind: to talk about how we might create a sense of community among ourselves and other women in Louisville.

Several Loretto sisters agreed to share with us their insights about community life and women. Any group that's survived as a community since 1812, as they have, surely has weathered some difficult discussions. We wanted to know how they handled them.

Eleanor Craig, a Loretto nun whose job experience includes teaching and organizing farmers in Kentucky, said she and her sisters over a period of about 20 years developed a way of dealing with hard topics.

The key to it, as I see it, is a commitment to listen. It is simple enough that a child can do it, yet it goes against the grain of the contemporary American conversation.

We're talking about waiting—letting precious time pass—before speaking after another person. This small step has helped to ease tensions and made group decisions easier to make, Craig told us.

About five years ago, some members of her religious community decided to "lay down rules" for how they, as a small group, would deal with difficult questions. They decided that for every serious discussion, they would meet in groups of no more than six and allow each person to speak for about four minutes. A short period of silence followed each speaker's comments, giving everyone a chance to think about what had been spoken. Only after every one had a chance to speak did the sisters respond to what had been said, Craig said.

This way of listening and talking wasn't something they invented. It grew out of several community experiences, including some members' participation in 12-Step programs and the sharing of knowledge gleaned by one of the sisters, Elaine Prevallet, when she studied with the Quakers at Pendle Hill, Pa.

The Quakers' brand of silent worship and group decision-making is easily recognized in the approach that evolved. So is the A.A. technique of letting people tell their stories, safe from the "cross-talk" of others.

Of course, not everyone likes this style.

While some members of our group were energized by the mere thought of it, others felt it sounded contrived and would squelch the natural spontaneity of our conversations.

To be a listener in 1993 is to get little respect. Verbal aggressiveness is considered assertive; listening is dismissed as wimpy.

You can't help but laugh, for example, at one wag's recent description of Ruth Bader Ginsburg as "charismatically challenged."

But Craig admits she finds Ginsburg "very charismatic," adding it may be because "I'm used to the style."

It turned out that, while we never consciously decided to try it out, our group experimented with the technique Craig described to us. The pauses we allowed to come into the room were awkward at times. But they refreshed us too.

They made us aware of each other, not just our words. Like punctuation points in a conversation, they underscored our similarities and bracketed our differences.

Silence, we learned, can be as uncomfortable as confrontation. But it feels safer, and, unlike verbal sparring, it nurtures trust, the cornerstone of community.

"We give our children time-outs to think about what they're doing," someone said during a break, as we leaned against the kitchen sink, sipping lemonade together.

"Why not give ourselves some?"

August 1, 1993

Girls
At Work

I remember the first time my father took me to work with him. I was just out of high school. It was summer. We drove the Watterson Expressway from our home, near the Breckenridge Lane ramp, all the way out to what was then the end of the line, the Dixie Highway exit.

There we took a right, drove a couple of lights up Dixie and turned into a shopping center, where my dad was manager of a shoe store.

This was not a casual visit. I was to be his cashier that summer and, as it turned out, for several summers to come.

It was my first job outside the gender-correct security of my flourishing but hardly lucrative babysitting career.

That summer I would learn to compute sales tax (3 percent!) in my head, spot a fast-change artist in action and master the art of casually dropping into conversation questions like, "Need any hose today?" and

"Did you see the handbag that goes with that?"

It was also where I learned how to "not hear" the cracks the male salesmen made about women customers behind their backs.

I liked the guys I worked with. They were kind to me, brought me Cokes on their breaks, helped me decipher stock numbers on shoe boxes, made sure I got to my car safely at the end of each day.

In return, I never told them what I thought of their comments or gestures. Instead I pretended not to notice, busy at my counter straightening shoe-polish cans.

Eventually I stopped hearing their remarks. They'd go in one ear and out the other, like the Muzak and easy-listening tapes that fill the stores in malls today—grating to the ear, but not worth making a big deal over.

Or so I thought.

Flash forward: April 28, 1994, "Take Our Daughters to Work Day."

This Thursday marks the second annual national observance of an event created by the Ms. Foundation as a reminder that girls need special attention when it comes to career planning.

I don't have a daughter to take to work, only a son, so I wasn't concerned when I first heard rumblings that this year's "Work Day" might be opened to boys.

It made some sense to me. Last year the boys in my son's class and the few girls who didn't get taken to work had a holiday of sorts since no one wanted the absent girls to miss serious instruction.

But was that enough of a reason to change the basic premise of this event?

Did it pose enough of a hassle to warrant taking away the *one day* out of the school year when girls are singled out? Hardly! Not when studies indicate they get *less* attention the rest of the year.

Though more than a quarter-century has passed since my initiation into the work world, women are still bumping up against glass ceilings, still getting trapped in poorer-paying jobs, still not setting their sights high enough in terms of career, still facing harassment.

So why are we giving up so soon on "Take Our Daughters to Work"?

It's sure not because of encouraging news from researchers on self-esteem. Studies keep showing the same results: Girls who at 9 or 10 show great self-confidence tend to lose it by their teens.

Rather than risk loss of friendship with those who are otherwise nice to them, they start to doubt their beliefs, question their feelings, silence their anger.

Sounds accurate to me.

Harvard psychologist Carol Gilligan has charted this sad regression in several of her books, and the American Association of University Women's report on classroom gender inequities last year confirmed similar academic patterns in girls.

Doesn't that earn the girls even ONE DAY to call their own?

I rang up the folks at the Ms. Foundation to see what they thought about revising the project. One thing was clear: They weren't for making it coed.

"Sometimes you have to do something special for one group and not for another," said project manager Gail Maynor. "There are already many, many activities geared just for boys but very little focused just on girls."

Maynor said making it all-female gives girls the nerve to ask tough questions about what they see and hear on the job.

But she said she welcomes spin-offs.

"If 'Take Our Daughters to Work Day' has inspired corporations to open their arms to the idea that workers are something more than just these people who get up and come to work and go home and come back, that they have families, if the workplace wants to acknowledge that, we think it's absolutely terrific," she said.

"We're not interested in stopping anybody from doing anything. The only thing we ask is that they don't do it on 'Take Our Daughters to Work Day.'"

That first summer my father took me to work with him, he lectured me on how not to be victimized by a fast-change artist.

He warned me about the guy who hands you two $10 bills and asks for a $20, then, when you've given him the $20 bill, he changes his mind and asks for the two $10s back. He does this quickly, to confuse you, so you don't realize he never gave you back your $20. He usually has a sidekick who keeps the other employees distracted with some irrelevant argument.

One day my dad's lectures paid off. A guy tried to pull a fast one on me. I saw what he was up to and stayed cool. When it was clear I was on to his con, the guy signaled his pal and they bolted.

The lesson I learned that afternoon seems especially relevant today in light of efforts to take the "daughters" out of "Take Our Daughters to Work Day."

I can't help thinking of what my dad told me 27 summers ago: If you don't watch out, somebody's going to get shortchanged.

I fear I know who it will be.

April 24, 1994

The Land Of
Yes-And-No

They were seated around a dining room table, a group of friends sharing a meal, when the conversation shifted to the tragic marketplace shelling in Sarajevo and how the U.S. ought to be responding.

The usual "either-or" scenarios came to mind. *Either we get in there and fight fire with fire, or we get out and admit we can't police the world.*

Simple. Black and white. Easy to understand. This is the broad-brush headline-news way of thinking about potential horrors that none of us really wants to contemplate in too much detail.

Extremes are easier to understand.

It's the murky middle ground—the place where the "right" path and the "wrong" one get tangled up in the overgrowth—that we intuitively recognize as dangerous territory. To survive there, you've got to pay attention.

So it was refreshing when someone at the table made a confession: "I'm not sure WHAT we ought to be doing over there," she said, looking up from her plate. "But then I don't even know if Tonya Harding should be in the Olympics."

The others laughed—a collective sigh of comic relief. Finally: someone without an opinion on Skategate.

But the relief ran deeper than that.

Her comment made it obvious how addicted we are as a culture to the collective assumption that there's a right and a wrong, a black and a white, an "either" and an "or," even in the most complicated situations—from world tragedies like Bosnia to media circuses like Harding's case to volatile issues like school reform.

In fact, discussions of education reform are almost sure to bring out the "either-or" in people. It doesn't matter if you're at a school meeting or an office party. There's an expectation that you're either "for" it or "against" it.

Either the Kentucky Education Reform Act is the long-awaited savior of Kentucky schools, or it is a demonic plague on education.

Either academic tracking is the only way to keep bright kids challenged in public schools, or it's an elitist effort that necessarily cheats other students out of a quality education.

This legalistic view of the world may work in court-rooms, but it's a crippling strategy in everyday life, where fear of lawsuits or prosecution is becoming a prime motivator of ethical behavior.

For example: Either Tonya is guilty of breaking some law, or she's got every right to skate. *But what if she didn't break a law, yet crossed an ethical line?*

Either she's a helpless victim of an abusive husband and bears no responsibility for lying to cover up for him, or she's a perpetrator of crimes of her own and, like all criminals today, ought to have the book thrown at her. *What if she turns out to be both?*

Either she's a good girl or a bad girl. A tough cookie or a wounded child. Or to put it in terms that any true sports fan can understand: Either she's a winner or she's a loser. *But what about how she plays the game?*

In truth, we're all losers when the great questions of the day—even the not-so-great ones—are viewed this way.

Either you're pro-life, or you're anti-life; pro-choice, or anti-choice. Somehow none of these ways of addressing abortion legislation seems helpful. It certainly doesn't open up the discussion.

But that's one of the disturbing by-products of dualistic thinking: It cuts off true debate, reduces complex issues to code words and eliminates any hope of understanding the other viewpoint.

In some ways, admitting to mixed feelings, or ambivalence, is un-American. We like our opinions hard and fast, preferably reduced to easy-to-read percentages in a graph or chart.

Network news polls reported for weeks on how the citizenry viewed the innocence or guilt of Harding. There were no open-response questions here, KERA fans. This was strictly true-false: Guilty or not? Worthy of a trip to Lillehammer or not? Quick, tell us your response and, please, don't bother to give the details of how you arrived at your conclusion.

Even without any outside pressure to see things black and white, most of us react to ambivalence the way the proverbial out-of-towner reacts to New York: We don't mind visiting now and then, but heaven help us if we have to live there.

One of the most encouraging news items I've read lately was in a story about Ray Suarez, host of National Public Radio's "Talk of the Nation," a Washington-based, live talk-radio show carried by 80 of the network's 489 affiliates, though not Louisville's.

Suarez is one talk-show host who shuns the black and the white and wants to hear the gray. He cultivates listeners, callers and guests who are eager to explore all angles of an issue, not just spout off about their own and dismiss and demean anyone on the other side.

His topics are not wildly controversial (he let callers talk for an hour about Trappist monk Thomas Merton's legacy), yet his ratings have risen by about 25 percent since last summer.

A radio colleague described Suarez's show as "a safe place for listeners who aren't sure how they feel about a subject to try out their ideas." How civilized. Will somebody please pass along this radical concept to Mr. Limbaugh, the King of Either/Or?

Meanwhile, maybe more of us ought to be willing to stake our claims in that swampy area where we like to pretend only the wimps reside—the land of the open-ended question, the province of yes-and-no, the place where opposites attract and influence one another,

rather than repel and revile and reject.
  Do you get what I'm saying?
  Either you do, or you don't.

February 27, 1994

Peace
Talks

"We are great at counting warts and blemishes and weighing feet of clay. In expressing love, we belong among the underdeveloped countries."

Saul Bellow, the author, said that. I suppose he was talking about the U.S. media, but he could have been referring to any of us—professional social critics or amateurs.

Bellow's phrase came to mind often during the middle week of September. During those dramatic days, we seemed, for a change, to greet news of peace-making and fresh starts with a healthy sense of trust.

That's a switch from the usual second-guessing and skepticism.

You remember the week: It began with the historic handshake of peace on the south lawn of the White House and concluded with the sudden surrender and guilty plea of '60s student-revolutionary Katherine Ann Power.

PLO Chairman Yasser Arafat and Israeli Prime Minister Yitzhak Rabin, former bitter adversaries, took a first step toward peace in the Mideast—apparently believing even a shaky move in that direction is a better risk than continuing to fight.

Power, a fugitive from murder and robbery charges for 23 years, turned herself in after deciding that living a lie, no matter how comfortable on the surface, was a worse hell than living in prison could ever be.

"She wants to be whole," her husband said.

Both these situations called for all of us—some more than others—to make peace with the past.

If you listened carefully during those days last month, you couldn't help but notice some uncommon themes playing their way into conversations and news reports.

The value of offering peace to your enemy, for example.

Now there's a rare topic on the afternoon deejay shows or, for that matter, at the family dinner table. Can you imagine Oprah or Geraldo pumping panelists for the nitty-gritty on how they came to live in harmony with people they once despised? I can hear the channels switching.

But many of us *were* nurturing that vulnerable virtue in the days after the handshake. And how could we not? There is something irresistibly powerful about witnessing sworn enemies clasp hands, if only for a moment and however hesitantly.

And what about the value of public apology?

How rarely do we acknowledge the courage it takes to

admit mistakes, as Power did—not as a ploy for dodging consequences but as a step toward accepting them?

When such confessions are made, which is rarely, they tend to be mistrusted and scrutinized. A formal apology, like the one Power is expected to offer at her sentencing this week, is rejected as "too little too late" or cynically dismissed as a gimmick to sway judicial opinion. No one, the prevailing attitude implies, "surrenders" unless coerced.

What's more, if you—the innocent bystander—are so bold as to accept an admission of guilt as genuine or, God forbid, offer forgiveness in exchange, you are viewed as a co-conspirator in whatever crime was committed or mistake made.

There's a peculiar brand of emotional correctness abroad in the land that demands we leave our compassion at the door when responding to perpetrators of crimes or political foes who summon the courage to change.

Sure, we've all been burned. Individually and as nations. But what if Arafat and Rabin had allowed past betrayals to forever preclude that first clumsy handshake?

Power was led into court in shackles on the eve of Rosh Hashana, the Jewish new year.

The next morning, at the synagogue where I attend High Holy Day services with my family, Rabbi Gaylia Rooks gave a sermon entitled "A New Beginning" that consisted of five letters—to hawks and doves alike and finally to God.

To Israeli Foreign Minister Shimon Peres, a longtime advocate of peace, she apologized for her own youthful "arrogance and cynicism" toward his efforts to achieve harmony with Egypt in the '70s.

"I marvel at your chutzpah to believe that peace can ultimately be won. From your lips to God's ears, may it be so!"

To God, she asked for "the strength, the trust, the patience, the love, the courage, the forgiveness and the vision we will need to build a world of peace."

But it wasn't just in pulpits that you found a greater willingness to trust overtures of reconciliation during those days in September.

I found one example on the back page of The New York Times in a story about the family of Walter Schroeder Sr., the Boston policeman and father of nine who was killed in the bank robbery Power fled in 1970.

Francis Schroeder Jr., a nephew, was interviewed for the story. Like Power, Schroeder comes from a big Catholic family and was opposed to the Vietnam War.

But he loved his uncle dearly, and even now not a week passes without memories of his murder. There was a time when Power's capture would have prompted him to say, "Put her up against the wall and shoot her," he told a reporter candidly.

And who can blame him for being bitter? It was a senseless murder. Even while trying to explain her role in the robbery in the context of the anti-war zeal of the era, Power has called his death "shocking" to her.

Yet when Schroeder learned of her surrender, he realized time had tempered his desire for revenge and another attitude, more generous and healing, had grown up in its place.

"For 49 years, I was taught to forgive—by my church, by my father. It gets embedded in you more and more as you get older," he said.

"We have a very short life to live. There's no use hating people. I want my children to forgive."

October 3, 1993

Playing
With
Fire

No sooner than you find out you're pregnant, the decisions begin. Which pediatrician to hire? What prenatal test to take? Cloth diapers or plastic? Breast or bottle?

Somewhere along the line, especially if you're the parent of a boy, you will also face the Toy Gun Question.

And it's a killer.

To buy or not to buy: That *is* the question.

If you're male, chances are you owned a stash of toy guns as a kid and you did not grow up to be a serial killer. You may not even own a real gun today. You may be a pacifist. Maybe even a rabid gun-control advocate.

"What's the harm?" you ask yourself as you wander past the well-stocked weaponry shelves at your local toy store, your kids in tow.

If you're female, you probably never owned a toy weapon—other than a plastic squirt gun. If you're like me, you may have tried out your brothers' cowboy pistols and rifle replicas and wondered, "What's the big deal?"

But walking the toy-store aisles today, be you man or woman, you may experience a change of heart.

Suddenly recalling a gruesome headline or a terrible statistic, you may feel this business of playing with guns is, indeed, a very big deal.

It is not kids' stuff at all.

If you have spent much time around children, you know how they learn what they learn. It's by practicing. Going through the motions. Rehearsing the moves.

Think of the kid in the driveway, poised for a jump shot, getting used to the feel of the ball in the palm of his hand, the flex of his knees just so.

He stands there, posing before the garage-door hoop, long before he's tall enough or strong enough to make the shot. He does it to get used to it, to make himself at home with the motions so that when the time comes, he can shoot at a moment's notice.

Without missing a beat. Almost without thinking.

Now step back for a moment, and imagine this scene with a toy gun instead of a basketball.

Watch the child pose with the gun. Imagine him on the pavement, feet planted far apart, arms outstretched, hands together, gripping a pistol or a rifle or a semi-automatic, aiming it at his target. See his finger pull the trigger. Again and again and again.

Now ask yourself, what's he rehearsing?

The answer, no matter where you stand on the gun-control issue, is disturbing.

Crime statistics spell it out: Kids are hurting themselves and others with guns at an alarming rate. Sometimes it's accidental: 5-YEAR-OLD CRITICALLY WOUNDS COUSIN, 6, WHILE PLAYING WITH GUN. Other times it's not: HIGH SCHOOL SENIOR KILLS TEACHER, JANITOR WITH MOM'S PISTOL.

I know, I know: Toy guns don't kill people. Real guns kill people.

But toys do teach. And play does prepare. And rehearsals do, for the most part, lead to live performances.

We accept this as fact in most areas of our lives.

If you've ever tried to change a habit or master a new one, you know that rehearsing the behavior over and over, with props that are realistic, is one of the best ways to do so.

A standard remedy for people who suffer from fear of flying, for example, is to "desensitize" them by repeatedly walking them through the process—from boarding to debarking—until their natural inhibitions fall aside.

Why then, when it comes to playing with guns, do we have a blind spot?

Years ago, when my brothers strapped their cowboy guns to their holsters, their gun play was clearly fantasy. There were no gunslingers in their classrooms. No shoot-outs on our streets. Their pretend gun battles were far removed from daily life.

Today Justice Department data indicate that 100,000 students carry guns to school each day.

In Jefferson County, public school officials have confiscated handguns from nine students since classes began last fall.

Firearms are so prevalent that in 1990 Congress passed a Gun-Free School Zones Act, making it a federal crime to possess a firearm near a school.

Let's at least be honest about it. When kids play at gun battles today, it's not fantasy. It's real life they're imitating.

Some day-care centers, like the one my son attended for five years, make the decision easier for parents. They enforce a firm no-toy-guns policy. As a result, the children are never exposed to mock weapons during the hours they spend at the center.

I can testify that absence does not necessarily make the heart grow fonder when it comes to toy guns. Kids who aren't handed a toy gun to play with do not automatically, as one theory predicts, develop a craving for the forbidden weapon.

On the other hand, kids will "create" their own guns. They will make them out of sticks, out of blocks, out of their own fingers. I have seen them fashioned from bars of soap, paper-towel tubes, even peanut butter sandwiches!

But that's imagination—not training.

And it's a far cry from waving a plastic facsimile of an AK-47 at a neighborhood pal.

There's much talk about television blood and movie gore. But I have a far harder time with the idea of children mimicking violence than watching it on a screen.

Over the years, I've observed these fine lines being drawn by my husband and me, and by our friends who are parents. Each of us seems to have our own boundaries on the issue of toy weapons.

Some give their stamp of approval to toy swords because they're "historical" and rarely used to hurt people in the 1990s. Others split hairs by allowing squirt guns in a swimming pool. But even these are banned by other parents.

Lt. Gene Sherrard, of the Louisville Police Department, recently told a Courier-Journal reporter that while some kids carry weapons to commit murder, many pack them as "status" symbols.

I never played with guns, but I played with "pretend" cigarettes in the days when smoking was a status symbol—a sign of sophistication instead of self-destructiveness. I had a paper cigarette with a red-foil tip that looked remarkably real. As a little girl, I would put it in my mouth and feel terribly grown-up. I'd look in the mirror and see myself the way I perceived the adults around me—in control.

Years later, when I chose to light my first true cigarette, it was to reclaim those feelings I had as a child posing before the mirror.

I imagine boys who played with make-believe guns had similar strong feelings.

When you put the illusion of power and control into the hands of a kid who is angry, confused or lonely— as all kids are at some time or another, and more today than ever—I think you've got big trouble.

What concerns me most are the children who end up dying or killing a friend while playing with a gun in their own homes. The ones who were showing Dad's rifle to a friend or demonstrating Mom's pistol, feeling safe doing so.

I wonder how many of these children had felt important and secure with a toy gun in their hands.

And I wonder how many—like me when I graduated from toy cigarettes to the real thing—were unaware, as they tightened a finger around the trigger, that they were suddenly playing with fire.

January 31, 1993

Growing
Old Together

Remember when magazine ads for diamond rings invariably featured glamorous young couples dreaming of their future?

Well, look again. Today's diamond sellers are pitching to an older crowd.

One ad shows a bespectacled man gazing tenderly at a woman whose chin line appears to be sagging at about the same rate his hairline is receding. These two are not dreaming of the future but appreciating the present. "We have come so far together," he says. "Now is the time to celebrate."

Amen. We have come a *long* way, baby, when men and women the age of these two are selling something besides prunes or nursing-home insurance.

At a time when anyone who has anything to peddle is supposedly obsessed with appealing to the "youth market," I keep stumbling upon evidence to the contrary.

It's true one of the hot movies now is "Reality

Bites," a comedy about the restless, rootless 20-Something Generation.

But the picture playing down the corridor from that one, pulling in respectable crowds and an Oscar nomination, is "Shadowlands," an unlikely love story about an improbable pair. He's a shy, scholarly bachelor in his 50s. She's a middle-aged divorced mother, dying of cancer. Neither character, played by Anthony Hopkins and Debra Winger, is made to look younger or healthier than plot demands.

Though hardly a Hollywood formula for success, the film's become a modest one.

The change is surfacing in popular fiction too. Consider the new short story by John Updike in The New Yorker last month. It's called "Grandparenting."

The title alone signals a change for the author whose literary reputation was built on chronicling suburban America's marital infidelities. This is the story of Richard, a divorced man in his 50s, whose daughter has given birth to his first grandchild. When he visits her at the hospital, he encounters his first wife, Joan, and her current husband.

In a scene where Richard gives the couple a lift in his car, Updike creates a distinctively middle-aged dilemma for his hero.

Richard suddenly wants to kiss Joan goodnight as she scoots out behind him from the back seat, then just as quickly rejects the idea, remembering "his neck doesn't turn as easily as it used to."

The humor here is found not just in the arthritic

joints Updike alludes to. There's also irony in the fact that not so many years ago The New Yorker was notorious for publishing stories that focused on the detached and disconnected lives of baby boomers who were then in their 20s and 30s. Aging was rarely a topic for exploration. It was, if anything, irrelevant.

Today there's an acceptance of time moving on, bodies growing wider and softer, lives becoming more settled, physically if not spiritually. Perhaps it reflects a subtle shift in the culture as a whole. For women, certainly, there's much being written about age bringing with it a certain freedom, a relaxing of external standards of beauty and performance, a surrendering of other people's expectations, a sense of relief.

Feminist author Betty Friedan has written a book about it. Carolyn Heilbrun, a university scholar and mystery writer, lectured on the topic at the University of Louisville last year.

Even TV's Murphy Brown is tackling it in her no-nonsense way.

On a recent episode of the sitcom well-known for tapping into political trends, one of Murphy's old friends was complaining about not having as much time with her now that she was raising a child.

"I thought we were going to grow old together," he said.

"Frank," she replied, "we *are* growing old together."

When all's said and done, could it be that the collective graying of the baby boom generation—a group often accused of dragging the rest of the country through whatever developmental stage it's facing at the time— is now pushing us all toward a more balanced and healthy view of life and its inevitable cycles?

If so, it's a view that's liberating to all of us, from folks already calling themselves "seniors" to young people looking at the long road ahead.

I find these signs of change in our attitudes toward aging both encouraging and comforting.

Age has always seemed to be a state of mind to me. On a recent birthday, when some of my women friends gathered around a table to help me celebrate, the difference in age between the oldest among us and the youngest was more than 25 years.

When you stop typecasting people by age, whether it's in a diamond ad or around a dining room table, you begin to dash the stereotypes that restrict both groups and see the links—rather than the gaps— between generations.

When you think about it, it's fitting that boomers should be the catalyst for reforming rigid attitudes about aging.

We were, after all, the generation responsible for one of the silliest slogans to come out of the '60s: Never trust anyone over 30.

March 6, 1994

The Language
Of Violence

Once, years ago, a young waitress stopped by our table at a restaurant to tell my son he had "killer eyes."

She said it sweetly, as if praising his table manners. I probably thanked her. I'm sure I took it as a compliment.

But I wonder now how he took it.

Killer eyes?

I cringe to think what images came to his mind, or how confused he must have felt seeing me beam at the news that he looked like a murderer.

Killer eyes. Eyes to die for. Eyes that'll knock 'em dead.

This incident came back to me, in a flash, the other day when someone called attention to a phrase I'd used in a recent column. She wondered if I had thought about the violence it reflected.

The phrase in question was a familiar figure of speech: "killing two birds with one stone." I used it to suggest efficiency: accomplishing two goals with one action.

Frankly, I had not considered the literal meaning of the phrase when I typed it into the column. Dead birds were not at all the image I was after, just as murder was surely the last thing on the mind of our waitress.

So what's the point of using such deadly images? Why do they crop up so frequently (and unconsciously) in our everyday speech? And, most important, what effect do violent words have on those who speak and hear them?

These are not thumb-sucker rhetorical questions.

They are urgent and critical concerns as we search for ways to deal with the problem of escalating violence in our homes and schools and on our streets.

In the frenzy to blame movies, TV, rap music, computer games, talk radio and war toys for creating a climate of violence, it's easy to ignore the role played by our own tough talk.

Judy Schroeder, director of Jefferson County's Peace Education Program, works in local schools, training students to resolve conflicts non-violently.

"We talk about what escalates violence and what de-escalates it," Schroeder says. "One thing that can de-escalate it is choice of vocabulary."

In other words, when faced with an explosive situation, you're more apt to defuse it by using calm, soothing, non-aggressive words than by talking trash.

Tell that to skater Tonya Harding.

Regardless of her guilt or innocence in the savage attack on competitor Nancy Kerrigan, Harding's on-camera vow to "whip her butt on the ice" surely had a chilling and vicious effect on their relationship—and their sport.

But which comes first: harsh language or harsh actions? Does hostile imagery *encourage* violence or simply *reflect* it?

Harding, as we all know by now, grew up in tough circumstances, then married into tougher ones. At age 5, she had her own gun, a .22 her dad gave her. At 19, she was married to an alleged spouse abuser.

"When you are experiencing a lot of violence in your life," says Schroeder, "your language will express it."

Today, when even the simplest interaction can feel like an explosive situation, maybe it's time to call for a kinder, gentler national vocabulary.

We could start with an overhaul of our speech about politics.

The night of the president's State of the Union address, I listened closely to the way each network introduced its coverage, as I flipped channels.

On CBS, Connie Chung predicted Clinton would use the speech to "punch up" his legislative agenda. NBC's Andrea Mitchell? She said he'd "kick start" it. To his credit, the most aggressive verb the president used—albeit with emphatic body language—was "veto."

But the news biz has always relied on aggressive verbs to grab its audience. Sports reporting has the rep for being the worst offender (teams routinely stomp/crush/clobber and cripple their opponents), but here's a business page headline from The New York Times: "JAPAN STOCKS DEALT BLOW BY POLITICS."

Even in the University of Louisville campus newspaper, programs left out of a budget "GET THE AX."

Nobody's saying let's outlaw trash talk or stop using "action" verbs, as they're euphemistically called.

But some are calling for a grassroots boycott of brutality wherever it arises.

On a recent TV special on violence, I heard African-American actress Alfre Woodard tell a reporter she didn't believe we could or should "legislate against" violent talk or violent images.

"What we *can* do," she said, "is make it unpopular." I think that's beginning to happen.

Some argue that violence is an unavoidable fact of life, a recurring theme throughout human history—therefore an integral part of our language.

Words aren't the problem, they say. Actions are.

But words are powerful. We can choose to use those that resonate with brute force or those that nurture and comfort.

In the past, the shock value of violent words was useful for getting people's attention. Today they're so common, we're desensitized. We don't even hear ourselves "killing two birds" or "popping" a president or "whipping the butt" of the competition.

Perhaps what it takes to get the ear of America is no longer tough talk but quite the opposite.

Call it soft talk. It's worth a try.

February 6, 1994

Resolutions

My nomination for the most depressing family photo of 1993 (and, yes, the competition was stiff this year) is a picture that ran in newspapers a couple of weeks ago.

It was a portrait of a Palestinian father, just released from Israeli custody, making his young son kiss his pistol.

If this peculiarly '90s public display of affection isn't obscene, then I'd like to know what is.

If this father's intimate message to his son doesn't make it clear to all of us how the cycle of violence perpetuates itself within families, communities and nations, then I wonder if any message will ever wake us up.

'Tis the season, like it or not, when news magazines and tabloids like to run the most memorable photos of the preceding 12 months. If holiday glitter is unavoidable in December, viewing "The Year in Photos" is January's inexorable rite.

This year's roundup of pictures appears especially

grim to me and provides final, irrefutable proof (if anyone still needed it) that 1993 was not a good year for families.

Consider these images: two brothers on trial for brutally killing their parents; a mother mourning a daughter kidnapped from her bedroom and murdered by a stranger; soldiers accused of raping mothers and daughters in the line of duty; a husband mutilated by his wife, who claims he abused her; schools held hostage by gunslingers; a pair of little boys luring a smaller boy away from his mother and into a deadly trap; mug shots of parents accused of suffocating a child in a plastic bag, tossing a baby into a garbage container, setting a daughter's bedclothes on fire.

At what point do we stop and ask ourselves: What's wrong with these pictures?

It's true, as an FBI expert pointed out in a recent story on the national outbreak of kidnappings of children, that strangers are the least of most kids' worries. The odds of your child being accosted by unknown assailants—as Polly Klaas was or as the little British boy in the mall was—are slim.

It's the people our children know well who are most likely to hurt them, the experts tell us.

I think that's supposed to be a comfort. To me, it's a sign we're in even bigger trouble than we thought.

But human beings being who we are, our New Year's ritual of looking back has a therapeutic flip side to it as well.

It's called Making Resolutions.

We all do it at some level, usually a pretty mundane one.

When we look back and see we've overindulged and gained weight since last January, we vow to eat less chocolate in 1994. Or we resolve to walk the neighborhood with a friend three mornings a week, regardless of the weather.

This year something less private may be needed in the way of resolutions.

Instead of coming up with a list of personal reforms, what if we created some community resolutions and worked together to bring them about?

I have one to offer here. Maybe you have some to recommend, as well. It's never too late to add to the list.

Mine is simple: STOP STEREOTYPING.

The easy way to deal with a complex world is to place other people in neat boxes. Life becomes predictable then. You don't have to waste time trying to understand what people are saying. You already know.

White males, for instance. They rule the world, right? And they're all alike. Power hungry, insensitive. And what about children of alcoholics? We know what they're like, don't we? There are shelves of books that will tell you exactly what their characteristics are. You know one, you know them all. Same goes for single mothers. Parish priests. Yuppies. Gays. Gun owners. Parents of children in Advance Program classes. Pro-lifers. Pro-choicers. College basketball players. AIDS patients. Baby boomers. Feminists. Small farmers. And, yes, big farmers.

This is not an easy thing to do, this letting go of stereotypes. It means staying open-minded about some people you would rather not open your mind to. It means trying to understand—even if you don't condone—the behavior of some unsavory characters, like those featured in "The Year in Photos."

It means putting yourself in their place for a moment and wondering what made them who they are and what might have changed the course of their lives.

The man making his son kiss his gun. The woman attacking her sleeping husband. The little boys murdering one of their own.

If there's a corollary to this resolution of mine, it's this: Get to know the people you would be likely to stereotype. Listen to them. Look for something you might have in common. Then make the most of that connection.

A reader I've never met wrote to me last month. Her letter is an illustration of what I'm suggesting. She admitted she'd been reading my columns all year but only recently did something "click" between us, as she put it.

"I kept reading, though, thinking since you're a woman with a 9-year-old son—same as me—that we should have something in common."

At the end of the letter, she made it clear she is an African-American—a difference between the two of us that she obviously did not let get in her way.

Her letter made me think of a line I read in an interview with Maya Angelou last year, shortly before the inauguration of President Clinton, where she read one of her poems.

"In all my work," she said, "I stress that we human beings are more alike than we are unalike."

One year and many, many grim photographs later, I still find that sentence hopeful and sobering and, perhaps more than ever, the key to a happy new year.

January 2, 1994

The Art
Of Dying

June 22, 1994: My grandmother is dying. She's 97, so it's neither a surprise nor a tragedy. She shut her eyes a few weeks ago and hasn't opened them since. She looks like she's sleeping. Like I could shake her and wake her. Just a calm, peaceful sleep.

A few days after her death last month, I remembered a story my grandmother once told me.

It was about the birth of my father, her oldest son. She delivered him at home, in an upstairs bedroom, knowing that downstairs in another bedroom her mother was dying.

Life coming and going in a two-story house. Great joy colliding with terrible sorrow, each intensifying the other.

Today, of course, babies are born in hospitals, and grandmothers die in nursing homes. We keep our major life events at safe, sanitized distances from each other.

In the course of my grandmother's lifetime, birth and

death came to be viewed as medical conditions, to be dealt with by appointment, rather than natural stages of life that arrive on their own schedules.

What was once a private family affair became, for many, a high-tech horror.

So I was enormously relieved and grateful to learn that my grandmother's death on June 28 was as private and uncomplicated as possible.

She died in a nursing home, it's true. But she was surrounded by family—her sons and their wives.

She died with dignity in her own good time. Nothing speeding up death or slowing it down.

She died without extraordinary efforts to "save" her from the ordinary process of dying. Without tubes or needles or sticks or drips or pain medication. Without anyone pounding on her chest, opening an artery, shooting her with morphine.

I've seen the other kind of death: the last minutes of a life spent in a frenzy of buzzers and beeps and disheveled bedclothes.

I've come to expect it, dread it.

But this was blessedly different. My grandmother had been lying in her bed, appearing to sleep, not moving other than to inhale and exhale, for weeks.

"About 4 o'clock, she started breathing harder," my father told me later. "I leaned closer and I heard a rattle."

He knew the sound, what it meant.

"And then she died."

On Mother's Day, when we visited my grandmother, she thought my 10-year-old son was my mother, who died in 1978. A few weeks later, she began to see her own mother. The dead visited her regularly in the days before she lost consciousness. It was the living she couldn't recognize. Why is it that at times of birth and death we are most attuned to the mystery in life?

Victoria Giacalone Aprile was born in Sicily in September, 1896. Around 1900, she left her homeland with her mother to join her brothers who had settled in Louisville.

It was, like today, not an easy time to be an immigrant.

In a recent Courier-Journal story on U.S. attitudes toward immigration, a reporter quoted a letter from President Herbert Hoover, describing Italians as "predominantly our murderers and bootleggers...foreign spawn (who) do not appreciate this country."

Hoover was president when my grandmother and my grandfather, who was also Sicilian, were raising their family, building a small produce business in Jeffersonville, Ind., that would ultimately be lost during the Depression.

She was a survivor.

She outlived her husband, two of her four children, most of her friends, all of her siblings and, to some observers, every shred of her usefulness.

The priest at her funeral addressed that issue. Who are we to judge whose lives are useless and whose are not? he asked. She prayed, he said. Isn't there value to that?

Certainly, the people who spent $100 or $1,000 to hear the Dalai Lama speak this spring in Louisville would never call him "useless"—though his life ideally would consist of little more than prayer and meditation.

But an old woman in a nursing home saying her rosary is another story. She had no kingdom, no followers, no status.

It's true, she told us she was ready to die for years before she did. She selected her burial outfit long ago.

Why the rush, I remember wondering. Looking for an answer, I once copied these words from Sicilian novelist Elio Vittorini: "We are a sad people, we Sicilians. Always hoping for something else, something better and always despairing for being able to attain it."

The sadness could have come from the generations of Sicilians who were subjugated by landowners and nobility. In my grandmother's case, it may have come from being uprooted from one culture and taken to another, then deserted by a father who returned to Europe after finding he couldn't adjust to the New World.

We speculated at the wake about what kept her alive so long. Was it her "healthy Italian diet," touted today by nutritionists? Was it her distaste for butter and love of olive oil? Or was it a stubborn streak, a will of steel, a survivor's instinct, that kept her going?

A week before she died, her veins refused to accept any more needles, even the ones keeping her alive with glucose and water. The IV tubes were taken away. Grandma was allowed to die.

The other night I was with Dad and my stepmother when the priest came to anoint Grandma. We stood in a circle as he put his hands on her head and prayed. They say the dying can hear even when they can't respond. I hope they are right.

The morning my grandmother died, a few hours before I got the call from my dad, I was leading a "writers camp" for 10 girls, mostly 12-year-olds.

One of them had written a piece she wanted to read out loud. It was, coincidentally, about the death of her grandmother several years earlier.

As she read, Katie started to cry. We comforted her with hugs and tissues, and I reminded the girls that it's by writing about the people and events that trigger strong feelings in us that we teach each other life's truths.

I used Katie's tears as a way to make a point: "Never shirk the hard part." I told them to follow her lead and write about sorrows, losses and fears, even when others might not want to hear it because it makes them uncomfortable.

Newspapers do this for the communities they serve.

Individuals do it for their families and friends.

And sometimes, like right now, the circles overlap, and the audiences merge.

The night of my grandmother's funeral and wake, my husband and I attended a Jewish sabbath service.

It was the night—would the coincidences never end?—when his father's mother was to be remembered in the Kaddish, the prayers for the dead.

The service, though, was anything but mournful. A young couple who were getting married that weekend came forward to read prayers and to receive the rabbi's blessing. Smiling well-wishers crowded the chapel. Their affection for the bride and groom was contagious.

I felt a powerful mingling of hope in the future and reverence for the past.

I felt the energy and confidence that marriage bestows on a community.

I felt gratitude for the traditions that give meaning to the crazy way joy and sorrow collide in our lives, as they did for my grandmother 74 years ago in the two-story house where her son was born and her mother died.

I felt the absence of grandparents for the first time in my life.

But what I felt strongest of all were Katie's tears, hot and sticky, reminding me of my own advice: never to shirk the hard part.

July 10, 1994

Dianne Aprile writes a weekly column that appears Sundays in The Courier-Journal. She also writes fiction and is the recipient of a Kentucky Arts Council fellowship and a Kentucky Foundation for Women writer's grant. Her reporting on domestic violence, mental health and women's issues has been singled out by the American Bar Association, American Psychiatric Association and Society of Professional Journalists (SPJ). Her columns earned first-place awards in 1994 from The National Society of Newspaper Columnists and from the Louisville chapter of SPJ. She lives with her husband, Ken Shapero, and their son, Josh, in Louisville, Ky., their hometown.